I0669392

SNAKE PIT

The First Assassins Anonymous Novel

AV IAIN

Chapter One

Gorgeous — *delicious* — smells rise up in Mark's kitchen. Garlic.

Onion.

Olive oil . . . it all lingers on the air.

And wafts up my nostrils.

A saucepan bubbles away, boiling potatoes. The lid chatters, barely keeping the contents sealed within. The meaty, filling scent of cooking sausages seeps from the oven. I can hear the crispy *crackles* as their juices begin to flow.

Sat on one of the kitchen chairs which Mark crafted with his own hands, I lean back and breathe in deeply. Before me, I have a glass of orange juice mixed with fizzy water . . . about as close as I'll ever get to a Screwdriver.

I take in Mark. A sensible, beige apron is tied on about his wide, muscular — *tall* — frame. His long, thick black hair hangs down the back of his neck. He has loosened it from the ponytail he usually has it put up in; while he's putting in a shift in his workshop.

The things the man can do with his hands . . .

Standing beside him is his adopted son, Nathan.

If I hadn't known for a fact that Nathan was adopted then I never would've believed that Mark wasn't his father. Nathan has the *exact* same raven-toned, sleek hair which seems to get longer and longer by the day as he ventures further into teendom. It's something of a wonder to watch Mark and Nathan working together; to see how they silently ebb in and out of one another's way, taking part in the various tasks which make up the dinner preparations. Their understanding is one which I know can only be developed through the father-son bond.

For a few seconds, I find my mind reeling — *getting away from me.*

I turn my thoughts to my own children.

Living with my ex-husband, Arnold.

Then I forget about it.

What's done is done.

The past can never be repaired.

Feeling as though I'm doing very little to help out with the dinner-making, I push my chair back and rise up; feeling distinctly wrongly dressed in my v-neck over a pair of raggedy blue jeans. I guess if I'm going to help out in any serious way I'll need an apron too.

"Is there anything you need doing?" I ask.

Mark gives some sort of a muffled grunt. He looks at me over his shoulder, eyebrows raised. Then he glances to Nathan. It strikes me as a touch funny to think that the two of them are pooling metal resources so that they might find some useful work for me to do . . . God knows I've been lying about the house for long enough. Finally, it's Mark who turns his attention to the kitchen bin. He shifts back to me then gives a wry grin. "Guess it's looking a little full. Probably best to put it out now — looks like it'll drop below freezing later."

Feeling a touch regretful that I volunteered to help at all, I venture over to the bin. Then I go through the rigmarole of pulling out the rubbish bag; of tying it into a knot. That done, I hoist the bag over my shoulder and tread steadily out of the kitchen.

"If I'm not back in an hour send a search party."

Mark and Nathan laugh politely at my joke.

————

My warm breath forms icy clouds as it meets the chilly, November air. I squeeze the filled-to-bursting rubbish bag in my grip; hearing the plastic crackle. It's heavier than I imagined, and I can't help wondering if it's because I've allowed myself to go somewhat soft . . . if I've neglected what were once — *reasonably* — hard muscles.

I unlatch the front gate and step out into the night.

The street is silent.

Sky clear of clouds.

Streetlamps illuminate the houses with their vaguely miraculous orange light.

I have one of those dizzy thoughts about just how this street might've looked a hundred years ago. Would it all have been gas back then? Or would it have been plunged into darkness . . . just another anonymous field on the London periphery; not yet scalped by the never-ending — *ever-expanding* — urban sprawl.

Right away, I can tell that Mark's comment about the

temperature pitting out at zero wasn't too far off the mark. Almost immediately, I regret not having slipped a fleece on over my shoulders, or anything more substantial than a pair of sandals on my socked feet.

I can't wait to get back inside.

To the *warm* house.

If I play my cards right, Mark might see his way to lighting up the fireplace.

He may even stretch to whipping up some hot chocolate by way of dessert . . . marshmallows would be a great, unexpected — *and highly appreciated* — bonus.

A girl can dream.

The only items which occupy the street are the wheelie bins standing out on the curbs. Their sombre silhouettes suggest they have some more ceremonial purpose than their coldly pragmatic one.

The rubbish dropped in the bin, I take in the street for a final time.

There's something vaguely magical about Sunday evenings in the grips of winter. Everyone at home. Warm light spilling out from around drawn curtains. Cars parked in driveways. Utter silence out in the streets.

A kind of witching hour.

An unmistakably *northern* wind blows and I tremble all over as my skin erupts in pimples. I rub my hands together and decide I'd better return to the kitchen before that search party turns to reality. And it's just as I turn that I get an uncomfortable feeling.

That *unmistakable* sense that someone's watching me.

Usually, when I head out late in the evening — *again to take out the rubbish* — it turns out that some cat is observing me from where it perches on a nearby fence. Its ghostly, reflective eyes fixed upon me . . . watching my every move . . . daring me to make a *mistake*.

A couple of times it's even turned out to be my own cat, Lizzie.

Standard procedure has me scooping her up under my arm and taking her back inside. I've never been one to trust cats going out at night. Not with the kinds of drivers we have around here . . .

But tonight there's no cat.

It's something *far* more dangerous.

It's AA.

Chapter Two

"Miss me?" AA says with a smile, as he emerges from the hedge he was lurking behind. He wears a thick overcoat with the collar popped up to conceal his neck. He looks strangely pristine: his hair sheening with gel, his eyes with a wicked glint, and his mouth filled with pearly, recently whitened teeth.

Although the obvious answer is, *No*, I say nothing by way of reply.

To be honest, I'm in shock.

It's been a year since we 'took care' of Brian Mathewson.

A year since we ducked out of the killing business . . . or, at least, it's been a year since *I* ducked out of the killing business.

Another freezing-cold breeze blows in from the north. I wrap my arms across my chest, unsuccessfully keeping out the chill, and trembling all over as a consequence.

AA only smiles wider at my discomfort. "Not think to put a jacket on?"

"I just came to put the rubbish out."

AA glances to the wheelie bin, as if he needs to see the evidence. When he turns his attention back to me, he seems somewhat more reserved — somewhat more *pensive*. "So you're all signed up for the family life, huh?"

I think about my life at present.

About how I just hang around the house, not really doing anything.

If Mark has one fault then it's that he's too kind; that he's been *too patient* with me.

He knows *some* truth about what I am — *what I was* — about what I do — *what I did*.

Maybe he's secretly afraid that if he hands out advice willy-nilly he might find himself on the wrong end of a firearm. Or maybe it's because his employment, for want of a better word, is *non-traditional* also.

Granted no one gets *killed* in his 'non-traditional' employment.

I tried to find a job — I really did.

I attended a few dozen interviews, but I was never able to answer the questions about the large gaps on my CV with any degree of confidence.

I look back at AA, deciding that I don't have the patience to deal with him right now considering that (a) I'm freezing my arse off and (b) that there's a warm meal waiting for me back in the house. I've had more than my share of nastiness in my life.

Now it's time for *nice* things.

Only nice things.

So why am I so tongue-tied?

Why can't I whip up the courage to tell AA where to go?

There's only one conclusion to draw . . . I'm curious about what he has to say . . .

"What is it?" I ask, finally.

AA's smile disappears for good and I know that this is the closest he's going to get to being 'serious'. "I was just wondering if you wanted in on something." He shrugs. "If you wanted to do something with your days."

I resist the urge to pick up on that comment; to press him from details — to try and establish whether or not he might've been keeping an eye on me. If I know anything about AA at all, then I'm pretty certain I know the answer to *that* question.

"A hit?" I ask.

AA's familiar smile returns. "No, it's not a hit. The opposite, actually." He pauses for a second, glances off along the street as if someone might be surveying us. There's no one there. "I received a letter — "

"A 'letter' ?"

"Are you going to let me finish or are you going to keep parroting every little thing I say?" He gives his shoulders a little wiggle. "If you're going to draw this out then might I suggest you invite me inside for something hot to drink?"

"No chance."

There's no way I'm going to jeopardise my relationship with Mark. The two of them have met, but that doesn't mean I want AA to become a 'family friend'.

When I shudder again, it's at this thought rather than from the cold.

"Look," AA says, "if you're interested — if you're looking to make some *cash* — then meet me at Brent Cross tomorrow morning. Bright and early."

I do some swift mental acrobatics to work out the location of that particular Tube station. Having been a Londoner for a decent portion of my life, I get there quickly enough.

I think long and hard about what I'm about to say, and then, surely *without* giving the matter the thought it truly deserves, I reply, "What's bright and early?"

"Nine."

"All right," I say, then instantly regret it as AA begins to walk away.

For all his failings, AA has never been one to mince words.

To waste time unnecessarily.

Nine o'clock tomorrow morning it will be, then.

But not to kill.

Chapter Three

The next day, I peer out through my bedroom window, into the back garden.

Grey skies dominate.

Beads of rain skitter down the glass.

Everything about today says, *Go back to bed*.

But I refuse.

I've made my mind up.

The alarm clock on Mark's bedside table shows that it's just gone seven in the morning, so I have time to jump in the shower then throw on a smartish outfit and a pair of sensible shoes. Since AA hasn't given me any extra details on what he has in mind, I have no real idea how I'm supposed to doll myself up.

So I decide to err on the side of caution.

My tortoiseshell cat — *Lizzie* — brushes past my leg as I make my way down the staircase. When I get to one of the middle steps, I can't help the thought which crosses my mind. The one which concerns the gun I have buried in the back garden. I know it's a stupid thing to do — *to keep illegal firearms about the house* — but it's something which I've decided is unavoidable.

I can't help myself.

It reassures me to know it's there.

Of course, I quickly discard the idea of going digging about in the back garden for the gun. Aside from anything else, I don't want Mark to become suspicious; to believe that I've reverted to my Bad Old Ways . . . particularly since I'm acting strangely already today; up and out of bed before ten.

When I step into the kitchen, I expect to find it deserted — for Nathan to be getting in another five or ten minutes sleep before absolutely *having* to get up for school; and for Mark to be in his workshop. However, as I cross the threshold, I find myself staring at Mark's back almost right away. He stands at the sink, running water through the espresso maker, apparently getting it ready for the first brew of the day.

He turns, looks me over.

I track the development of his expression as he begins with curiosity, moves swiftly onto confusion, before finally ending up stuck on politeness.

That seems to be Mark's default mode for most interactions.

But especially awkward ones.

"You're up early," he says.

"Yeah," I reply, agreeing with him, as I cross the kitchen then root through one of the cupboards.

"If I'd known I would've rustled up your porridge earlier."

"Think I'll cope," I reply, digging out a box of cereal, and — with a shake — deciding that it's still good for one or two portions.

Only as I pour out the cereal, splash on some milk, and prod the first mouthfuls in, do I realise I'm being blunt; that I can't simply smash the suburban bliss — for want of a better term — without some explanation.

I swallow the cereal down then look Mark in the eye . . . those *beautiful* hazel eyes.

"It's a business opportunity," I say. "I think it could be good for me."

"Oh," Mark replies, his expression neutral for a second too long. "That sounds . . . promising."

Throughout the time I've been living with Mark, I've remained vigilant to all those little signs that he might be becoming tired of my slapdash, lazy ways. Surely he wants me out of the house more than I currently am.

Not that he'd *ever* say so much out loud.

He's too *nice* for that.

I finish my cereal without any probing follow-up questions.

Once I've dumped the bowl in the sink, and when I'm readying to disappear up the stairs to go brush my teeth, he calls me back. I linger in the kitchen doorway, eyes fixed on him, and his — *understandably* — confused expression.

"This isn't . . . you know?" he says, as if this makes all the sense in the world.

And, strangely, it actually does.

He's talking about killing.

He's talking about *AA*.

I drop my voice in case Nathan might be listening in upstairs. "As far as I know it's all above board." I pause, think about what to say next, then add, "If it looks bad, I'll just say no . . . you know that I can put my foot down when I want to."

With that done, I tread back towards him, give him a kiss on the cheek, and then disappear upstairs to brush my teeth.

The problem is that when I tell Mark I know when to 'put my foot down' I don't even believe it myself.

Chapter Four

I reach Brent Cross station at about half eight in the morning — a full half an hour early. I give silent thanks to Mark for handing me the umbrella on my way out the door.

For some reason, I've never been good at those practical things.

He's good for me in that way.

And, while getting myself onto that particular mind track, I wonder in just what way I've been good to *Mark* . . . there must be something otherwise he would've tossed me out the door long ago, if only for his son's benefit.

The rain skitters down on the umbrella, and I watch with — *I'm sure* — a slightly hypnotised expression, as fat droplets tumble off the rim. Although the skies are as oppressively grey as they were when I woke up — and the chill seems to blow in more fiercely — I can't help but feel positive.

Positive about the future.

Although I wouldn't go so far as to admit it out loud, it's clear enough that I've been at a loose end for the longest time now. With no clear direction for my life, I've become lost.

Reduced to becoming a stay-at-home slob.

Numbing my mind with daytime television.

Senseless internet-browsing.

Far too many cups of black coffee.

Now, this could prove to be a dead end; it might turn out to be one of these high-profile, morally questionable 'jobs' which I've sworn never to become involved in again. And if that turns out to be the case then I'll simply walk away.

Yeah, just *walk away* . . . as easy as that.

When I reach the end of the platform, and the station exit, my mind switches to where I'm headed next. And I can't help but feel somewhat excited by the prospect.

It seems almost like old times.

Almost like I'm back to how things were.

Keeping myself dry with the umbrella, I slip my mobile out of my jacket pocket.

AA sent me the address.

And I consult the screen.

After about five minutes' walk, I arrive outside a dilapidated-looking block of flats.

I eye up the façade, wondering if there's anything particular about it . . . but — if there is — I *can't* see what it is; it looks just like one of any of the Victorian-era terrace houses along the road. The instructions tell me to hit the buzzer for the third-floor flat, so that's what I do. A voice comes over the intercom and I realise right away that it's familiar.

It's Amy.

Amy Douglas.

My heart hangs in my throat.

I think what it means . . . and then think about what AA said the previous day; when he referred to a 'we' . . . I suppose this was who he was referring to.

I wonder what other surprises are in store.

I head up the spiral stairs, listening to them creak all the way.

It takes me off guard to feel a drop of water against my cheek.

Cold.

Slightly salty.

When I look up, I see there's a hole in one of the tiny windows in the stairwell. One of those tiny breaks I've always wondered about. Was someone carrying furniture up or down the stairs carelessly? Or was some directionless teenager looking for diversion?

Any diversion.

When I reach the third floor, I'm confronted with the entrance.

I hesitate.

It feels as if this should be some sort of an emblematic moment. One of those times when, in films, they might say, *There's no turning back now.*

I think about turning back, and then tell myself that I need to stop being ridiculous.

That my life *isn't* a film.

I can quit — *get out of this* — any time I like.

I rap my knuckles evenly, steadily, against the thick door.

When the door opens, I find myself staring at three faces from my past.

And *three* faces of my future.

Chapter Five

To say the room is Spartanly furnished would probably be to give it a little too much credit. To give someone the credit of actually having *sat down* and thought through how they might arrange the furniture. Putting it straightforwardly, the flat resembles a charity shop . . . nothing matches with anything else. The wallpaper — to start — is a patterned, snot-green shade, while the Persian rug thrown across the bare floorboards looks like any of a million others.

The air smells distinctly of dust.

And *damp*.

There are three armchairs — all of them completely different shapes, sizes, colours, and textures — and the sofa seems so enormous that it dominates an entire wall of the room. A large series of windows looks down on the street below.

I suppose it would be a good vantage point if there was anything at all to look at.

And then there are the faces.

The ones *occupying* the cobbled-together assortment of furniture.

First I take in Amy — sitting on one of the armchairs. The one who answered the intercom when I called up from downstairs. She has blond hair, and one of those ageless faces. I've always pinned her as being about ten years younger than me; so in her mid-twenties. *Please don't do the maths.* She could probably have made a good go of being an actress; her eyes, in particular being a magnetic, searing blue.

Because I'm tactless when it comes to social graces, my eyes slip down to her hands, and to the finger she shot off while working a job with me.

It's almost impossible to make out a scar, but if I squint in just such a way I'm pretty sure I can make out the line of the stitches. Brian made sure she got the very best in plastic surgery.

Next, I shift over to the woman I recognise as Tabby, sat in another of the armchairs:

Stewardess . . . *flight attendant* . . . whatever the PC term is these days.

She ran a variety of international errands for Brian — mostly involving blood and bullets; though not necessarily in that order. Shall we just say we met in 'dramatic circumstances' and leave it there?

She has flowing red hair, and a porcelain complexion. But beneath beats a heart of steel, or whatever other strong metal you care to mention.

Finally, I turn my attention onto the last person present:

AA.

He looks awfully smug, but I should probably have expected

as much. "You're looking *sensibly* dressed, Anna," he says, from his place on the sofa.

I pick up on the snide, sarcastic tone to his voice. And I look over the others; noting how they all seem to be a great deal more casual than I've turned out.

Amy wears a simple white v-neck over tatty blue jeans. She has on a pair of well-battered, once-white — *now-grey* — trainers. Tabby is slightly smarter, but not by much. She wears a scarlet turtle neck which, coupled with her flame-red hair, turns her into a fireball . . . either *too much* or *just enough* depending on your opinion. The black jeans she wears look like they've been recently bought or that Tabby has taken ridiculous pains to keep them in good condition; ironing and lint-harvesting and who knows what other material-conservation methods which have escaped my interest throughout the years.

Now that I look AA over, I realise he's wearing a tracksuit.

Jet-black . . . which, like Tabby's choice of costume, matches *his* hair.

AA looks as if he was on his way to the gym before this impromptu meeting.

I have to admit he has a point when he observes that I've come 'sensibly dressed' . . . but, then again, they all have the admirable advantage of knowing what this meeting is about. I just had to *guess*. I put the insinuated insult out of mind and switch my attention onto the two girls. "How've you been?"

Tabby gives a nondescript pout, while Amy — quite without warning — rises up from the armchair, rushes me, and throws her arms about my waist, hugging me as if she was nine or ten. "It's great to see you, Anna," she says, her face half buried in my jacket.

Her voice is one-hundred-per-cent sincere; something which seems to be somewhat at a premium these days. For a moment, I feel almost sentimental, and then I reply, in a practised, cool tone I reserve for such occasions, "Good to see you, too."

I second guess myself as to whether or not I really mean that.

Didn't I fool myself into thinking that I came here out of simple curiosity?

That I just wanted to *see* what I was in for?

I think again about that turning-point . . . about there being *NO TURNING BACK.*

"Why don't you take a seat, Anna?" AA says, an enthusiastic hop to his voice which makes him sound almost like he's leading a group therapy session.

'Group therapy', or not, I do what he says. I peel Amy away from me and choose the only free armchair; one which is threadbare and which was originally either red or brown — depending on your guess — but which is now a washed-out orange.

When I actually sit, I'm surprised at how comfortable it is.

All those years seemed to have softened the springs.

I glance about again, as if half-hypnotised by my surroundings. "This is a nice place," I say, with heavy sarcasm.

"Thanks," AA replies, with an exceptionally dirty smile. "I keep this place for *discreet* entertainment purposes." He puffs on his fingernails and then polishes them on his tracksuit front. "A good investment all told."

I know 'discreet entertainment purposes' really means man-on-man hardcore action; that this, for want of a better word, is his Sex Flat. The place he brings his lays when he doesn't want to reveal where he *really* lives.

A strange seriousness descends over me. I cross my legs and sort of stare back into mid-air. "What's this about?"

AA casts a glance over Amy and Tabby.

I have to say that I don't much like the conspiratorial tone . .
.

AA's expression turns a touch sombre, and he reaches inside his tracksuit jacket. From some inner pocket, he withdraws an envelope. It's standard, letter-sized; 10cm by 20cm. Of course, the envelope has already been opened, the slit mercilessly torn. From within, he slips out a folded piece of paper. He *un*folds it. Through the page, I can see that tidy, black-inked handwriting scrawls across the paper. He eyes us over the page as if this is some sort of poetry reading and he wishes to take the temperature of the room before launching into his performance.

"*To Whom it May Concern,*" AA begins, quoting the letter in a hideously nasal, unmistakeably *posh* tone of voice.

I shift a glance off to Tabby and Amy, and, in spite of myself, can't help from sharing a silent chuckle with them. In a weird way, I've missed AA and his personal brand of humour . . . perhaps most of all when it's not directed at me . . .

AA goes on reading, "*You do not know me, and to let you know just how I got hold of your details would be to betray my own identity. Needless to say, I wish to remain anonymous. This is one reason why I have chosen to communicate with you via 'snail mail'* — AA wiggles his fingers to make quotation marks — "*so that I might lower the chances of our dialogue being intercepted . . .*"

"This all sounds very mysterious," Amy butts in. "When do they get to the point?"

I ask, "Neither you and Tabby know about this letter, either, then?"

Amy widens her eyes, tilts her head to one side. "All *he* told us is that there's money to be made." She exchanges a sidelong glance with Tabby. "He sold it to us like good, old business acquaintances . . . something compatible with our 'mutual skillsets'."

AA gives a sigh of contempt. "If you'd *allow* me to continue then perhaps you will see what this is *all* about . . ."

An elongated pause fills the decrepit little flat.

Outside the window, someone honks their horn.

Another person shouts across the street.

All three of us girls turn our attention back onto AA.

He gives another one of his prima donna puffs of outrage then continues. "*The funeral was six months ago. You will have read about it in the news. The inquest was finally closed just last week.*"

"*Whose* funeral?" Tabby puts in. "*Whose* inquest?"

This time, AA holds up a sturdy index finger like a conductor silencing an unruly member of his orchestra . . . or perhaps a worn-down pre-school teacher making a silent threat of 'No Playtime'.

"*I did not know where to turn for help. I feel as if the State has failed* me. *As if the system has failed* her. *There was something about 'going through the motions' with the whole inquest procedure. It seemed as if there was never any doubt about* his *innocence. As if* he *could not be allowed to fall. I did not know who to turn to; who might be able to handle this with discretion. And, if it so came to it, be ready to hand out the justice which is so surely deserved.*"

"So, what," I say, unable to stop myself. "We're *vigilantes* now?"

AA doesn't so much as glance up from the letter this time.

He goes on.

"*I am, of course, willing to pay all expenses — all such* payments — *that might arise. Money should be no object in the pursuit of justice, or at least that was what I once believed in my more naïve childhood.*

"*If you are indeed interested in taking on such a line of enquiry then please respond in writing to the PO Box address at the bottom of this letter at your earliest convenience.*

"I would be most grateful for any assistance you might be able to provide."

AA breaks from character. "It's signed '*One Concerned*'." He glances up. "What'd you think?"

Chapter Six

My heart goes *pitter-patter* in my throat as I try to get my head around just what all this implies. Just what all this *means*. AA passes the letter around, apparently so that we might be able to peruse the details for ourselves. Apparently also with the ulterior motive that one of us might be able to draw some extra meaning from the tidy handwriting.

One question — and one question *only* — plagues my mind. I look up at AA, see his beaming smile, and feel almost as if I'm about to crap on his party. "Why'd you bring us in on this? I mean, whoever sent this letter, they sent it to you."

AA clicks his fingers at Tabby — the one currently in possession of the letter — and, after a chiding scowl, she hands it over. AA theatrically clears his throat, and then scans the page. " 'To Whom it May Concern'," he reads, then pauses as if to continue, before finally laying the letter in his lap. "Can't say it's explicitly addressed to 'Adam Alderknot' . . ."

"The envelope?"

AA picks up the envelope — discarded at his feet — and turns it over so I can read it.

The front is entirely blank.

No address.

Not even a name or an instruction.

I pout. "But it arrived on your doorstep."

"Ah," AA continues, smiling now, "that's just the thing. I was at the gym one day and I just *happened* to find it in the outer pocket of my kit bag." As if it's required, he nods over at the kit bag which he's left dumped — in all definition of the word — against the wall.

"Well, then, they left it in *your* kit bag."

AA rolls his eyes, then shifts a knowing glance over Amy and Tabby.

It's something of a consolation that their expressions remain as blank as mine; giving me a much-needed sense of companionship in the feeling of bafflement I'm experiencing.

AA, though, is apparently unaffected. "The *gym* I go to isn't your standard needles-at-dawn affair."

I think about all those news stories I've read — along with mindless gossip — about how most gyms make a lucrative trade in performance-enhancing and sensory-enhancing drugs . . . I can't help but feel the snobbery oozing off AA's voice.

But I allow him to continue.

"It's a place where Brian *himself* wouldn't have felt ashamed to frequent." He pauses, allowing this particular observation to sink in. If there's any way of short-circuiting our group it's invoking Brian's name.

"Not Yawley's, was it?" I put in, thinking about how I once had a chance to visit Brian's health club of choice . . . it was certainly a memorable experience . . .

AA shakes his head then rolls his eyes for a second time. "No, *Anna*, I've a bit more style than somewhere as *base* as Yawley's . . ."

I look to Amy and Tabby, glad they are just as beleaguered as me. It's good to know there's people in the vicinity who're just as clueless about London's assorted high-class gyms as I am.

"Which gym, then?" I ask.

AA furrows his brow. "Does it matter? All you need to know is that it's the type of place where people of Brian's ilk are likely to frequent; those who go about in his circles."

"So," Amy says, "what you're saying is that you believe this letter to be legitimate? That it's someone who knows *of* you, and what you do" — she catches herself — "*did*, and for that reason we should take the offer seriously."

AA is about halfway through a nod before he catches himself, frowns slightly, then says, "Mm, kind of . . . what I *really* wanted to hammer home here, children, is that whoever slipped this note to me addressed the letter as 'To Whom it May Concern' . . . which seems to suggest that they didn't want to get in touch with *me* exactly, but those who are *like* me . . . those who might be able to look into this, uh . . . *interesting-sounding* case."

There was silence for a beat.

Then I said, "But *AA*, we know *nothing* about this case . . . and, I mean, I thought we'd all given this up . . . I thought we'd *all* given the killing up."

I look about the others, half expecting one of them to speak up, to go on in some sort of a Catholic-to-confession style about how they have sinned . . . and about how they are *truly* sorry for what they have done. Neither Amy or Tabby say anything, though, and I take their silence as confirmation of their adherence to a stricter moral code.

One which *doesn't* allow them to kill at the drop of a hat.

At the *ding!* of a cash register.

AA pouts. "Where does the letter say anything about *killing*?"

I sigh. "That bit about 'justice' ? . . . Oh, and the fact that they got this message to — how you put it — 'people like you' ?"

AA appears stumped for several moments.

But he soon widens his lips to reveal row-upon-row of pearly whites.

"We'll cross that bridge when we get to it, eh?" he says.

I measure the feeling of the room.

It's sub-zero.

AA gives his lips a lick, then casts another glance over us. "I mean, what's the worst that could happen? We write them, they send us our expenses, we do our very best with the case but ultimately get nowhere . . . *everybody's* happy."

"Everyone except the client," Tabby puts in.

"And whoever got killed," Amy adds.

I take a deep breath — right down to the pits of my lungs — and then say, "Someone will be left with blood on their hands."

When they all turn to look at me, I can't help feeling that it *is* already too late.

And that, what's more, the fear I've only just finished voicing is in extreme danger of coming true . . .

Chapter Seven

I show up outside the cinema, as I always do, half an hour early.

I've brought a book with me, deliberately leaving my mobile phone at home.

It's one of the *Rules* . . . one of the self-imposed ground rules I've set for these meetings. I guess that everyone can do with being radio silent for a while. Especially when one of your friends happens to be AA.

Within the shopping centre, I take a seat on one of the bar stools outside a faux Italian café. It's some place called — no joke — *Luigi's*.

Among the gentle *burble* of conversation between casual shoppers — the out-of-time plodding footsteps — I sup my cappuccino and think about my filthy caffeine habit.

Then I try not to think about it.

One good thing I've found about having a non-specific amount of Time Away is that it's given me the chance to do things which I've always *said* I would do but — *in reality* — with the daily hustle-and-bustle, never get around to. And one of those is reading through a collection of classical literature; a library which was gifted to me by some long-forgotten great auntie, or second cousin, back when I was a baby. Back before I was old enough to read.

This week's tome — and, for shame, it really does take me a week to slog through a decent-sized book despite having an infinite amount of time — is *Madame Bovary*. I'm about halfway through and, I have to admit, there're certainly some life lessons that I'd do well to absorb. And some other elements which strike *way* too close to the bone.

"Hi Mum."

I glance up from my book, instinctively pressing my finger down on my current line so that I don't lose my place.

It's my daughter, Josie.

She has my mousy-brown hair; and her father's black eyes.

Today, she has her hair neatly tied back in a ponytail.

She wears a hooded sweatshirt with a unicorn. Lots of glitter . . . rainbows blasting out of the pristine paradise behind said unicorn. Josie is at the age — *twelve* — where I can't quite tell if her dress sense is ironic or sincere. Every time I see her, I resist the urge to tell her how much she's grown. What keeps me from doing so is the implied self-criticism.

That I see so little of her — *and her brother* — that I have the chance to be surprised by large changes in appearance.

I fold over my current page, and then slip the book away in my bag.

I slug back the last of my cappuccino, then ease myself down off the bar stool.

The spotty adolescent behind the counter wishes me a good

day and I wonder if his politeness is authentic, or if he's still coming to terms with his first job.

Most likely he hasn't yet had a chance to be worn down by the world.

All the same, I appreciate the sentiment; smile and nod by means of reply.

"Where's Ben?" I ask Josie, as we pad away from the café.

Humming to herself, already having apparently submitted to a world all of her own, Josie blinks back her daze and looks me in the eye. "Hmm? Oh, he wanted to go to the arcade with Josh."

" 'Josh' ?" I repeat. "Who's *Josh*?"

Despite myself, I can't help but feel a sort of playground envy that Ben's attentions are being directed onto some unknown quantity — this *Josh* — rather than onto his own Dear Mother. But, then again, I suppose that's *teenagers* for you . . . I suppose I would've had to have been crazy not to expect some sort of insolence from a fifteen-year-old.

And especially one who has more legitimate reasons than most to hate his mother . . .

Josie just gives me a nonchalant shrug by way of reply, as if the only thing she has in common with her brother is their geographical proximity.

"Well," I say, finally, "do you want to go fetch him?" I glance up at the film times above. "We've only got about five minutes before it starts."

"But it never starts on time. I mean, there's always the adverts which come on first. We've still got half an hour, twenty minutes at least."

I suppress the urge to respond in some way.

That's another thing that I've gradually had to grow more and more used to; children talking *back* to me . . .

30

"Fine," I say, glancing again at the ticket booth. "As long as Ben knows that we're here — that we're going to see *this* film — he can come in his own time."

Still feeling distinctly bitter, I pay for the tickets, instructing the bored-looking, forty-something behind the glass to be on the lookout for two fifteen-year-old boys, and to hand them the tickets which I've paid for and left behind.

He stifles a yawn, taps a few times on his keyboard, and then a printer begins its mechanical *whine*, spewing out the tickets.

As me and Josie pace away from the booth, I can't help wondering if the man there is some sort of a version of that adolescent back at the café, only in twenty years' time. I almost have the urge to have the two of them meet so they might exchange experiences.

One might be able to infect the other with new-born enthusiasm.

Or perhaps just the opposite . . .

Either way, I've learned to leave the world more or less alone by now.

As me and Josie file into our assigned screen, I can't help but remark at the build-quality of the tickets. Nothing more than one of those plasticky-feeling paper receipts. I have some vague memory from my childhood when cinema tickets were a far more solid *cardboard* . . . I guess that times change; costs must be cut; prices must rise . . .

———

After we've got through with what feels like the sixteenth — or perhaps *seventeenth*? — trailer for a 'Forthcoming Feature!' I wish I'd listened to Josie; that I'd paid her attention when she'd said that it'd be nothing but adverts for the first twenty minutes or so.

Then again, if I'm totally honest, my attention hasn't been all that thoroughly fixed on the screen itself, but rather on my surroundings. More specifically, I've been keeping a watch on the doors to the screen, wondering just when they might be thrown open to reveal a pair of surly, fifteen-year-old boys coming trudging through.

But the doors aren't thrown open.

And neither boy trudges on through.

I have to admit the motherly urge in me leads to self-doubt; to the question of whether I should've taken a firmer stand; if I *shouldn't* have ventured off to the arcade and dragged Ben by the ear to the cinema — his street cred with Josh be damned . . .

But I tell myself to be reasonable.

To *not* cause a scene.

In many ways — *so many ways* — I've abdicated parental duties to my ex-husband, Arnold. If there's discipline to be dished out it only makes sense that he's the one to do it.

I'd be too afraid that both Josie and Ben would *laugh* at me if I so much happened to raise my voice. And, believe me, the irony of the two of them having an ex-assassin of a mother who's afraid of *raising her voice* isn't lost to me.

The film has started up by the time the doors do swing open.

A brief flurry of light shimmers across the seats.

I turn in my seat, and see, sure enough, that Ben — and the Youth-Known-Only-as-Josh — have arrived. I think that I catch Ben's eye — I'm *fairly certain* that we cross glances . . . but I'm not certain enough to call out over the half-full auditorium.

Whatever happens, Ben and Josh shrug their shoulders at one

another and make a determined stride for the back row. I watch the two of them with narrowed eyes.

'Josh' wears a baggy chequered shirt, untucked, of course, and hanging almost to the cusp of his kneecaps. A metal chain dangles from his belt, which I'm sure makes an obnoxious *tinkle* with each step.

From what I can gather in the half-light of the cinema, he has shoulder-long, brown hair. And that it's in need of a good wash. As he lopes up the last few steps to the back row of the cinema, I can't help but notice a glint of something in his left earlobe.

An *earring*?

I cast it out of my mind for the time being.

Does anything say 'stereotypical rebellion' more than an *earring*?

I only allow them to leave my glare when Josie tugs on my sleeve, implores me to turn my attention to something playing out on the screen. For some reason I mutter to myself, "Whatever happened to Kevin . . ." Ben's *previous* best friend.

Josie, apparently overhearing me, and believing that I'm asking the question in all sincerity, replies in a whisper, "Ben and Kevin fell out."

I don't follow up this observation, deciding that to probe any further will only serve to infuriate me.

Still reeling from my son's snub, I find it difficult to absorb much of the film. When I tire of going round and round, trying to figure out the deeper implications of the snub, I turn my attention onto the meeting I held with AA, Amy and Tabby the other day.

It sounds like an intriguing proposition — of course it does — but, then again, was there ever a job I did for Brian which *didn't* sound intriguing from the outset . . . and which didn't turn into an unmitigated disaster by the end?

Then I think about what AA said.

Or, more exactly, what he *highlighted* from the letter.

That it would be *all* expenses paid.

Kind of like a job . . . and isn't that what I've been looking for?

It would be nice to no longer be drawing on my savings; to be having some other form of income. It'll put off that inevitable day when I have to go to Mark, not simply content about him allowing me to share his home, and ask him for some sort of a bail-out . . .

And that'll surely only speed up the arrival of the day when he finally sucks up the guts to sit me down for an Important Chat.

One which shatters this near-perfect world I've created.

By the time the film is over, I feel as if I'm oversaturated with explosions, gunfire, squealing tyres, and — *above all* — my own thoughts.

When I turn my attention to the back of the cinema I realise that Ben and 'Josh' have already departed. I look around, suddenly panicked, afraid somehow that I might've neglected my motherly duties. And then I remind myself that Ben is now fifteen years old . . . he hardly needs a helicopter parent.

With Josie striding alongside, chirping away about something or other, I do my best to push down the rage I can feel building. It's as if I'm going to break a rib.

Once out in the foyer, I scout around, soon coming across Ben and Josh; the two of them standing by a wall; *Josh* casually leaning with the sole of one trainer firmly pressed against it.

They both wear wry smiles, and that does nothing to improve my mood.

As I come upon them, I force myself to calm down.

I *demand* that I approach this with a cool head.

God knows that after the years I've spent killing people, I would've thought a cool head would be acquired as part of the experience.

I'm almost standing nose to nose with Ben when he finally decides to look me in the eye. In the end, I strike a sarcastic tone . . . I guess that's marginally better than fire-and-brimstone. "Nice to see you," I say. "Remember me? Your *mother*?"

The smirk disappears from Ben's lips.

He looks sheepish all of a sudden.

And I feel fairly certain I haven't yet lost him to the Dark Side.

That he hasn't yet gone Full Male Adolescence.

Feeling sufficiently contented with the reaction I've elicited, I drop the sarcasm. I nod to Ben's companion. "And who's this?"

"This is Josh."

As I study Josh, I get a better look at his earring. A silver skull and crossbones dangles from his earlobe. He scratches somewhere underneath his thick hair, revealing — *very briefly* — a tattoo on his neck. I just about manage to catch a glimpse of it . . . a coiled cobra.

I resist the urge to roll my eyes, reassuring myself that when Josh hits his early twenties and decides he wants to be an accountant, he'll have to take special measures to avoid that tattoo from being seen by job interviewers.

Josh gives me a smarmy grin by way of greeting, then says, "Howdy."

"Oh," I reply, looking at Ben. "I didn't realise your friend was a cowboy."

This gets a chuckle from Josie.

But not from either of the boys.

Deciding the time's right for me to break up the meeting, I take a quick glance at my watch. "Well, looks like we should be getting the two of you home." I give Ben a decidedly *burning* stare, and then add, "It's almost bath time."

It gives me some sort of sick pleasure to see him burning with a blush.

When I study Josh, he just gives an eye-roll, as if to say, *Typical parent.*

"It was *delightful* to meet you, Josh, and I do hope you enjoyed the film very much." I give the falsest smile I can muster. I turn back to Ben. "Come on, let's be off, shall we?"

Ben gives a heavy sigh and his shoulders sag, putting me in mind of a balloon which suddenly has all the air bled out of it. He and Josh share some sort of an elaborate handshake ritual then they bid one another goodbye.

I watch on as Josh does that odd, slinky-slidy teenage-boy walk that seems all the rage these days. I guess that some *rapper* must think it's cool . . .

I take the kids back to their father's house in the car — *Mark's car* — and then I allow myself a well-deserved exhale.

Chapter Eight

T he weather is somewhat brighter than the day I went to meet with the others at the Brent Cross flat; at AA's Sex Flat. I'd think that spring was just around the corner if I didn't know for a fact that it was mid-November and that all the weather had in store for the foreseeable future involved overcast skies and — if we're lucky — *sleet* . . .

I have my toggle jacket done right up and a scarf stuffed into the collar for good measure. All things considered, I feel decidedly cosy.

Amy walks alongside me with an impossibly bright-eyed expression smeared all across her face. If I didn't already know it for a fact, I'd find it difficult to believe that we were going to pick up some mysterious letter from a PO Box address which might — *hopefully won't* — end up in a murder taking place.

We all got together about a week ago and decided we would see what the sender of the letter had in mind. We decided we would come in pairs to check for a reply every day. It seemed only sensible that since the sender had gone to such lengths to conceal their identity, we should do the same. Also, given the strong — some might say 'unhealthy' — sense of mistrust which hangs between the four of us, it seemed a good measure to take so that we could all be reasonably satisfied that no one was holding out information on anyone else.

Since it only seemed to make sense, the Sex Flat having become our de facto base, we opened a PO Box in a place just down the street. I guess this will act as our 'office address' for the duration of . . . well, whatever it is we've taken on.

In the reply to the letter, we were brief, and we were certain not to go into extreme detail about the arrangement we had reached; no matter what the intention of the sender might've been. From our point of view, it made sense that the less we told about the four of us, the more chance we might have of getting to the bottom of this mystery.

A little enigma can go a long way at times.

The PO Boxes themselves are staffed by a gentleman with an Indian appearance. He has a bushy, frizzy beard and a baseball cap screwed down tightly over his balding head of hair. He wears a lime-green shirt which looks like it might belong to a football team, but I have no way of divining which . . . for all I know it might be a *cricket* team.

He is polite and professional as he goes about checking our PO Box for any incoming correspondence. I have to admit that, after the first few days of coming here, of us checking the post, I've almost started to believe that it's some sort of a not-so-elaborate hoax . . . and I can't help but get the strong feeling that AA is behind it.

Wouldn't it be just his sort of humour?

The man turns back, bearing an envelope. On the front, I make out the PO Box address. Without needing to look any closer, I can tell it's the same handwriting.

The reply to our letter.

I take the letter and thank him, then me and Amy stride outside into the midmorning sunshine. There're Christmas decorations in a few of the shop windows but we're still several weeks ahead of the Yuletide madness so there aren't many people on the streets.

Amy bounces beside me, like some overexcited terrier.

I decide that she's not going to last till we get back to Sex Flat, so I take a diversion into a nearby park. We stand close together on the damp grass as I pry the folded letter out from inside the envelope.

What surprises me most is the weight.

I realise, almost right away, that there are *several* pages.

I hand the bundle to Amy, whose wide eyes are eager to get a glance at the contents.

I study her as her eyeballs roll back and forth, drinking the entirety of the letter in; skimming back when she clearly wants to confirm something for herself.

As she finishes up a page, she hands it over.

And I get a chance to read it for myself.

There are instructions.

Lots of instructions.

The last piece of paper which Amy hands to me is a blank cheque, mentioned in the letter. This is supposed to be how the client will pay us. We just need to fill in whatever we need for expenses and it'll be paid directly into an account of our choosing. As specified in the letter, we are to say if we need anything further . . . if we need another blank cheque.

Amy glances up at me, the enthusiasm somewhat drained from her expression, replaced by more of a sense of anxiety. "I think we should tell the other two . . . right away."

I nod in agreement. Then I pull out my phone.

And we agree to meet as soon as possible at Sex Flat.

Chapter Nine

They say that absence makes the heart grow fonder, but I don't think that old cliché holds true for Sex Flat. Actually, to be honest, as I step in over the threshold, I truly believe that it's only got worse. There's this revolting *unplaceable* stench of rotting fish today.

Having used one of our freshly cut keys to get access, me and Amy — alone for the time being, while we wait for AA and Tabby to arrive — set about trying to discover the source. We finally pin it down to the kitchen . . . specifically the sink.

A coat of rust surrounds the plughole and an odd *green* liquid is stuck to the bottom of the sink. Neither me or Amy have any intention of contracting radiation poisoning so we halt our investigations.

We make ourselves as comfortable as seems to be possible in Sex Flat, which entails leaving our heavy winter coats on and sitting down on a piece of the mismatched furniture each. That done, we sort of rock back and forth, trying to keep warm. I have the urge to go exploring — if only to keep myself warm — when I hear the gentle *creak* of staircase floorboards. Soon enough, Tabby and AA come stomping in. With the grins on their faces, and the obvious excitement just *steaming* off them, I feel almost nostalgic for the silence which dominated the flat only a few seconds previously.

AA clicks his fingers at me, and then at Amy.

Amy hands the envelope over and AA snatches it from her grasp. He reads it with Tabby looking over his shoulder. The two of them stand there — in the middle of the flat — a somewhat surreal sight for them to be reading silently while me and Amy watch on.

It takes them five minutes to read the letter. When they're done, I slip the letter free of AA's grip. It feels better to have the letter in my possession. Almost as if *I'm* the one in control. The tricks we play on ourselves . . .

In a kind of daze, AA murmurs, "Cuthbert Gonderberry."

We all know who Cuthbert Gonderberry is, of course. An actor. Or, more accurately, the latest, hottest British export . . . at least that's how they refer to him in Hollywood.

There's unlikely to be so much as a soul on the planet who doesn't at least *recognise* the name Cuthbert Gonderberry. It's one of those names which seems almost impossible to forget. And when his name fails to do the trick then his image surely *does*.

Even in my mind's eye, it's easy to summon his classical features; those hallmarks of Good Breeding. The straight-edged, yet gently *curved* jawline; the penetrating blue-green eyes . . . that tussled, never-quite tidy, inky black hair. And how, despite Gonderberry being well into his forties, he still wears an expression of childlike innocence.

Although I don't make a habit of reading the gossip rags —

goodness knows I've had enough of gossip rags to last a lifetime, courtesy of Brian Mathewson — even I haven't been able to escape the rumours about him being thirtieth or fortieth in line to the British Throne, and a hundred or so to the Danish one. Whether or not those rumours come anywhere close to the truth remains to be seen . . .

If I was judging on looks alone, it's safe to say that it's difficult to have any doubt.

He just seems unmistakeably *regal-looking*.

I breathe the sour air of Sex Flat.

I wonder if it's a good or bad thing that I've become accustomed to the odour.

Does that mean the odour's soaked into me?

That me and the odour are now one?

When I glance about the others' faces, I see that they're still reeling with the shock of who we're dealing with. It came as a total surprise that Cuthbert Gonderberry's name appeared in the letter; that the letter-writer's Big Reveal was that he's the one they want us to investigate. But, to be honest, I suspected something of the kind.

Of course, we've all heard the story.

The *big* story in the past year.

It concerned Cuthbert Gonderberry's fiancée.

In a way, it's reassuring that it takes me several moments to summon her name; that I've somehow managed to keep my mind more or less cleansed from the constant barrage of 'celebrity' gossip. But the name *is* there, lodged in amongst the grey matter.

Isla Darrington.

Of some royal stock I really couldn't much care for.

I turn my thoughts back to the bright-red, popup bars which

adorned the screens of the various news websites I browsed that day.

BREAKING NEWS: ISLA DARRINGTON FOUND DEAD

I think on that phrase 'found dead' over and over . . . think about the vaguery it suggests; the questions which it conjures in the mind.

These days it seems as if 'news' has become a first-past-the-post business.

Who can be quickest to the broad strokes.

Do we even ever *really* need the details?

Or the facts . . .

Feeling myself beginning to sink into the floor of Sex Flat, I draw myself back from the brink. And I think about the case as I remember it.

Isla Darrington was found dead in Cuthbert Gonderberry's city house . . . what would be termed — at least by my definition — a *mansion*.

The house itself, at least for me, became something of a fascination as the news reports filtered in. The constant photographs of it from all different angles.

It is located nearby Hampstead Heath; about an hour's walk from Sex Flat.

The first photos which made it through to the media were clearly taken from files; scavenged from internet image searches. Soon, though, photographers began to raise their cameras up and over the surroundings. And, in one memorable case — as the news story blew up to international proportions — to take pictures using either drones or helicopters from above; to show off the gorgeous, expansive grounds.

I will always remember the delightful lawn. The large, glistening lake. The ornately crafted bushes. Then there were the discrete lines of elm trees which ran around the periphery, partially concealing the sturdy ten-foot high fence about the circumference. The house itself was known as Parisianer Hall, although, if it was indeed named in honour of some Parisian, there was little evidence of francophone involvement in the architecture.

The main house itself had those distinctive Tudor-period wooden beams. There's always been something about that particular design which has brought out a cosy feeling in my heart. Almost as if it seems like a spiritual home to me. What do I know, maybe there is some aristocratic blood lingering in my veins from some time long past . . .

Like most of his kind — which is to say the *aristocratic* kind — the house was an heirloom, passed down to Gonderberry from his deceased parents. I know, from somewhere, that his father had been an Admiral in the Royal Navy; that his mother had been some sort of politician, before they died in a plane crash about ten years earlier.

I shift my attention back onto the others.

The problem is that there seems nothing to say.

We all know the details.

We all *know* that Isla Darrington was found strangled.

The very fact of who these people were — the grandness of the setting where this event took place — wasn't the reason the news story found international-level coverage.

It was the *circumstances* surrounding the death.

That Isla Darrington was strangled to death by Gonderberry's Burmese python.

Although I've never been much of a biologist — to put it

lightly — I can still remember all those sidebars in the media outlets; how they flagged up the precise qualities of the snake. There was one particularly memorable news 'feature' which went into detail about each one of the 'specimens' which Gonderberry has in residence at his home. How he has made collecting exotic snakes a pastime.

I can't quite bring to mind the exact species — or the exact *quantity* — of snakes present in Gonderberry's home, but if memory serves, they easily numbered in the dozens.

When I think back to the inquest, I recall that it centred around the question of *why* Gonderberry allowed the snake free . . . why the python hadn't been safely housed in its enclosure. It was one of those things which was brushed beneath the carpet.

Left unsolved.

Sometimes things aren't neat and simple . . . sometimes there *isn't* a straight-forward answer. Sometimes a mystery will *never* be solved. However, if the letter is serious — and the blank cheque suggests it is — then there might be a little more digging to be done before the mystery is so swiftly written off.

The silence in the room continues while each one of us — no doubt — rakes up our own personal memories and observations surrounding the case. As I take in the various expressions, I realise that one thing is for sure.

Not one of us will let this go.

We want to see this through to the end.

Chapter Ten

Wdecide on breaking up our meeting soon after.
Tabby and AA apparently have places they need to be.

Perhaps they've got other jobs they're running on the side.

I suppose that others aren't quite as fortunate as I am . . . they don't have the same cosy situation I have. Or maybe it's just that they have higher living expenses than I do; it could be that their parents never taught them how to make pennies sing.

And I still have *substantially* more than pennies . . . even if I did lose my home and gained nothing in return.

As I accompany Amy to Brent Cross station, she witters on about how we should be firming up our communications strategy; that it's something of a Luddite point of view to assume that snail mail is more secure than a digital alternative. That she has ways of making electronic communication perfectly safe. I just tell her to take up the issue with AA; after all, he seems to be the de facto leader here.

Once we've wished one another goodbye, we board our respective trains; returning to our respective places of residence. I only think to check the time on my mobile when I ready to insert my key into Mark's front door. It's just gone five in the evening.

Perfect.

Just in time for dinner.

Sometimes I wonder if my stomach exercises some sort of subconscious control over the rest of my body. It seems to have a real knack of making sure that it stays fed; and in decent time.

Sure enough, as I step over the threshold, I find myself almost overpowered by delightful smells. I can tell, even before I've set foot in the kitchen, that it's hamburgers. There's also the wonderful scent of potatoes and oil cooking in the oven.

My heart does a loop-the-loop.

Mark stands with his back to me, working away at the stove, flipping burgers, apparently unaware that I've even come home.

With a wicked smile, I decide to take my chance.

I slink slyly up behind him, pause, and then whip my hands around, covering his eyes with a swift gesture. It's something that I've always seen happen in films and on TV and I just want to see if it actually works in real life.

I expect Mark to do one of two things.

For him to leap out of his skin in fright or to give an elongated *groan* at such a clichéd act. But he does neither.

He stays very still — patiently waiting for me to remove my hands from his eyes.

Realising the fun's over — if it can really be called that — I peel my hands away. He gives me a gentle, sleepy smile, but I can tell from the dark bags which cling to the bottoms of his eye sockets — the webbed, engrained lines about his eyes — that he's not in the mood to be sociable. That he wants to be left alone.

"You're back," he says, a plain, dull statement.

I take the hint and shift away, taking up my position at the kitchen table. "Yeah," I reply, and can't think of anything to add. I half think about traipsing upstairs and grabbing my copy of *Madame Bovary* — I've kind of stalled about three quarters of the way through — but I decide I should do the mature thing and stand my ground.

Try and *understand* my partner's feelings.

Something which I'm guilty of failing to do more often than I want to admit.

"Is everything okay?" I ask.

"Hmm?" Mark replies, as one of the hamburgers gives a *hissing* sizzle.

"Is everything all right?"

Mark flips the hamburger yet again then tilts his head back over his shoulder to acknowledge me. "Uh, yeah. Everything's fine."

But I know better than that.

Then again, I know better than to go bothering a man when he's got Something on his Mind . . . that's a hiding to nothing if ever I saw one.

In the end, I decide I'm better off leaving the kitchen — leaving Mark to sulk about . . . whatever it is he's sulking about. But I don't go for *Madame Bovary*, instead settling down in the nook on the first-floor landing which houses the computer.

I have to admit, it's going to take an awful lot to rip my attention away from this case; from finding out just what happened to Isla Darrington. And just what Cuthbert Gonderberry's involvement in the matter was.

I fire through a good few articles, hoping I might turn up

something which will catch my eye; something which might offer us a breakthrough.

I bring up the various photos of Gonderberry's house once again, and lose myself for several minutes in fantasy, wondering how I might've turned out if I'd been born to a house just like that one. I do my best not to delve into too much detail, knowing it will only cause me pain to think of where I would be as opposed to where I am *now*.

Most of the images, of course, have links to articles related to the investigation of Isla Darrington's death. I try to stay away from those just as long as I possibly can.

But, soon enough, I can no longer resist.

The news story has the sort of coverage — the sort of associated background information — which is common with such an event. Just from perusing the screenful of links, I can't quite fathom that there can be anything surrounding the case that hasn't been roundly held up for inspection; examined from every possible angle.

And yet, if what our client says is correct — if our client's *hunch* proves correct — then there *must* be something. There has to be something more.

When Mark calls up to say dinner's ready, my brain already feels near to saturation from the details I've absorbed surrounding the case.

While I descend the stairs, becoming hypnotised by the succulent odours, I wonder if the others have become similarly obsessed with the case; I wonder if they're putting in the same amount of groundwork.

I take my place at the dinner table, the hamburger and chips laid out on the plate before me. Nathan is already at his place, his head down as he concentrates wholeheartedly on his food. Mark soon comes to join us, continuing to wear his apron while he eats in an endearing, almost motherly way.

I know that there's not much 'motherly' about him in the bedroom.

It seems almost as if it's a travesty to refer to it as 'hamburger and chips' when this dish is — *clearly* — so much more.

The bread for the hamburger is seedy and fluffy. And the meat itself is sweet and tender; just how it should be. The chips are *really* potato wedges; there's none of that extra layer of grease which seems to be the requisite to *really* refer to them as 'chips'.

We wash it all down with a perfectly concocted fizzy water with squeezed fresh lime. I can almost *feel* my guts becoming cleaner as I take sips of water.

"Is it all right if I leave the table, Dad?"

I glance up to Nathan.

Mark is still stuck in whatever weird funk he was in when I arrived.

He looks to Nathan briefly then gives him a nod.

Nathan keeps his head bowed — not bothering to look me in the eye — as he picks up his plate. As he heads into the kitchen, I can't help noticing the *shining* black eye he has. I wonder if it was a harmless accident or if there is something *more* to it. Still, it's not for me to pry into . . . this is something between Nathan and Mark.

I hear Nathan's plate land in the sink with a metallic *thunk*. Then there's the sound of his footsteps on the staircase as he returns to his bedroom.

A silence drapes down over me and Mark like a damp blanket.

I feel a skitter up my spine.

And I suppress the urge to ask, *Is everything all right?* all over again.

Instead, I chew my way through the rest of my dinner without saying anything at all.

Mark seems just as keen to reciprocate.

When we're both done — and the two of us are leaning back contentedly in our respective chairs — I decide that enough is enough . . . I've never been much of a fan of the softly-softly approach.

"What's wrong? Is it my mysterious disappearance? Are you *worried* about me?"

Mark slowly shifts his gaze onto mine.

Our eyes lock.

And that static electricity seems to crackle between us.

It's impossible to deny the chemistry we share.

Impossible and *foolish.*

Mark's eyes flash for a second, then he shakes his head. He looks down at his plate where only smeared-on ketchup remains. "I'm sorry, Anna. I didn't mean to piss you off."

"Yeah, well. You did a good job of it."

He looks up from his plate.

Smiles.

"Sorry."

I wonder if I should press for the reason, but decide against it.

One step at a time.

For the time being, I'll settle for being on good terms.

If he wants to tell me the details then that can come later.

With full-blooded insistence, I force him to leave the dishes to me. As I don the bright-yellow washing-up gloves the vague cynical thought bumbles through my brain that he wanted to make peace before it came time to do the dishes. Most likely it was just a coincidence. For all I know, something's bothering Mark in his workshop . . . some piece of wood which refuses to slot together with another.

There is one good thing about hamburger-and-chips dinners, though, and that's that there's hardly any washing-up to be done. I get through in something approaching record time, slotting all the dishes into the machine within two or three minutes while leaving the baking tray to soak in hot water overnight.

I guess the dishwasher has something to do with my sharp efficiency.

When I get to bed, I feel fatigued. And then — considering my sum-total of the day's events consisted of picking up a letter, meeting with the others at Sex Flat and then slotting items into a dishwasher — I wonder how a *real* job would treat me.

I take one long look at *Madame Bovary* and decide that I've earned the night off.

Before I go to brush my teeth, to pry myself in under the covers and drift off to sleep, I think to check my mobile which I left lying on the bedside table.

I tap the screen to wake it several times but there's no response.

Finally, the screen blinks into life.

The backlight bright in the near-dark of the bedroom.

I cast a glance over to Mark, see that he's already out for the count, breathing profoundly, his eyelids twitching as he gets his forty winks. When I shift my attention upwards, to the landing, I see that Nathan's bedroom door is firmly shut.

It seems that I'm the last one standing tonight.

Then again, I always was a night owl.

I turn back to my mobile screen.

A single message appears there.

Written out in simple, block capitals:

APPLICATION SUCCESSFULLY INSTALLED

I squint at the screen, uncomprehending, and then notice a new icon at the bottom.

The one which reads: AA.

I glance up again, somehow feeling self-conscious that Mark might be witnessing this whole situation. He sleeps on, dead to the world.

I tap the icon, wondering if I might not be making a huge mistake.

If I might not be about to tumble right into some sort of digital nightmare.

A hacker's dream.

No time for regrets now, though.

Too late for regrets.

The phone seems to think to itself for a long few moments, and I feel the casing growing hot. I start to believe that I really *have* made a terrible mistake. But there's little that I can do about it; what's done is done.

It's then that the whole mobile screen turns white.

It simply becomes *awash* with white.

A single line of text appears:

Hi Anna! Isn't this cool? Amz

Chapter Eleven

W e're all piled into one of AA's cars.

For AA, it's something of a comedown.

While I'd grown accustomed to AA driving the very latest and greatest in sports cars, this particular motor looks more like something which Mark would drive.

Not to get on Mark's case . . . his car is an *insanely* practical estate.

Just like what AA drives now.

Although there's really no need to ask, I suppose that AA selected this car for this particular job to lend us a note of anonymity; so that we wouldn't standout. So that we wouldn't prove to be *memorable*. The car seems to be second-hand, too, judging from the smushed-in chewing-gum marks which appear on just about every single one of the floor mats. I guess that AA's budget no longer stretches to a personalised valet service. Not on a weekly basis, anyway. It feels almost like a family road trip, what with me and Amy sat in the back seats, and with AA and Tabby — our Mummy and Daddy — up front.

Just the thought of us being anything *like* a family sends a shiver up my spine.

It really is a scary thought.

AA trundles us up the road which leads to Cuthbert Gonder-berry's home.

Beside me, Amy clutches her camera to her chest.

Tabby has a camera too.

No prizes for guessing that we've been putting the generous, no-holds-barred expense allowance to good use . . .

Back when the three of them dropped by Mark's house to pick me up, Amy took it upon herself to explain — in terms a toddler would understand — just what she did with my phone. The upshot of the whole deal is I now have an application — an *app* — which will encrypt any sort of message I send. Amy tries to downplay her genius by telling us all that it was a very simple thing to do given there're only four of us. But — as far as the rest of us are concerned — it might as well be witchcraft.

She goes on to say that she learned about the ins and outs of the technology back when she was a copper working in Cyber Crimes.

The plan over the course of the next week will be to get our client in on the system.

So that we're all very much working in the twenty-first century.

I suppose Amy can dream a dream . . .

Amy then informs us that 'AA' isn't a reference to the de facto leader of our team, but, in fact, something of a dry joke:

Assassins Anonymous

Ha-*bloody*-ha . . .

AA eyes a parking space down a nearby cul-de-sac, and he takes his opportunity. He neatly parallel parks the car just within one of the Pay-to-Display spots on the road outside the countless Victorian-style terrace houses. There's a whole bunch of mumbling about who's going to pay the — admittedly *extortionate* — parking fee, but in the end I point out this is what the expenses are for . . . looks like we're going to need another cheque, after all.

Once we've all alighted from the car, we set about heading off in the direction of Cuthbert Gonderberry's home. Already, I can feel a strange churning feeling in my gut. A slight sense of apprehension. I tell myself that I'm being stupid for feeling anxious about this; I've already done so many other *far tenser* things than lurk on the periphery of some celeb's home. And it's not even like we'll be suspicious, either; I'd imagine that Gonderberry's only too used to paparazzi trying to get snaps of him.

As we close in on the elm trees which droop over the fence marking the periphery of the property, I can't help the butterflies which flutter in my stomach. I spent so much time on this case; so much mental energy in examining all the angles. And I have so many images of the house stowed away in my subconscious that it seems almost unreal to see it materialising before my eyes.

I look to the others, wondering if they're similarly affected.

AA is beaming widely.

Amy too.

Tabby seems to be the only one who's at all twitchy.

The camera dangles about her neck on its strap. With seemingly every third step, she glances back over her shoulder, and then does a sweep of our surroundings . . . apparently expecting a police car or perhaps private security to come trundling up, demanding what it is that we're doing here.

We make an entire circuit of the property, trying to find a decent vantage point — even a hole in the fence where we might be able to take some snaps. But it seems Gonderberry has taken care with his privacy. If he didn't before the whole episode surrounding his fiancée, then he has certainly done so following it.

The circuit brings us back to the front gate; a spindling iron-embedded, hardwood affair which seems at odds with the otherwise warm façade of the mansion as I've seen it in countless photographs. Then again, a front gate isn't *supposed* to be welcoming when you possess Gonderberry's level of fame and wealth.

Gates are meant to keep the common people out.

To keep the common people's *questions* out.

"What now?" I say, deciding that someone needs to break the silence.

It seems like an almost ridiculous image; to have Amy and Tabby with cameras hanging down from their necks. And with AA just sort of standing with his hands on his hips, as if he's the director of this whole sorry expedition.

We really *do* put the amateur in 'amateur sleuth'.

AA's glance, I note, is fixed on the buzzer beside the gate; the means through which commoners are expected to communicate with the man of the house. Before I can stop him, he reaches out and presses the button, causing a distorted ringing to emerge from the speaker. There's a long pause, and then, "Hello?" comes the reply on the other end.

Even through the static — through the *distortion* — I recognise the voice.

Cuthbert Gonderberry.

It sends a shiver through my gut.

"Who's there?" he says, his voice hurried, but unalarmed.

AA casts a glance between all of us.

It's around that point when I note the camera lens at the intercom.

And I realise that AA has had the foresight to hold his palm flat over it.

When AA speaks again, it's all I can do to stop myself from laughing.

He affects the worst American accent I've ever had the misfortune of hearing.

"Heya, pal, we're tourists."

AA flashes us a glance, wiggling his eyebrows as he does so.

Perhaps he thinks he's Humphrey Bogart.

Maybe one of us should tell him — quickly — that he's very much mistaken.

But it seems too late.

"Uh," AA goes on, "we were just a wonderin' if we could come take a look around the place — y'know, we're *awful* interested in these *cosy* homes you English got."

My chest tightens.

A laugh dies at the back of my throat.

We're *done* for . . .

What seems like the longest few moments in my life plays out; static spewing from the intercom, letting us know that Gonderberry is still very much on the line.

And then the reply comes:

"Just a second."

I wonder to myself if Gonderberry is consulting with some member of his private security team. If there's one thing I've learned about exclusive homes situated in and around London, it's that they take their security *very* seriously.

And surely Gonderberry will be somewhat jumpy following his own recent past.

He no doubt wants precisely *nobody* coming sniffing around.

I draw a sigh, readying myself to hit a sprint if I absolutely have to.

I wonder if we'll be able to make it back to the car before being knocked to the ground by heavies. Or if it'll be police who arrive on the scene.

Now that we no longer have Brian Mathewson's long arm stretched around us — keeping us safe from the more *base* elements of reality — we have genuine reason to fear for our safety. And what checks into our past might reveal.

This feeling seems to be shared between all three of us if the jittery glances being passed around are anything to judge by.

I expect the subtle appearance of two large men in suits. Or for a half-crazy rant to crackle out of the intercom, decrying us, demanding that we *go away*!

However, what I'm least prepared for is the mechanical *whine* on the other side of the gate; and for the gate itself to gently wind back.

Like the others, my jaw latches open as we observe the entirety of the property stretch into view before our very eyes.

Chapter Twelve

AA gives me and the others a knowing wink.

As if he knew this would work . . .

To be honest, I'm still more than a little tentative about proceeding. I can't help but think on the cynical angle, consider whether this might just be a trap . . . if what Gonderberry most wants is for us to be caught *trespassing*. But there's no time to think this particular aspect through seeing as AA is leading us on along the path, headed on an unshakeable course for the front steps of the house. I'm rendered dazed by the whole experience. As if I have literally stepped into a living photograph. The two girls following at my heels are similarly stunned.

"Let me do the talking," AA says, dropping his faux American accent.

Thank God.

Ahead of us, everything seems to happen in slow motion. The mansion's sturdy oak doors slowly pull back to reveal a yawning blackness within.

A figure stands in the doorway.

In the hard daylight, it's almost impossible to believe my eyes.

Almost impossible to believe the image which they show me.

It's Cuthbert Gonderberry.

Today, he wears a simple, baggy white shirt. He has the buttons undone so that it exposes his carved pectoral muscles, and his flat stomach. Underneath, he wears a pair of stark, close-fitting black trousers. Nothing on his feet.

I can't help but think that he looks something like the stereo-typical thesp.

He seems almost like the Danish prince himself, lost in the modern age.

His hair is a little longer than I remember from pictures; from films. His face, too, seems an awful lot leaner.

I only realise that we've come to a halt on the pathway when he breaks into a wide smile, as if beckoning us forward, into his home, as if we have a written invitation.

Still, I can't quite shake the feeling that we might be about to fall into a trap.

If actors are good at anything then it's *acting* . . . putting on a show.

Faking it.

Of course it's AA who's first to shift off the spot, and to proceed on his way along the path, headed for the doorway, and Gonderberry standing there, ready to receive us.

The three of us have no option but to follow.

Gonderberry smiles from ear to ear and I have an extremely tough time speculating just how authentic he is being. I certainly can't detect any sign of ill-intent. But, then again, I've never been the best when it comes to judging character. I've spent a good portion of my life seeing other human beings as nothing more than lumps of meat . . . it's a way to live, I suppose.

"Hello, there!" Gonderberry says, reaching out to shake AA's hand.

His accent is ridiculously posh and projected.

It's almost as if he feels that the world truly *is* his stage . . .

I cringe internally as AA replies, "Pleased to meet you," in that turgid American accent of his. But if Gonderberry detects anything odd, he makes no outward showing.

When he turns to take us three girls in, I try to detect any sign of him judging us, working out which one he might best be able to *pluck* from the herd.

But, if he does, he does it awfully quickly.

Too quickly for me to notice.

Instead of the handshake he deals AA, he gives each of us a pair of kisses on the cheek. He doesn't linger longer than necessary. But neither is he cold. His etiquette is just right.

At least when it comes to women.

All of us thoroughly greeted, he slinks back onto his doorstep, claps his hands together, and then says, "Where're you visiting us from, then?"

AA glances back at me, as if I'm able to help him out of the hole he's gone and thoroughly entrenched us in. Somehow, it's right then that inspiration strikes me.

Or — perhaps more accurately — a hare-brained reaction.

"*Belarus*," I reply, hurriedly, attempting the same mangled American accent.

Gonderberry lifts his eyebrows, but, unlike AA, he does it in a manner which I can really believe in. He actually looks *charming* when he does it. He smiles wider too, and the smile leaks warmth into his voice. "Minsk is a wonderful city — did some filming around there. Once upon a time." He wrinkles his nose, as if searching for just the right expression — I think darkly to myself that he must be so used to having people put words into his mouth that it *really is* an effort. "A very . . . *vibrant* part of the world."

For the first time since our arrival, an uncomfortable silence settles in.

But — it seems — Gonderberry is most at home with uncomfortable silences.

"So, would you like to see the gardens? Take a stroll?"

When his eyes settle on mine, a freezing sensation seizes hold of my gut.

I do my best to conceal my discomfort before his attention shifts onto Amy.

"Actually"— his American accent has shifted into what he believes passes for Eastern-European-inflected English — "We would very much to see house. See the inside house."

Gonderberry pauses for a moment. He pouts.

And I fear the worst.

That he's discovered us.

I *knew* this was too good to be true.

However, right when I expect him to bark to some unseen *security guard* he breaks out his winning smile again. "A bit of a sticky wicket, that. Cleaner's off this week, you see?"

My chest tightens.

I resist the urge to glance over my shoulder.

I can show no outward signs of paranoia.

Finally, he holds up a finger as if having plucked the answer from the air, and says, "Just promise you won't judge an unkempt pad."

I hardly have time to catch my breath before AA has replied for all of us — a shit-eating grin smeared all over his lips.

"We shall do no judging."

Chapter Thirteen

If it was surreal to find ourselves within the grounds of Cuthbert Gonderberry's home, it's far more surreal to find ourselves within the mansion *itself*.

I take in the floor beneath my feet; the chequered, regal-red and royal-blue tiles. I'm sure my mouth is latched open as I shift my gaze upward, as I take stock of the wooden beams — the stone *pillars* — which support the interior. Then there's the large staircase which could easily fit half a dozen walking up it side by side.

As I suspected, Gonderberry's throwaway comment about his maid having the 'week off' was just that . . . the place seems spotless. A strong scent of polish cuts through the air.

When I slip Tabby and Amy — standing at my heels — a glance over my shoulder, I follow their gaze and find myself staring — like them — at the ceiling.

At the gorgeously cursive designs etched in plaster.

Then, of course, there's the chandelier.

"Please," he says, with a wide smile. "Feel free to take any photos you wish . . . goodness knows there're enough of them out there already."

By the time I'm done mentally casing the hallway, Gonderberry is already leading us towards a side passage. As he walks, he throws his hands about his head. "You would never *imagine* how much trouble it is for the upkeep of a place like this." He gives a profound sigh and his shoulders rise and fall with its force. "I suppose the Admiral never thought all that much about his children; about what would become of the joint once he finally snuffed it."

I know — from one of the countless gossip-rag interviews I read — that when Gonderberry refers to 'the Admiral' he means his father.

One of those amiable *quirks*.

He leads us through a corridor, and then into a smaller, cosier room.

Bookshelves occupy all the walls.

Each shelf is stuffed to bursting with leathered volumes.

Yellowing pages.

He gives a smirk and meets my eye for the fraction of a second. "This has always been my favourite room in the whole house — ever since I was a child, really . . . I find that things can get awfully *lonely* with one person in a home such as this. I need a place to *compartmentalise* . . . to burrow myself away."

I turn my attention to the fireplace, and to the log which is currently crackling away atop the gentle flames. It's then that I feel the warmth of the fire versus the draught biting at my heels. When I look out of the window, across the grounds, I see that the sky has turned dark; that night is already setting in.

Despite the situation — despite knowing that we all need to

have our wits about us — I can't help but feel a slight sadness pour through my veins.

There's always something about the winter which makes me sentimental.

"Tea?" Gonderberry says, still smiling widely, and staring directly at me.

I glance to AA, Amy and Tabby, as if they might be able to help out with this request.

As if I wouldn't be able to answer the question myself.

When I turn back to Gonderberry, I decide I have to keep up this idiot game which AA has started off . . . how else are we going to manage to *stay* in the house?

"Uh, yes," I reply, severely unconvinced as to my Belarusian-English accent. "That would be *good*."

Gonderberry presses his hands together then grins at each and every one of us in turn. "In that case, I shall be right back." As he turns on his heel, he waggles his finger in a matronly way, and adds, "Don't go running off, now, will you?"

"Oh, no!" AA replies.

Gonderberry soon slips from the room, apparently off to go and make the tea.

Not one of us speaks until Gonderberry's footsteps have completely faded away into the distance. Now that we've set up this story of us being dewy-eyed tourists, it brings on new complications. Such as the one which supposes that we should speak among ourselves in our *native* language . . . not in accented English, like in Hollywood.

Apparently feeling that we're in the clear, Tabby speaks up, though keeping her voice to a husky whisper. "He's so *charming*," she says.

There's a murmur of agreement from AA and Amy.

I reserve judgement for the time being.

I know that I've never been a natural when it comes to giving an opinion on character and I want to have time to make up my mind.

To be quite honest, I'm still not completely convinced as to whether the offer of tea was a genuine gesture or an opportunity to sneak away and consult with some member of his security team. One thing is for certain, we have fallen into Gonderberry's trap this time; he has us enclosed in a small room of his own home.

Maybe the next noise we'll hear is the *whine* of police car sirens.

I cast off that unpleasant thought, turning my mind back to the present.

I take in the room again; able to do so with a touch less pressure now that I don't have to contend with Gonderberry breathing down my neck . . . keeping a firm eye on each and every one of his *visitors* . . . checking that they are indeed having a 'jolly good' time.

It's then that my focus falls onto a rococo-style side table.

On the surface, I make out what looks like a bound manuscript.

Seeing that the others are all occupied absorbing the details of the room — of this *library* — I tread towards the table. Then I glance down on the manuscript.

On a whim, I cast a quick look about the room and see no obvious surveillance equipment — no obvious CCTV camera.

I pick up the manuscript.

It has been folded back to about three-quarters through.

I read over the lines of dialogue, instantly recognising the form of the text as corresponding to some sort of a play. I look over the names:

OCTAVIUS CAESAR
MAECENAS
MARK ANTONY
DOMITIUS ENOBARBUS
CLEOPATRA

Something twigs in the back of my brain.
Something *familiar*.

I glance about, see that the others are occupied with their own observations — that Tabby and Amy are taking snapshots of various things.

I flip through the manuscript pages; arriving to the title page. I skim the hastily — *yet elegantly* — scrawled title and author:

Antony and Cleopatra by William Shakespeare

And then — just below:

AUBURN THEATRE

I give a pout, and a whole bunch of unpleasant memories return to me; mostly involving under-heated classrooms and *unending* class-readings of the Bard's work. Going through *A Midsummer Night's Dream* for the eighth time, purging every last simile and metaphor from the bone-dry text; trying to cobble together something intelligible to say . . . or, in my case, something *unintelligible*.

Wondering if time might have had some effect on my ability

for concentrating on Shakespeare, I turn to the first page. And I flip my way through the beginnings of the play, savouring the warmth from the fireplace, and, on some level, able to delight in my surroundings.

The *tinkle* of porcelain brings me back to reality.

My heart skips a beat.

I look up.

Gonderberry stares back at me.

Those sea-green, sky-blue irises — what colour *are* his eyes? — glisten.

He bears a tray which he lays down on a coffee table just in front of the fire.

Before I get a chance to explain myself, he nods to the manuscript I hold in my hands. He gives a wry smile. "You know native English speakers have as much trouble as anyone else in truly understanding the depths of Shakespeare."

Dumbstruck, I make a vague sound at the back of my throat.

Finally a very British, ". . . Sorry," makes its way out past my lips.

Gonderberry makes no comment on my apology. He pours the tea into cups. As he does so, I have a chance to fully absorb the eggshell-blue designs which sprawl over the sides of the teapot and cups. I faintly wonder to myself just how many *centuries* old this crockery might be. If this was anyone else — if I'd found myself in any other situation — I'm fairly certain I'd have taken such a display as an obvious sign of showing-off . . . as it is, though, I'm beginning to get the feeling Gonderberry is just as genuine as he comes across.

And I wonder if this is going to be a simple job after all.

If it's not going to be the complicated — not to mention *dangerous* — matter we'd all pinned it as being.

I surreptitiously lay the manuscript back down on the table after what seems like a polite period of time. I take my tea from Gonderberry. When he hands over my cup, I can't help but glance up, thinking about sugar . . .

Seeing none, I decide to take the plunge, having a sip.

And I can see why sugar is not necessary.

The flavour is faintly fruity — something between elderberries and strawberries — and the milk seems to add body to it.

When I glance up, I see Gonderberry holding his own cup in its saucer; clearly wanting to see how his guests fare with the brew he's concocted before drinking himself.

Again, our eyes meet for a brief moment.

This time I break off eye contact.

And, feeling awkward, I decide to make conversation.

"Are you" — after the first two syllables I catch myself; remind myself that I should be speaking with an affected accent — "I wish to say," I continue, "you plan to have a play? To make a show?"

I catch Gonderberry's single narrowed eye but by the time I've blinked his expression has shifted. And he's smiling all over again. He sets his teacup in its saucer and then places it down on the coffee table. He draws in a deep breath, as if this reply will require special effort, and he says, "It's all very much up in the air at the moment. There has been an issue with the production; one of the actors is having health issues." He cocks his head to one side, then shifts a glance off at AA, Amy and Tabby — all of them listening attentively to Gonderberry. "But," he continues, drawing out the word as he turns back to me, "if it does happen to come off then you would be my special guests." He gives a wide smile, exposing all his healthy, *strong* teeth. His rosy-red gums. "It would be my *pleasure*."

My heart goes *thump-thump* in my throat.

I feel a sudden chill pass over my skin.

I try to tell myself that it's because of the draught sneaking into the otherwise baking-hot room . . . but, in truth, I know the real reason.

That Gonderberry intimidates me.

And I'm not sure *why* . . .

I'm not certain if AA detects my discomfort, but he draws Gonderberry's attention away from me and onto himself. "We were wondering," AA says, "we have read some stories — *stories* about some of the . . . uh . . . animals, the . . . uh . . ."

"*Pets?*" Gonderberry suggests, smiling wryly.

AA beams back, setting his teacup and saucer down on the coffee table. "Yes."

Gonderberry casts his glance over all four of us — and I can easily imagine him standing in the middle of the stage, taking in the entirety of the audience with that stare. It's electrifying. It feels as if he's peering into our soul — peering into *all* of our souls.

"And you would like to see?" Gonderberry asks.

"Oh yes," AA replies. "*Very* much."

Chapter Fourteen

W e head down a spiral staircase, leaving the cosy, warm air of the library behind us.

At the bottom of the stairs, the plaster walls give way to stonework.

The air becomes decidedly chilly and I can't help wondering just *how cold* it must get down here in the middle of the night.

Leading us along the passageway, Gonderberry points to a doorway then mutters, "The wine cellar." As we pass by it, I take a quick glance. All things considered, it's just as I expected; an assortment of wine bottles all neatly slotted into wooden racks.

He pauses before continuing on along the passageway, then he turns to address Amy and Tabby with a rather grim expression. "I will ask you *not* to use any flash photography beyond this point." He keeps up the same expression for another second before it cracks about the edges. His easy smile returns. "Sudden bright lights might *startle* the creatures."

I slip Amy and Tabby a glance, and they each give me a shrug.

We head onwards — following Gonderberry along the passageway.

I get a strange, otherworldly feeling when the air turns turgid.

A twitch which begins in my gut and moves steadily up through my body.

The air smells just like I *thought* it would.

Just like any of the reptile enclosures I've visited at a zoo.

There's the gentle *buzz* of high-intensity heat lamps.

The devices which keep the creatures charged up.

Gonderberry leads us through the doorway, and into the sparse, subterranean room.

When I arrive on his heels, I take it in for myself.

The enclosures.

Beyond the glass, I take in the sawn-off logs; and the — *I suppose, given the lack of sunlight down here* — fake greenery.

Skitters pass across my skin.

And my eyes — almost unconsciously — go searching for the creepy-crawlies.

I've never thought of myself as being squeamish but I guess most of us — deep down — have a fear of the *different*; and especially, at least in my case, the *cold-blooded*.

I look to Tabby, then to Amy, and finally settle on AA.

The all wear something like hypnotised expressions.

Each one of them fascinated by whatever it is that's coming next.

By what Gonderberry will *do* next.

The first enclosure Gonderberry brings us to has a pool of water at its centre.

Actually, it seems more like a *pond* than a pool.

Something about the sight makes me want to say that it's *lovingly* arranged . . . that Gonderberry — who surely *was* the designer — spent a great deal of research and development time in getting the habitat *just right*.

And that sends a fresh shudder through my ribcage.

"*Laticauda colubrina*," Gonderberry says, and then — for the zoologically challenged among us; and I'm most certainly one of them — "Colubrine sea krait. A *sea* snake."

Tabby, the only one among us who looks genuinely eager to get an eyeful of the specimen beyond the glass, leans into the enclosure, squinting to better make out the interior. She brings her camera up and takes a picture.

Gonderberry, too, bends into the enclosure, getting a closer look.

I take a sharp breath then decide I'm not going to be able to put it off any longer.

Within, sure enough, I make out the snake.

It lies at the bottom of the clear pool.

A zebra-like design adorning its body.

For some reason I get it into my head that it looks pensive . . . as if it's looking us over and wondering which one it should bite first.

"Can you see its yellow lip?" Gonderberry asks.

I wonder if this is a good opportunity to reinforce the foreign-tourist routine. "Its . . . 'lip' ?" I repeat.

Gonderberry smiles paternally then indicates with his index finger — pointing to his upper lip. "Just here," he says, then points down at the snake again.

Although I have no intention of getting any closer than I already am, I can certainly make out the yellow lip . . .

Perhaps the snake has those famed hypnotic abilities, because

I only realise the others have moved onto the next enclosure several moments later.

I come up behind them, and I take note of how Tabby is still standing the closest of all of us to the latest enclosure. Maybe she *wants* the snake to bite her . . .

Gonderberry stands with his back to the enclosure. "This here is a *very* special species of mine; an Egyptian cobra."

His eyes travel across us all. And then, suddenly, with a rapid jerky movement of his hand, he prods the glass.

The snake — the Egyptian cobra's — hood pops back. It leaps up forming an S-shape, bearing its fangs. It hisses so violently that we can hear it even through the — *hopefully* — reinforced glass.

"See those beautiful markings," Gonderberry says, casually tracing the glass with his finger to illustrate the thick blue-grey stripes which wrap around its body. "Those are the *bands*. This particular specimen is known as an Egyptian *banded* cobra."

"Venomous?" AA puts in, with a decidedly *English* twist to his voice.

When I glance to Gonderberry, I wonder if AA's gone and put his foot in it, but Gonderberry seems so swept up in his snakes that he doesn't currently have the capacity to register such details.

"Oh yes," Gonderberry replies, staring at the snake. "*Very*."

I glance back over my shoulder, to the first snake we saw.

Before I get a chance to ask the question, Amy gets it out.

"And that one?" Amy asks. "The sea snake?"

Gonderberry smiles wider still. "Very much so . . . in the wild, of course." He remains that way — looking quite manic — for several seconds. In the end, though, he can no longer constrain himself and he gives a hearty chuckle. "These ones have their venom glands removed."

This time it's Tabby who turns to Gonderberry with a wide-eyed expression. "*Not* venomous?"

"No," Gonderberry replies with a slight laugh in his voice.

He seems to lose himself in the moment for a long while, then — *slowly* — he slips back to consciousness. Back to the present moment.

When he paces forward, showing off more of his collection, I can't help but fix my attention on the enclosure across the room. The one which is covered by a black cloth.

I say nothing but when Gonderberry gets through with showing off another half dozen or so — *very venomous* — snakes, Tabby decides to take the initiative.

"What's that?" she asks. "Over there?"

Gonderberry pouts, stretching all his neck muscles as he does so. " 'Over there' ?" he repeats, with a strangely distant quality to his voice. He looks across all of us and in the moment I'm quite sure that just about anything could happen.

That he might be ready to call us out for the pretenders we are.

What is it they say about it 'taking one to know one' ?

Finally, Gonderberry throws up his hand as if to dismiss the question. "It's a . . . ah . . . *long* story," he replies. Then he gives a wincing smile. "Why don't I show you all some antiquities? There's *so much* to this house and I've no doubt been boring you with my little hobby." He spreads his arms wide as if greeting a great friend following a long absence. "You can see snakes *anywhere* . . . even in Belarus, I'd imagine."

And, with that, he ushers us out.

With the same glimmer in his eye which seems to have been

present the entire time, he shows us about his house with great gusto. He takes time to explain all the various intricacies of the medieval weaponry found in one of the upper rooms, and he tells us all about his ancestry; that a great deal of the equipment belonged to either his ancestors or to the ones who they vanquished. He allows Tabby and Amy to take all manner of photos of the various 'antiquities' and then offers to take a group-photo of all four of us . . .

When AA asks for Gonderberry himself to stand with the girls for a photo, he blushes profoundly and mutters some apology about 'the light not being quite right' . . . but none of us push him, of course. Not one of us has let on yet that we know just who he is, after all.

By the end of the tour, I can't help feeling just a little guilty about the deception we've spun. From everything I've taken in from Gonderberry so far, he seems genuine and *enthusiastic* . . . if not a touch lonely. It's not every superstar actor who would be pleased to show uninvited foreign visitors around his home.

I begin to suspect the person who sent the letter.

Could it have been some scorned lover?

Someone with an axe to grind?

After what has been three or four hours — and with darkness now having fully set in — Gonderberry leads us back to the front hall. Already, I find myself becoming depressed just thinking about the cold weather awaiting us outside . . . the short, but chilly, walk to where the car's parked. Right as we're on the point of leaving, and with Gonderberry gushing with thanks for us 'stopping by', he reaches out and takes hold of AA's elbow.

It stops everything dead.

Brings a silence crashing down upon us.

My heart hangs in my throat.

And my pulse hammers my temples.

"Tell me," Gonderberry says, smiling as he has throughout our visit, but now with more than a small bite to it. "I'm curious . . . I was thinking about my visit to Belarus." He rolls his eyes up in their sockets as if physically searching his brain. "Trying to *pin down* the year." He meets AA's gaze, then says, "I do recall that it was just after Belarus had declared independence . . . which year was that?"

Every muscle in my body seizes tight.

My brain freezes.

When I switch a quick glance about the others — about Tabby and Amy — I see that they, too, have been caught unawares by this question.

The tension in the air could be cut with a knife.

And then all our eyes fall on AA.

Some bitter voice at the back of my head tells me that it's his mess.

He'd better clear it up.

AA swallows hard — we all witness his Adam's apple bobbing in his throat.

I note how Gonderberry's grip on AA's elbow seems to strengthen.

Suddenly I realise that Gonderberry has quite powerful forearms.

And I catch a quick glimpse in my mind's eye of him shirtless in some forgettable film, or other. I suppose, like all superstar actors, he has a demonic personal trainer; someone to make sure his body stays in the very best condition.

Would he be able to take AA in a fight?

AA licks his lips. He casts a quick glance over us, as if one of us is about to help out — as if one of us has had the opportunity to tap the required details into a search on one of our phones to bring up the answer. He switches his attention back onto Gonderberry and I hope against hope that he's not going to fuck up.

"Nineteen ninety," AA responds, somehow remembering to put on that mock . . . whatever-accent-it's-supposed-to-be.

We all turn to Gonderberry, waiting to see whether this is going to be the end of the road . . . perhaps even legal charges; if charges for this sort of thing even exist.

Gonderberry stares hard at AA now. "That's funny," he replies. "I could *swear* I was in Minsk in nineteen ninety-one." He gives a wicked smile. "In fact, I was digging through my old passports. I'm *certain* the date stamped there was nineteen ninety-one."

My whole body goes rigid.

And my heart just *stops*.

I snap my head up to look over the other two.

Tabby and Amy look just as taken aback as me.

As I thought, this was all just an act . . . maybe even Gonderberry's best performance yet.

AA opens his mouth again, and I wish that he'd just shut his *trap*. "I believe you are mistaken," AA says, somehow managing to remain calm and collected despite Gonderberry's firm hold on his arm. "The independence was made, how you say — "

" 'Declared' ?" Gonderberry suggests, with a flaming expression.

AA brings out another smile. "Yes, yes. It was *dee-clare-ed* in nineteen ninety . . . but it was no official until the following year . . . until the nineteen ninety-one."

We plunge into another chilly silence.

Gonderberry holds himself very still, and then, without any sort of warning, he releases his hold on AA, allowing him free.

His complexion is *ashen*. He doesn't seem angry any longer. He seems more . . . *afraid* . . .

His eyes whip between us. "Who are you? Who *are* you people? Journalists?"

AA shakes his head. "No," he says, keeping up the same faux accent, as if our game hasn't already been rumbled. "We are not journalists."

Gonderberry says nothing at all.

I can tell now that he's trembling.

That beneath the baggy white shirt he wears — and the well-sculpted pectoral muscles I just can't help noticing — he is unable to keep himself still.

I try to tell myself that it's from the night-time breeze, but, in reality, it feels as if this encounter has crossed the line. That after the initial high-jinks this has turned decidedly serious. Now it feels like we've trodden where we shouldn't have.

That we've raked up *trauma* that should've been left alone.

I act on instinct. "Mister Gonderberry," I say, speaking with my standard-issue Londoner's accent. "We're really sorry about this. About coming here. It was a *stupid* trick . . . a stupid act. *Deception*."

When Gonderberry shifts his attention onto me, it seems almost as if his eyes are lost to a fog; as if he's looking out through thick mists. He makes a distant sound at the back of his throat — something like a groan.

I look to the others. "Come on. It's time we left."

The others are apparently in such shock about what I've dared to do that they obey.

With Gonderberry seemingly present but *not* present, he watches us out through the door. Several lights have blinked on to illuminate the pathway. Darkness shrouds the surrounding gardens. When we reach the gate, I glance back over my shoulder.

I see Gonderberry standing there, still absorbed by us . . . and yet — *seemingly* — not seeing us at all. When we are finally out on the road beyond the mansion, I allow myself to draw a deep, cleansing breath.

"Well, that's enough of that," I say, mostly to myself.

Chapter Fifteen

The *whumpf* of a pillow to my forehead brings me around.

Morning sun streams down through the skylight.

I have just about enough time to blink before I'm struck with the next blow.

When Mark readies to strike me a third time, I'm prepared.

I wait till he brings the pillow down then grab hold of it, wrestling it from his grip before he can snap it back and take aim once more.

I'm surprisingly strong when I want to be.

Grinning maniacally, I grab hold of Mark.

He wears only a pair of boxer shorts.

His *ripped* chest open to the air.

Time for me to take full advantage of those famous carpenter's hands . . .

The two of us lie back in bed.

A layer of sweat clings to my skin.

My chest rises and falls as I try — *mostly in vain* — to get my breath back.

I peer up and out through the skylight, to the clear-blue skies.

There aren't many things that feel *cleaner* than a bright winter's morning.

"Well," Mark says, the bedsheet draped over his waist the only thing preventing him from being stark naked, "I guess that's *one* benefit of Nathan's Saturday-morning training."

To be quite honest, this little bed-ritual has become something of a routine ever since Nathan got himself pushed up to the 'A' selection of his school football team; ever since he has had extra training sessions. Being, like Ben, fifteen years old, he's easily mature enough to trudge his way off to the park just around the corner where training takes place.

Me and Mark remain lying beside one another — neither of us saying anything — for another few minutes.

In the end, my mobile breaks the silence.

It gives a *rumble*.

On instinct, I glance over to where it lies on the bedside table.

A notification shows up on the screen.

That 'AA' application which Amy installed.

When I look over to Mark, I catch him staring at my mobile as if it was some kind of ticking bomb. He meets my eye, gives a roguish smile, then shifts out from beneath the bedsheet. "Guess I'll get myself showered. No good lying about in bed all day."

I can't help but track his progress across the bedroom, becoming somewhat hypnotised by his muscular buttocks as he heads for the en suite bathroom. As he brings the door shut behind him, he gives me a wink.

I wait till the water begins flowing before I flip through the screens, tapping the 'AA' icon to bring up the messenger application. I've always been suspicious about having a device with both video and audio recording capabilities *just lying around* . . . and I certainly have more to hide than most girls; more than simple decency.

There's a new message from Amy, who seems to be the chattiest of all of us on this encrypted messaging service. Then again, since the technology is her own, she most likely has more reason to trust in it . . . to trust in its confidentiality.

As for me, I've never felt all that comfortable about recording any sort of communication; anything which can be held up and used as evidence later.

But, according to Amy, these messages will simply *disappear* . .
.

It's a group message.

Amy wants to pin down a meeting date.

A time for the four of us to discuss the latest developments.

The latest developments with *Cuthbert Gonderberry*.

It's been a week since we went to his house, since we put on that idiot show pretending to be Belarussian tourists. Even thinking about it makes me wince.

There're few things I'm ashamed of — *all right, perhaps* more *than a few* — but that encounter with Cuthbert Gonderberry is certainly one of them. What I most disliked about the encounter was the dishonesty; the *deception*.

It's weird that I've never felt this bad after a hit.

I've always been able to compartmentalise . . . to somehow tell myself that whoever was my target had it coming. Now, though, this just feels as though we were tormenting some fragile, exposed human being who only wanted to show kindness towards strangers.

To show them his *home*.

And we took full advantage.

The more I think of it, this whole sleuthing thing — whatever it is that AA wants to set up with the four of us — just doesn't seem to be for me.

Perhaps I should return to the whole ordeal of bundling CVs off here and there; waiting to see what will happen.

Maybe that'll give some direction to my aimless life.

Downstairs, I hear the *crunch* of a key in the front door.

My whole body goes rigid beneath the bedsheet.

Gut instinct beats logical thoughts.

I know Nathan shouldn't be home until midday.

And — glancing to my mobile screen — I see it's hardly gone ten.

Suddenly frantic, I look about, discover the baggy t-shirt I was wearing the night before, discarded in an untidy bundle in the corner of the room. I slip out from beneath the bedsheet and pick my way across the carpet. I yank it on over my head. As I pass by the full-length mirror, I catch a quick glance at the beige colour, at the design on the front which declares: *Bydersbrudge Ceramics Factory*. This is one of Mark's t-shirts, of course. One which he's leant me for sleeping purposes. I locate a pair of jeans hanging off the back of a chair and quickly thrust them on.

Feeling as if I'm less exposed — and with the water of Mark's shower still flowing — I sit on the edge of the bed and stare at the door, listening for the *creak* of each step as Nathan climbs the staircase. It's strange, although Mark makes me feel *more* than at home in his house, I can't help but feel sometimes that I'm an intruder . . . as if there's something inextricably *foreign* about my presence here.

This is Mark and Nathan's home above all else.

And they already have their engrained routines.

Their particular *things*.

And one of those *things* is that Nathan appears to have no issue with *not* knocking on his father's bedroom door. From my observations, I've been able to cobble together a mental rule-book. It goes along the lines that between the hours of seven a.m. and ten o'clock at night, Nathan is perfectly within his rights to walk right into his adoptive father's bedroom. Needless to say, ten a.m. on Saturday morning is fair game.

I continue to concentrate on the bedroom door, hoping that Nathan will just *keep on walking*; that he will make his way directly to his own bedroom.

The landing floorboards creak just outside the door.

I imagine him there, thinking over whether or not he should knock on his father's bedroom door. I will him to *carry on* . . . but, if there's anything I've learned from 'willing', it's that, more often than not, it serves very little purpose in reality.

And so proves the case right now.

I watch in horror as the doorknob turns. As the door opens.

Nathan stands there, in his football kit. His boot bag hangs down at his thigh.

The shirt is a washed-out red. The shorts are an inky blue-black.

He wears the socks scrunched down around his ankles, exposing his bare and — I realise belatedly — *bloody* shins.

Feeling the frown lines etch themselves in my forehead, I take in Nathan's look of complete surprise. "Oh, uh, I didn't think . . .

I thought you were . . . uh, your coat . . . I didn't see your *coat*. I didn't know . . . realise . . ."

"You're home early," I say, unable to think of anything else.

"Uh, yeah," Nathan replies, with a slight jabbering quality, as if this whole episode is unfolding in a dream. "I . . . uh." He glances down to his shins as if this explains everything.

I manage to raise a smile. "Come on. Let's go get you cleaned up."

Nathan hesitates, lingering in the doorway. He casts a glance off to the en suite, as if Mark might impulsively flip off the shower and come out to see what the matter is.

Finally, Nathan looks back and gives me something resembling a smile. "Okay."

———

Once I've wrung my first-aid knowledge thoroughly dry — and not feeling all too badly about how I've done in applying iodine to Nathan's gashes — I watch the kettle come to the boil.

Outside, I see that the sky has turned grey, and that a fog is beginning to settle in.

Almost midday and I haven't made it out of the house yet.

Talk about *laid back*.

As I set about pouring out the cups of tea, breathing in the warm, wafting, *sweet* scent, I shift a glance over Nathan, to where he sits at the kitchen table. "Milk?" I ask.

"Okay," he replies with a slight smile.

I do as he wishes.

Then I bring the cups of tea over to the table.

Upstairs, I hear the shower click off.

Like always, Mark uses approximately ten times more force than is necessary to slide the shower door open and bring it shut. I glance over the lip of my mug at Nathan and the two of us share a smile at this silent joint observation. "So," I say, after we've been quietly supping at our tea for several moments, "just a bad tackle?"

Nathan blinks a couple of times, gives an unconvincing smile, then nods.

I think hard.

Think about that black eye Nathan came home with a few weeks ago.

If I choose to say something then it will mark a turning point in our relationship; surely it will see us treading fresh ground in terms of what is or isn't on the table for discussion. A level of frankness which has, thus far, evaded us.

Upstairs, the two of us seem to be tracing Mark's movements across the bedroom floor. He treads heavily — like always — and he whistles as he goes about setting his clothes out for the day ahead. This time I don't feel like smiling, though. Decided, I glance up from my half-finished cup of tea. "Have you spoken to your dad about it?"

"About what?"

"Don't play stupid, Nathan."

I note the bite to my tone . . . and I can't help wondering just where I get off speaking to Nathan like this. But, then again, for me to be bringing up this topic at all, don't I need to strike some sort of a parental tone?

Nathan retreats into himself; his eyes seeming almost to sink back into their sockets. His shoulders wilt. When he speaks again, he bows his head to address his mug of tea. "Yes," he says. "He knows about it."

'Bullying' is a situation I've never been aware of . . . well, one which I've never had *personal* experience of; either as the 'bully' or the 'bullied'.

So I feel a long way outside my comfort zone.

I drop my voice to a lower tone, although the chances of Mark being able to overhear our conversation from where he is up in the bedroom is remote at best . . . especially with all that out-of-tune whistling he is doing.

"What has he *done* about it?" I say.

Nathan shrugs. "He said it's up to me . . . that — if I like — we can keep it a secret, between the two of us." Nathan finally glances up. "He says there's no reason the school needs to know about it; no reason to make the issue *worse*."

I think about this.

All things considered, this seems to be a remarkably aware approach from Mark.

Nathan will only be attending school for the next year . . . then he will cut free and go onto sixth form college. He will get his preparations underway for university. However, it's the sort of *watchful inactivity* which I've never been able to quite wrap my head around.

There *always* seems as though there's something more that can be done.

Why must we put up with the present for some — *theoretically* — better future?

But this isn't me we're talking about.

This is *Nathan*.

"And are you happy about that?" I ask. "Are you happy to *put up* with it?"

Nathan continues to stare into his cup of tea. He gives a hard sigh, his shoulders rocking back, and then he glances up. "I guess."

His tone *sounds* just as unconvincing as the answer itself.

I hear footsteps on the landing above.

Mark leaving the bedroom.

And mine and Nathan's conversation coming to an end.

I get up from the table. "Let me know if there's anything I can help with, okay?"

When I turn my back to him, set about rinsing my mug out in the sink, I hear him reply, in a downbeat, defeated voice, "Okay."

Chapter Sixteen

I t's eleven o'clock at night — in the middle of the week — when I turn up back in Brent Cross. When I pad my way along the streets which have quickly become familiar. I trace my footsteps to the building which houses Sex Flat.

The others are already there when I arrive.

Tabby. Amy. AA.

We all arranged the meetup through Amy's app.

It seems to have worked out . . . at least to the extent that a battalion of police hasn't yet shown up to intercept us. But, then again, I don't suppose we've done anything technically illegal just yet; our criminal impersonation of Belarussian tourists aside . . .

As soon as I cross the threshold, I have the opportunity to sample the atmosphere; to sense the slightly serious mood. I know there's been some development.

Something which has the potential to *change everything*.

"So," I say, deciding that it comes down to me — *as the latest arrival* — to thaw the frostiness, "what's the big news?"

Amy takes it upon herself to respond. "Our client got in touch through the app — we now have a direct line of communication with her." She gives a slightly smug grin. "We have a way of communicating which is just a touch quicker than snail mail."

So it's a 'she', I think to myself, as if that means anything at all.

"And?" I reply, deciding to cut through Amy's self-satisfaction.

"We filled her in on the visit — about us managing to get into Gonderberry's mansion."

"Was she surprised?"

Amy pouts. "No, not really — she claims he's always been outgoing; friendly to an almost insane degree. She implied that that's how he's managed to get so far in show business. In an industry where there're so many egos; so many prima donnas, I suppose that someone with a human touch is highly valued."

I wait a beat, glancing over AA and Tabby, seeing if they've got anything to offer. Assuming they don't, I say, "Any idea *who* our client is? Has *she* given anything away?"

Amy shakes her head. "Nothing that I've been able to fathom."

I give a sigh then peer out of the window.

A single ray of winter sun licks the scene below.

Down on the street, I see that there's a pair of men of Middle-Eastern appearance. Both of them are bundled up in Army-surplus overcoats; zippered all the way up to their throats. As they rub their hands together and jog from one foot to the other, they beckon the passing people to stop by. When a woman of about sixty does, one of the men unfolds his fist to reveal a pair of dice lying on his gloved palm. He mutters something by way of explanation, and I watch as she hands over a twenty-pound note. Still jogging from one foot to the other, the man shakes the die, then tosses it down onto the pavement. Hypnotised, I watch as the plastic die bounces a couple of times, finding equilibrium. The man and woman stoop over, taking in the number displayed on its side.

With a wry grin, the man digs into his pocket and produces five twenty-pound notes — *one hundred pounds*. He hands it over to the woman with a nonchalant shrug which makes me almost certain that the notes must be forged.

However, the old woman isn't just any old mark. She takes the best part of a minute to inspect the notes, before, with a wide smile, she nods to the man and wishes him a good day. She picks up the pair of canvas bags — filled with shopping — and continues along the pavement; apparently headed home.

And — *apparently* — eighty pounds richer.

"Anna?" AA says. "*Earth* to Anna?"

I glance up.

Realise the three of them are staring at me.

"Sorry," I reply, "I was miles away."

"*Obviously.*" AA gives me a reprimanding look. "We were discussing our next *move.*"

I cast a final glance down at the Middle-Eastern men, and then put them out of mind. I look over the others. "I . . . I've been doing a lot of thinking over the past week. About this whole situation — this whole *job.*"

"And?" AA says, his expression creased-up, apparently sensing what I'm about to say.

I meet their concerned expressions.

All *three* of them.

"Well," I begin, "I feel kind of . . . I don't know . . . *bad* about it?"

There's a definite pause as the whole room reflects on this observation.

And then they break out in laughter.

Although I feel something like fury burrowing in my gut, I force myself to press on a smile, waiting for them to gather themselves together.

With tears in his eyes, AA raises his head. "So, let me get this straight . . . you used to be a hired killer — you used to kill *without* a thought . . . and now you've gone and got your knickers in a twist over playing a simple little deception on someone who — as far as we can tell — could easily be a murder suspect?"

I hardly need AA to point out the irony.

I've turned everything over in my mind constantly . . . or so it seems.

Tabby speaks next. "If it makes you feel any better, Anna, I don't think that we did much to fool him — and you certainly did your best to own up to what we'd done."

I think about how my conscience wouldn't allow me to leave his house without owning up to the truth. And I think about how that *same* conscience has led me to this point; to wanting to back out of this job altogether. That same conscience which — *somehow* — reasoned that killing for money was no big deal. That it was just like any career . . . can I really trust my conscience?

"Then it's over," I say. "I laid it all out for him — our cover's blown."

Already, AA is holding up his hand. "Not so fast."

I draw a breath and feel myself beginning to shake. It's not because I'm *afraid* of pulling out of this job . . . it's that I don't think I'll be able to live without it.

For better or worse, these few weeks have given my life some sort of meaning.

Some sort of direction.

To back out now would be akin to pulling the rug out from beneath my own feet.

AA continues, "I *believe* that this has only served to give us another opportunity — a *fresh* chance."

"And how's that?" I reply, unable to keep the sarcasm out of my tone.

AA shrugs. "It gives us a chance to apologise; to come *clean*."

I turn back to the window, look down into the street.

The Middle-Eastern men have gone.

Upon closer inspection, I can see the reason why.

A pair of policemen — dressed in smart navy-blue uniforms — plod along chatting absent-mindedly.

Still staring down into the street, I say, "I want to know who our client is . . . I don't want any more of this mystery. It makes me feel . . . *uncomfortable*."

A long silence lingers in Sex Flat.

Then — to my surprise — AA says, "Okay. We'll work on it."

As I watch the police tread out of view, I wonder if I'll soon have cause to fear them too.

Chapter Seventeen

R ich, thick smells of chocolate rise in Mark's kitchen.
I stir the gorgeous, thick sauce with a wooden spatula.
And I resist the temptation to lick the melted chocolate.

I remind myself that we're doing this for a purpose.

That we're baking a chocolate cake.

The result will be worth all this patience; all this *force of will*.

In the background, I'm somehow aware of my phone buzzing. I never bother to activate the tone since the vibration feature is loud enough. I glance to Mark — apron fixed about his waist — and I excuse myself, leaving the chocolate behind for the time being.

When I get up to the bedroom, I glance to the screen, half expecting to see a notification from Amy's app . . . that Assassins Anonymous has a new report; perhaps AA has come through for me and revealed the identity of our client.

However, I soon see that it's a missed call.

Seven missed calls, to be exact.

No sooner have I glanced down the list, and absorbed the seven-times repeated unknown number, when the phone begins to vibrate again. I stare in a kind of shock, seeing that this is the eighth time this particular number has called me.

I catch hold of myself.

Then answer.

"Hello?"

"Mrs Harris?"

"*Miss* Harris," I correct the speaker — *a male* — without thinking.

"This is Constable Ashton of The Metropolitan Police."

My heart bounces up to my throat.

Nausea grips my stomach.

All of a sudden, I lose that sickly sweet taste of chocolate in my mouth.

It's replaced by something bitter . . . *deeply unpleasant.*

Somehow I regain my composure.

"Yes," I reply.

"It's about your son, Miss Harris," he says. "Benjamin Hammond?"

I think quickly, trying to get my head around this. "I'm sorry . . . I don't understand."

The man — *Constable Ashton* — clears his throat.

I get the impression that I've said exactly what *every* parent says upon having a police officer announce their child over the phone.

Well, I've never been anything if not predictable . . .

"This evening we brought your son into the station for shop-lifting."

" 'Shop-lifting' ?" I echo, continuing my ditsy streak.

"Yes, Miss Harris." His voice begins to sound a touch weary.

"The owner has decided against pressing charges so we have decided to release Ben with an official warning. We need you to come by the station to pick him up."

I snap back to reality.

Get my head around what's going on . . . at least in a pragmatic sense.

The constable gives me the address, and I make a note of it.

With a quick apology to a bemused Mark, I slip out of the house, catching the Tube.

Somehow I've managed to make it through life this far without spending too much time in police stations, or prisons, for that matter. But, to be honest, the police station is everything I might've expected.

Too-bright strip lighting.

Shining floors stinking of polish.

Scuff marks all over the walls; chunks taken out of other places . . . all of those subtle signs of struggle; of suspects resisting arrest.

The young male officer on the desk gives me a form to fill out.

When I've done so, I'm escorted by a female officer through a labyrinth of nondescript hallways. I note the tiny tinted windows which peer into the lockup cells and my heart sinks as the truth hits me . . . that I'm *here* to pick up my *son* . . .

The officer pauses at the cell, fishes through her set of keys, then opens up. When I peer inside, it takes several seconds for my eyes to grow accustomed to the gloom. I'm of half a mind to complain about the lack of lighting before some sense hits me, reminding me that these sorts of places aren't supposed to be pleasant.

The room is sparse, only a concrete bunk built up out of the floor with a thin mattress on top. There's a stainless-steel seatless toilet.

Ben sits on the edge of the bunk hunched over, head in his hands, tufts of hair sticking through the gaps between his fingers. He remains totally still, as if he hasn't heard the door open.

"Ben?" I say, my voice sounding dry, and quivering slightly.

He doesn't move.

"*Ben?*" I repeat.

Finally, he brings his hands down; away from his face.

I expect him to be crying . . . to be covering his tears so that I don't see.

But he's not.

Dark circles hang down from his eyes, and he has a distant look about him, but other than that he seems unmoved by the experience. *Worse,* I can't help thinking, *he looks as if this is all just some routine procedure.*

"Come on. They say you can go now."

Ben glances to me, and then to the officer. He gets up slowly, as if he's in no hurry at all. Perhaps he wants to put off the world of pain he is about to enter . . . the inevitable consequences which are going to follow this 'experience'.

I repress the urge to say or do anything when he slips out past me, through the doorway. I know that I need to remain in control; that I *can't* lose my temper.

As we pad along the corridor — out of the lock up, the police officer on our heels — I sneak a glance into one of the windows of the holding cells, see a familiar face within.

Josh.

That *boy* who came to the cinema with Ben.

I only realise that I've stopped to look when the officer speaks up. "Madam?" she says. "Is something wrong?"

"No," I reply, and head on out of the station.

————

Once we're outside, in the cold winter air, I realise that Ben only wears a t-shirt and jeans. He pulls on a black beanie hat which the officer returned to him on leaving the police station. Hiding his hair, he looks far more like a thug than ever. I resist the urge to tell him to take it off.

We begin the walk to the nearby Tube station, and I remain at a loss as to what I should say. But, as I see the Underground sign approaching, I realise that I have to say *something*. "What did you steal?" I ask.

He remains silent, pacing along the pavement.

His head bowed.

I wonder if he's just going to pull this silent routine with me; if he's going to hope that if he just keeps his head down and ignores me then this will all go away.

Yeah, fat chance . . .

"Just some biscuits," he says.

" 'Biscuits' ? *Why* were you stealing biscuits?"

He replies with that most teenage of gestures: a *shrug*.

It's then that I can hold myself back no longer.

I grab his t-shirt sleeve.

Bring him to a halt.

Something passes over the surface of his eyes.

I see it for what it is . . . a *snap* decision . . . him deciding *not* to wrestle out of my grip.

Him deciding *not* to fight back.

Smart choice.

"Bored," he finally replies, as if this explains everything.

"Listen," I say, staring at him, even though his gaze drifts somewhere up over my shoulder. "I don't know *what* got into your brain — *why* you thought you needed to do this — but I'm here to tell you now that if you ever do *anything* like it again there will be drastic consequences."

Even as I hear the words pass through my own mouth, I second guess just what I mean by 'drastic consequences'.

Oooh, scary . . .

I have no way of telling whether or not my words are getting through to Ben.

He just keeps on giving that same mid-air stare.

I decide that I might as well finish what I've started.

Content that he's not going to run away, I release my hold.

"Was this Josh's idea?"

Another shrug.

"Was it *your* idea?"

He shifts his gaze back onto mine. "*Dunno.*"

Again, I somehow manage to keep myself reined in.

When it comes to disciplining my children, that old cliché about people in glass houses not throwing stones has always been summoned to mind.

And I frequently have to tell myself that it's nonsense.

That my children know *nothing* about what I do.

About what I *did*.

"Why didn't you phone Dad? Why didn't you ask Dad and *Kate* to pick you up?"

No response.

"Ben . . ."

But I don't get much further than uttering his name before he's storming away; before he's making a beeline for the Underground.

Never one to be walked out on, I pursue him, determined to catch up.

I get hold of him again.

As it often does, my strength catches him off guard.

He struggles briefly and then gives in.

For the first time, I realise he has tears in his eyes.

"I didn't want them to *know*, okay?" he says.

I say nothing in reply.

I just allow it to *be* what it is.

He didn't want to ruin his 'reputation' with those who really matter.

Me? I'm disposable. *Nobody . . .*

I keep my tone clean and crisp.

Cool.

"And what makes you think — *for one second* — that I won't tell Dad?"

Ben looks me in the eye.

Behind the tears, I can see genuine fear.

The frightened kid has risen once more to the surface; vanquishing whatever teenage demon has brought on this behaviour.

"I'm asking you," Ben finally replies. "*Please* . . . just this once."

I hold his gaze.

And inside me something melts.

I can't help but cast my mind back to the twenty hours of labour. And then, after all that effort — all that *pain* — how he just appeared in my arms . . . bundled up in a blanket.

Through the haze of the epidural, and the gentle, mumbling voices of those in attendance, I recall staring into his sea-green eyes . . . and realising they were the same as my own. That I had given birth to myself.

I feel the gentle *thump* of my pulse in my throat.

I know that he's manipulating me — I know that my own *emotions* are manipulating me. My logical mind is telling me over and over that I shouldn't agree to anything right now.

That I should take time to think about it . . .

And yet, I find myself replying, "All right —*just this once.*"

Ben blinks. His tears are gone.

On instinct, he lurches forward, throws his arms about me.

Squeezes me tight.

And I can feel him trembling.

Chapter Eighteen

For a few seconds — as I study the message which has just
come through the AA app — I wonder if the encryption
function has gone faulty; if it has *forgotten* to decrypt the message:

MTSF2

When I check the sender, it informs me the message is
from Tabby.

I wonder if she — like me — isn't quite able to stretch her
trust in the app all the way.

If she feels that she needs to be somewhat cryptic in her
messages.

I remember an old saying I once heard off Amy: 'Garbage in
garbage out'.

Tabby's message doesn't prove to be *just that*. After I've turned
my phone upside down — sideways on — several times, I'm able
to make some sense of it.

Meet at Sex Flat. 2 p.m.

That's simple enough.

I go to grab my coat off its hook in the hallway, only to run into Mark just as he's coming up for air; just as he's emerging from his workshop. He's wearing his overalls, the sleeves are tied about his waist to expose the chequered shirt he wears up top. And he has half a dozen buttons undone, revealing his ripped midriff.

"Going out?" he asks, then, "Mind if we have a chat first?"

With my coat dangling off my finger, I do a mental calculation, thinking about just how long it'll take me to make the two o'clock appointment versus the time Mark will absorb with this 'chat' of his. Perhaps it's the mental sums, or the promise of that *glorious* abdomen, but I decide to hang around for a few minutes.

He shepherds me into the sitting room — closes the door.

I wonder why he bothers.

There's nobody else in the house.

A frantic — *crazy* — idea enters my head . . . that he's going to kill me.

That my wonderful, seemingly perfect, live-in lover will turn out to be some sort of psychopath. And, where psychopaths are concerned, two certainly is company.

Mark picks at some sawdust beneath his fingernails. "It's about Nathan," he says.

"Mm?" I reply, and then, realising that I might be playing it *too much* on the subtle side — trying *too hard* not to allude to the conversation me and Nathan shared, I add, "What's the matter?"

Mark gives me a slight smile, but it soon slips. "Just looking for advice, really."

I perch on the arm of the sofa.

This has to be the first time Mark has *ever* solicited advice from me.

I'd better make it count.

"I'm sure you've seen the bruises," Mark says, "the cuts and scrapes that Nathan's been coming home with." He pauses a beat then glances over his shoulder, as if Nathan might be poking his head around the door — as if Nathan might've arrived early from school. "Well, when I asked him about it, he told me that it's some *boys* involved; that they've been picking on him." He breathes a deep sigh, then scratches the back of his neck. "But we agreed not to kick up a fuss — that it would only make things worse. Now, though, I'm not so sure . . . it just . . . I don't know . . . it doesn't seem to be *stopping* any time soon."

Why anyone *ever* thinks things will stop just by doing *nothing* often beats me.

Then again, I suppose that accounts for a hefty portion of the world population.

Everybody wants to do nothing and see results . . .

"What should I do, Anna? I want to help . . . but I don't know *how*."

Unable to prevent myself thinking about my own son — and his delinquent urges — I can't help wondering if I'm really the best person to be asking for advice. Then again, I said nothing at all to Mark about Ben's shop-lifting. Maybe that's how I've managed to hold onto my role of being some shining beacon of parenthood.

"Well, I suppose you *could* speak to the school — just make them aware of what's going on . . . while making it clear you believe any intervention might make things worse."

"You think they'd really do *nothing*?"

I shrug. "It's worth a go, isn't it? I mean — if you're *really* that concerned."

Mark eyes the ceiling.

"Of course, you will be effectively allowing the matter out of your hands — you can't account for what the school will do next . . . they might decide to intervene anyway; as a matter of policy. They need to cover themselves — in a legal way . . . if anything happens to Nathan, and it turns out they *knew* what was going on, they would be liable."

Mark's eyes have become sunken in their sockets now. He seems to have shrunk. His shoulders are slouched. His chin almost touches his chest. I wonder if I've done the right thing — if I shouldn't have just kept my mouth shut.

When Mark speaks again, I'm almost certain that it's going to be to thank me in the nicest terms for my advice, while he trudges off to his workshop, still thoroughly mired in his mope. However, he raises his head, presses his lips together and then spits it out.

"Actually, I had an alternative in mind."

"Really?"

He arches his shoulders, and I hear a light *creak* as his muscles unknot. "I wondered if you'd be able to have a word with Ben — if you could ask him to look out for Nathan."

"*Ben?*" I reply, with a strong note of disbelief I'm sure Mark picks up on.

Ben and Nathan go to the same school.

Until about a year ago, the two of them played on the same football team.

Before Ben — it seems — grew tired of sport and turned his attention to delinquency.

Mark nods. "From what Nathan's told me, he's quite a strong

influence about school . . . not exactly popular, but nobody messes with him."

I think about this.

Hold up the observation and compare it with my own image of Ben.

School is like another world — a parallel universe.

And we, as parents, really have only the tiniest of ideas about what goes on.

I shift my attention back to Mark. "All right, I'll ask him — see if he can help out."

Mark grins. He plants a kiss on my forehead. "Thanks."

I watch as he heads back to his workshop — more of a spring in his step now.

For probably the hundredth time, I wonder why I didn't get into some similarly *meaningful* occupation.

I guess we just have to manage with the cards we're dealt.

Chapter Nineteen

I hang up the call as I climb the staircase to Sex Flat.

My mind continues to buzz with the conversation I just shared with Ben.

I wonder if it could be considered *blackmail*.

When I brought up the issue of Nathan — asked whether Ben might've seen him getting picked on at school — he gave that most teenage of answers; that he'd heard 'rumours'. But he reluctantly agreed to do what I wished.

To keep an *eye* on him.

And to report back.

Perhaps I should've aimed for a career as a spy master after all . . .

It's when I tread the floorboards outside Sex Flat that I can't help but overhear the voices from within. And not only that; the conversation seems so . . . *animated*.

My heart thumps a little harder.

Suddenly paranoid, I glance over my shoulder.

There's no one there, of course.

I take a second to collect myself and then tread onward.

Knock on the door.

Amy answers. She wears a wide smile. Her blue eyes *twinkle*. "Oh, hi, Anna," she says, as if she might be greeting me for some house party.

I attempt to steer a glance past her, to the occupants, and to the source of the incessant babble, but Amy makes a better door than a window, as they say.

When Amy does finally step back and allow me a look into the flat, I immediately take in the woman — in her fifties, if I guess correctly. She wears what appears to be a mink — or some other mammal's — hide. While she sits, she clasps her knees together. I can't help but notice the precarious pair of strappy high heels she has on . . . and I vaguely wonder just how she got up the staircase in them.

Her skin is leathered in a way which suggests she's made excellent use of tanning beds throughout her lifetime . . . or, perhaps, she has the sort of money which affords her the opportunity to get some 'winter sun' whenever she feels the urge.

As I tread further into the flat, I catch an unpleasant, overpowering stench of daisies.

The woman blabs out something more, apparently finishing her current train of thought, and then turns her attention to me, interested in the new-arrival. As I stand there, I can't quite help but feel myself being appraised; and found *wanting*.

The woman belatedly presses on a smile. "And you must be *Anna*," she says.

I flip a glance over AA and Tabby, the two of them looking just a little shell-shocked by whatever *experience* this woman has put them through thus far.

"That's right," I reply, unsure what else to say.

The woman remains seated but tilts her face upward, in my direction.

I indulge her, giving her a pair of air kisses — one on each cheek.

Introductions over with, I take a seat on the sofa beside AA.

Meanwhile, Amy perches on the armrest of Tabby's chair.

We all focus our attention onto the woman.

"Paula Stevenstar." She grins. "But I'm sure you know that already."

I do . . . I've heard the name before.

And I instantly realise how she got in touch with AA.

Quite simply put, she's an ex-client of Brian's.

I look about the others, then back to Paula Stevenstar. "Sorry for interrupting — I was running a little late." I glance to AA, Tabby and Amy. "Where were you up to?"

None of them reply.

But Paula does.

"Well," Paula says, "I was just explaining to your . . . ah . . . *colleagues* here about the details of the case; the details which might have escaped your attention."

"And what details are those?" I reply.

When Paula smiles, wrinkles emerge around her mouth and eyes. She looks across us, then says, "About Cuthbert Gonderberry's frequent flights of rage . . . about those little moments when he seems to . . . ah . . . *lose control.*"

That sends me back to the day we visited Gonderberry's mansion. Once again, I feel the sense of shame at what we did . . . it feels only marginally better that I came clean in the end; that I owned up to our deception.

"And what do you know about these 'flights of rage' ?" I ask.

Paula purses her lips. She squeezes her knees tighter together. Clasps her hands in her lap. "As I was just explaining, Cuthbert and I came up together . . . we shared many a function; many a *performance*. In fact, we shared something of a *fling* . . . in the early days, of course — before Cuthbert's career *really* took off."

I look over the others, trying to gauge the temperature in the room.

Trying to judge just what sort of credibility we're to give Paula Stevenstar.

From the various stories I've heard surrounding her, she's become a vicious kiss-and-teller; apparently propping up her dying acting career with a series of revelations surrounding those with a level of fame she failed to ever truly achieve.

I decide we need to get the facts down before taking any decision whether or not to continue with this case. I'm interested in *justice* . . . I'm not interested in giving people a dose of personal revenge; and especially when it's on Paula Stevenstar's behalf.

"You see," Paula continues, "when I read about what'd happened — about Cuthbert's *fiancée* succumbing to that snake of his — I knew there had to be more to the story." She draws a sharp breath through her nostrils; it acts to inflate her emaciated figure like pouring air into a withered balloon. "Cuthbert is always very conscious of what he *shows* to the wider world." She pauses a moment and I'm certain that I catch the glint of a genuine tear in her eye. "But he lets that façade down in his private life — he allows those he brings close to see who he *really* is."

Again, I shift a glance at the others.

When I speak again, I can't help the cynicism oozing off my tone. "Would you be kind enough to relate one of these episodes to us?"

If Paula senses my probing tone then she doesn't let on.

She's either a better actress than I previously envisaged, or she's constructed some sort of dream world to inhabit . . . a world in which she is always correct.

A world in which her memories and opinions take on the weight of *facts*.

Dealing with someone like this — a *deluded* person — can be one of the diciest propositions going. I can't help but wonder if the others haven't drawn this same conclusion. If they haven't *realised* just who we're dealing with.

Perhaps AA, Tabby and Amy — the mercenaries they are — have decided they're going to take full advantage of the situation — take the money — while they still can.

Paula glances up; a single tear running down her cheek. "He tried to kill *me*."

————

Although the room was quiet before — *at least in terms of the audience* — it takes on a new-found silence now. One of those profound, deeply felt silences which feels almost blasphemy to break. When my gaze slips past Paula, I find myself staring down on those Middle-Eastern men in the street outside. They're back again. Back with their dice.

Playing that game.

Cheating the punters.

I switch back onto Paula.

Her posture is almost frozen.

Whereas before she looked relaxed, as if she was at home; as if she was delighted to have an audience to *hold forth* with. Now, though, she seems afraid. She grips the seat of her chair tightly, sinking her fingernails into the fabric. Her complexion — previously so well-tanned — has now turned a decidedly *snowy* white.

As she relates the story, her dramatic tone of voice deserts her.

It's replaced by monotone.

"We were taking on a production of *An Inspector Calls*. I played Sheila Birling while Cuthbert interpreted Gerald Croft." She pauses to gather herself then smiles, despite herself — despite her rigid posture. "He was just so *dashing* . . . showing up to rehearsal in that leather jacket of his . . . with his ragged and ripped jeans." She shakes her head. "I thought he was such a *tear-away*." She glances up. "That was before I found out about his family, of course; before I found out who he *really* was. Where he *lived*."

My chest tightens.

I think back to the mansion.

To all those photographs.

And then to my own real-life experience of Parisianer Hall.

Is that what really defines us?

Who we're born to?

Where we live?

"I couldn't quite believe my luck," Paula continues, "when Cuthbert asked me out for a drink. I thought he wanted to go over our parts; I thought it would all be a professional matter." She draws breath again. "However, as it soon turned out, he had *far* greater designs than mere *rehearsal*."

I meet AA's eye for the longest moment.

For some reason, I expect him to press on a wry smile.

Or to slip me a wink.

He does neither, though.

He remains still.

Serious.

Drinking up everything Paula has to say.

I turn back to her, no wiser as to whether or not we're being taken in.

"I believed it to be serious when he brought me to meet his parents." She gives a shake of her head. "So *strange* how they lived, really. I can recall how Cuthbert briefed me ahead of dinner, about how I was *only* to address his father as 'Admiral' . . . an old-fashioned touch, but one which wasn't *entirely* out of the ordinary in those days. *Different times*."

I look back down to the men in the street, seeing they've got themselves another mark. This time it's a Japanese tourist, a long-lensed camera dangling from his neck. He smiles as the man takes his money and as the dice are sent tumbling.

I watch on for another few moments as the dice, apparently, come up wrongly and the Middle-Eastern man, with an apologetic shrug, ends up with the mark's twenty-pound note.

Still smiling, the Japanese tourist plods off along the street.

What he's doing in Brent Cross, I really haven't the faintest idea.

Whatever the reason, it's ended up costing him twenty pounds.

I shift back to the foreground.

To Paula.

"We must have been *together* for about six months" — she flushes — "perhaps a little longer, when Cuthbert invited me to that dinner with his parents. While I wouldn't go as far as to say his parents were *thrilled* to meet me, I at least believed that it had gone . . . *decorously*." She shakes her head and turns her attention to her hands, which still grip the seat. "However, that night, when we returned to our lodgings in Islington, I found out just what

Cuthbert thought of my performance. I can still remember the examples he brought up; how I had apparently not shown sufficient respect for his mother, how I hadn't *curtseyed* low enough . . . how I had addressed his father as 'Admiral' *instead* of 'sir', as I was apparently supposed to do following the first time I had addressed him as 'Admiral'. It was like meeting royalty. As if I had met the *Queen* and committed all manner of *faux pas*."

"And what did he do?" Amy puts in, sounding somewhat rude to break Paula's flow, but, at the same time, only speaking out loud what we all want to know.

Paula squints, as if she's peeling back the mists of time, bringing her memories just a touch sharper. "It was the strangest thing. Cuthbert was unable to shut up about our meeting for what must've been two hours — perhaps three . . . and then he just dropped the whole matter. He became all sunshine and rainbows. He asked if I wanted to go out for a drink and a bit of a dance." She shakes her head. "He was apologetic the whole time, and, you know how it is, you believe you might be able to change them . . ."

She shifts a glance about the girls, including me, as if we chime with this observation.

"Anyway," Paula continues, "we went to some local place — I forget the name, though it's most likely been knocked down by now — and we passed what I thought to be a wonderful evening. One which, to be quite frank, had me falling for him all over again."

She sucks up a deep breath then shifts a glance out of the window.

I wonder if she's keeping track of those men and their dice game like me.

"The two of us stumbled back to the flat, and I recall feeling a touch dizzy — wanting to have a lie-down . . . and I told Cuthbert as much." She grips the armchair cushion even tighter still. If there is any blood remaining in her hands then it has surely been squeezed out now. "I can still remember — almost as if it's burned into my mind" — she taps her temple — "the smile on his face. It was a *joyful* smile; a *carefree* smile . . ."

She trails off and I think long and hard about raising my voice to prompt her.

But, it seems, all four of us leaning into her is all the prompt she needs.

She is merely milking the moment.

"To be frank, I was a little *sauced*," she continues with a slight smile. "I slipped off to sleep. I was aware of Cuthbert *appearing* in our bedroom, but of little else . . . I know that I was lucky, that it was some instinctual reaction; that something buried within my subconscious gave me a nudge . . . told me to *wake up*. To take a look. And, when I did, when I opened an eye, I saw the blade reflecting the moonlight — the *knife* which Cuthbert held down at his side." She shakes her head. "I acted quickly then, I recall leaping up out of bed, fighting to get away from him. As I stumbled out of the bedroom, and away through the flat, I glanced back over my shoulder, saw him still standing over by the window. The knife down at his side. He didn't give chase." She pauses another second, then adds, "I left the flat that night; thought I would never see him again . . . *hoped* I would never see him again. But ours is a small world, so we were bound to cross paths at some time or another. The two of us, though, seemed content to avoid contact."

The room drifts into uneasy silence. I wouldn't like to *imagine* what the others think . . . what the others have on their minds. As for me, all Paula's story has done is convince me that we're dealing with grave exaggeration; with someone who is out to seek attention. And, call me crazy, but I have no ambition to get involved in the professional world of publicity . . . or to touch it with a ten-foot bargepole, for that matter . . .

I decide to take the initiative. "Thank you Paula. It was . . . pleasant of you to come here and meet us in person. It's better to be able to put a face to a client; to know just on whose behalf we're working."

She inclines her head to acknowledge this.

I wonder if I can take another step.

I look about the others' faces . . . think this through.

"However, I believe I speak for us all when I say that this is an . . . *unusual* undertaking; one which we might not be ideally suited for. If you give us a week or so, we might be able to put you in touch with — "

AA cuts me off. "I think what Anna is *trying* to say is that we'll think about what you've told us and formulate a plan for getting to the bottom of this."

I feel strongly like telling AA — *in no uncertain terms* — that this is precisely the opposite of what I had in mind. But, as it turns out, 'Paula' beats me to the punch.

She tilts her head to one side and I see the tear tracks on her cheeks. "You don't believe me, do you . . . *Anna?*"

I glance about the others.

They're all telling me — with their stares — that I should *shut the hell up*; that I shouldn't be getting in the way of this nice-paying gig.

Fuck them . . .

"It's not a case of believing or *not* believing; it's just that I believe we all *remember* things differently . . . we are all prisoners to our own perceptions." I meet Paula's eye. "You said yourself that you'd been drinking; that you probably didn't have your full senses about you . . . Of *course* I believe you when you say that he was furious about how you acted in the company of his parents, but that doesn't mean that he was willing to kill you later. Again, as you said, he didn't give chase . . . you only *saw* him with the knife."

Paula continues to stare me in the eye for several seconds.

At the last, she blinks, as if breaking the spell.

Then she gives a faint nod and busies herself getting up from her chair. "I hear what you're saying."

I stay where I am.

Although it wasn't my intention to ruffle any feathers — *to smash any delusions* — I could see no other way of going about it. Sometimes a sledgehammer is the kindest tool . . .

Nobody says anything as she skitters across the room.

When she reaches the door, I expect her to go full-thesp, to rip it open, to shimmy through and then to slam it shut on her heels. However, she turns back.

Looks over us.

"All the same, I would like you to continue to investigate Cuthbert." She looks at me —*concentrates* on me. "It's just a gut feeling . . . that something isn't right. A crazy old bat's money is as good as anyone else's; why not take it?"

And, with that remark, she leaves, shutting the door behind her.

But not with a slam.

More like a barely perceptible *click*.

Chapter Twenty

None of us really say anything about meeting Paula Stevenstar.

We all seem fairly content to just allow the matter to drop.

To allow what's played out in Sex Flat to percolate.

On my way back home that afternoon, I decide to put my own spy network to the test.

I call up Ben and have a hurried conversation. When I push him for information on Mark's adopted son, Nathan, to begin with he feigns that he hasn't a clue who I'm talking about. Soon enough, though, the penny clunks in the mechanism; perhaps when I bring his attention to the dagger I'm dangling over his head . . . the threat of me telling his father exactly why he came home late that one night.

Ben informs me that 'everything's fine' with Nathan, and I decide that I have to take his word for it. At least I can honestly tell Mark that I'm on the case; that Ben hasn't seen anything to be concerned about as regards to Nathan.

When I get back to Mark's house, everything is quiet, so I drift on up to our bedroom where I find my cat Lizzie lying on the bedspread. She gives me a brief *chirrup* of greeting, deigning to flutter her eyelids fractionally before shutting them firmly once more and going back to sleep. Sometimes I wonder if I'd be cut out for the feline life.

Because I feel a little soiled after visiting Sex Flat, I give myself a quick shower, and put on a clean pair of jeans and a t-shirt. When I go downstairs, I see that about a quarter of the chocolate cake remains on the kitchen counter. I brew myself a quick coffee and snarf down a generous-sized portion. I've just about swallowed when I hear my mobile phone buzzing about upstairs, on the bedside table where I left it.

Feeling as if I might be about to burst at the seams, I dance my way up the staircase, sweep up my mobile and hold it to my ear. "Hello?" I say, simultaneously fishing a chocolate chip from where it's lodged between my bottom lip and front row of teeth.

"Anna?"

It's Mark.

"Hi," I reply, allowing myself a slight smile. "I just got home . . . where are you?"

"A & E."

My heart gives a hard beat. " '*A & E*' ?!"

"Yeah, there's . . ."

To start with, I believe there's something wrong with the connection. But then I realise Mark's curtailed his answer because he's placed his palm over his mobile while he speaks with someone. I hear his dampened voice, followed by rustling.

Then he shifts his attention back onto me.

"I was wondering if you could, uh, bring something for us to eat . . . a *sandwich* . . . something like that?"

" 'A sandwich' ?" I echo, as if he's speaking a completely different language.

"Sorry, Anna, I've got to go," he says, and then hangs up.

A little stunned at the whole exchange, I continue to hold my mobile to my ear for another few moments. I stare out through the kitchen window, to the darkened garden outside. As I stand there, I feel something up against my calf. When I glance down, I see that it's Lizzie — that she's rubbing up against my leg . . . apparently, in all this hustle-and-bustle, her dinner has been forgotten. I snap back to reality, make a mental itinerary.

And at the top — first things first — I serve up Lizzie her dinner.

———

Mark sees sense several minutes after he calls, sending along a text message with the exact details of the Accident and Emergency unit he is located at. When I get there, it surely looks just how any Accident and Emergency room on the face of the planet looks. Graven-faced people. Makeshift bandages applied and turned a discoloured brown by the assorted wounds. Others clutch their arms to their chests, while others still have their legs propped up on nearby chairs. The air reeks — *overwhelmingly* — of antiseptic and *blood* and *sweat*.

The only person in sight with a white jacket is an overworked doctor. Just from a quick glance about the waiting room, I can see that neither Mark or Nathan are here. Wondering just who I should speak to, an answer comes at me from out of the ether.

I eye the matronly woman sitting at a reception desk.

With a sympathetic pout she makes a call and then utters some incomprehensible directions about where I should head.

Someone with a wadded-up ball of damp cotton wool, and with blood dripping onto the floor, arrives beside me. They sound incomprehensible — *obviously drunk* — and I decide to take my chances with getting lost.

I'm sure that it takes me about five times longer than is strictly necessary to locate the examination room, but, when I do, I almost find myself getting thrown straight out again.

A doctor with tanned skin, and big bags beneath his eyes, attempts to turn me right around, but Mark calls out in time, telling him that I'm okay to go in.

That he *knows* me.

The doctor rolls his eyes then disappears out into the corridor, back into the mad, seemingly never-ending stream of doctors, nurses and porters rushing to get somewhere.

My attention shifts onto Mark, and I see that he's sat on the examination table.

Right away, I note that Nathan's sitting in a chair off to the corner of the room; *unscathed* and still dressed in his school uniform. It seems my gut feeling that Nathan was the one in need of medical attention was well off target.

I feel dazed as I absorb this fact, and turn my attention onto Mark, seeing that he holds his arm across his chest. I can see that he's got a bandage wrapped about a pair of his fingers and that the bandage is soaked with blood. He is strangely chirpy for someone who's clearly suffered blood loss. "They'll be by to stitch me up in a few minutes."

"What," I begin. "*How?*"

Still clutching his afflicted hand across his chest, he gives a shrug. Then he says, "I was working with the jigsaw . . . trying to get the cut *just right*." He shakes his head. "Weirdest thing how it happened. Can't really remember feeling any sort of pain; there was just this kind of *warmth* . . . and then, when I looked down, there was blood *everywhere*." He nods to Nathan, sitting attentively — if a touch *solemnly* — in the corner of the room. "Good thing that Nathan had just come back from school; that he happened to peep into my workshop a few seconds after I'd done it . . . otherwise the house might've resembled a slasher flick."

I flip a glance over to Nathan.

He gives me a sheepish smile.

That's one thing about Nathan which I've always admired — how he never likes to have the limelight. How he likes to *play down* his involvement in just about anything . . . anything which might be seen as an achievement; a sign of *maturity*.

I shift back to Mark, who continues.

"They wanted to check there wasn't any nerve damage. Seems my cut was as smooth, as clean, as the one I put in the wood." He gives a slight chuckle. "Shame that I won't be able to use that piece; not with all the blood I left on it."

I remember myself, the handbag which dangles off my shoulder. I fish through it, bringing out, from within, a pair of tinfoil-wrapped sandwiches. "I've got cheese and tomato or tuna mayonnaise."

Mark and Nathan exchange glances in a slightly eerie manner; one of those looks which makes me question whether they *might* not just be naturally father and son, and that some tenuous series of events has *somehow* brought them back together after all these years. "Toss him the cheese," Mark says, "I'll take the tuna."

I do as he says, though I restrain myself from 'tossing' anything; settling instead for handing them over sensibly. The three of us wait about in the room, me with nothing much to do, while the boys are chewing their way through their sandwiches.

Although the doctor and nurse are clearly unhappy about the extra person in the room, they make no verbal complaint; so we stand around while they set about sewing up Mark's fingers. Once they're through, and with another — *cleaner-looking* — bandage, we all head out of Accident and Emergency.

I drive us all back to Mark's house.

When we get there, as per standard, Nathan rushes off up to his bedroom.

Meanwhile, I hold the fort with Mark, in the kitchen, looking a touch guiltily at the dirty coffee cup and the plate I used to consume that piece of chocolate cake.

In all the drama of being called to Accident and Emergency, I didn't get the chance to slot the items into the dishwasher. I do so now, as Mark settles down in one of the kitchen chairs, his fingers all bandaged up. "I'd love a cup of tea," he says.

The dirtied plate and cup dealt with, I set about putting the kettle on to boil.

"I guess you'll be off cooking a few days," I say.

"The doctors said I need to take it easy for the next four or five weeks."

I give a pout. "You can't work?"

"No, I don't think they meant to say that."

"Then what *did* they mean to say?" I reply, a slight smile in my voice as steam puffs free of the kettle. I reach out, take it off its base, and pour the boiling water.

"Oh, just like they said, to 'take it easy'."

I give a shake of my head, splash some milk into each cup — remove the bag — and then bring the tea over to Mark. I take my place opposite, blowing on the surface of my tea, feeling the warm steam waft up against my cheeks.

When we've been sitting in silence for a few moments — after

Mark has talked *all around* the chocolate cake to such a point where I end up cutting him a slice — he peers up and says, "Good day today?"

I think long and hard about the question.

About what we were doing.

How we met our 'client' Paula Stevenstar.

I wonder about client-investigator confidentiality.

Does such a thing even *exist* with this kind of arrangement?

In the end, fairly certain my mind's made up in any case — that I'm no longer going to allow myself to be drawn into all this *nastiness* — I blurt out our client's name.

Mark almost chokes on his chocolate cake. " 'Paula Stevenstar' ?" he repeats. "You know, of *Temperance Square* fame?"

Not knowing what *Temperance Square* is, but feeling like I'm an idiot not to, I can only reply with a vague nod.

Mark cocks his head to one side. "What're you doing with her?" He catches himself after this remark; slipping back into what is really our standard mode of communication where my career is concerned . . . which, is to say, *no communication.* "Or . . . can you say?"

I hold myself still, feel the tightness form over my chest. More than anything, I want to be open with Mark — I want to open myself to him *fully* . . . and yet, at the same time, that's something which isn't so easily achieved after the life I've had.

After the *career* I've had.

A career which has been all about secrecy.

Then again, Mark knew *enough* about what I used to do . . . enough about my *killing-for-money* habit . . . why should this be harder for him to swallow?

I take the decision.

"With the others, you know, Amy, AA . . . Tabby . . . we all decided to take on some private-investigator work . . . to see if we might be able to help out with some . . . uh . . ."

"Cold cases?" Mark suggests, leaning in over the table, and looking decidedly interested in the turn of the conversation.

I nod. "Sure, something like that . . ."

He leans in over the table. Closer still.

He gives a slight wince as he does so — one of the only visible signs of pain he's given since his accident.

"And what bones are you digging up? Who're you looking into?"

I think long and hard about my reply.

Then decide that, since I've come this far, I might as well go all the way.

If I can't trust a live-in lover then *who* can I trust?

Certainly not AA . . .

"Cuthbert Gonderberry," I say, then give a shrug. "It's all public record — there's no *secret* about it . . . it's to do with his fiancée . . ."

Mark's eyes widen further still. "The girl who was squeezed to death by the python?"

"That's the one," I reply, staring down into my now-empty cup of tea.

"Wow."

"Yeah," I agree.

From upstairs, I hear footsteps; Nathan apparently making for the bathroom. Perhaps he's off to brush his teeth, to get ready for bed.

I try to recall a time when Ben or Josie ever took themselves off to bed voluntarily and can't think of one right away. Then again, I haven't exactly been the most *present* of parents.

"And . . ." Mark allows the remark to hang in the air, making it seem as if it's optional whether or not I choose to answer it.

I put him out of his misery. "We've been investigating the circumstances surrounding the death . . . surrounding Cuthbert *Gonderberry*."

"Are you qualified to do that?"

I shrug. "Last time I checked the entry requirements to working as a private investigator were about the same as those for shelf-stacking."

Yeah, and I wonder how many shelf-stackers have visited Cuthbert Gonderberry's *house*.

Mark seems to remember himself. He retreats into his seat. "Well, at least it's keeping you busy."

I don't have the chance to pick up on that remark — to *deal* with it in any way — because it's then that Nathan peeps in through the kitchen doorway.

"Hello," he says, with a slight smile.

I set about collecting the empty cups of tea, deciding that now would be a good time to put an end to this conversation.

Chapter Twenty-One

The next time I get a message through the Assassins Anonymous app, the text itself isn't encrypted. But that doesn't make the content any easier to devour.

The message has come through from AA, and it declares, quite simply:

5PM. Parisianer Hall. Come Alone.

Yeah, like I'm in the habit of going about with company . . . like I have a whole battalion of bodyguards all waiting in the wings, *watching*.

The message also comes as I sit in Mark's car — a sensible, rectangle shaped estate car; one of those which wouldn't look out of place sat on any street corner at any time — waiting outside Arnold's house. I always try my very best to *avoid* the awkward meeting on the front doorstep. It seems that Kate — Arnold's new woman — has some sort of a quest to make a friend of me . . . and that's despite me breaking her arm.

Perhaps people can't resist my charm.

Night is rolling in, and I can feel the nip to the air. I have all the heaters turned up to full, and I still feel as if I'm on the verge of shuddering all over. The clouds which lurk in the sky look as if they might be about to burst and bring forth snow. That would be nice. I suppose that if I had a real job it would be cause for concern, but as it is a gentle, white blanket over everything would be nice to look out on from my bedroom window.

Wrapped up in my duvet.

A purring cat lying on my stomach.

Mercifully, I don't need to shift my backside out of the driver's seat, and into the near-Arctic conditions, because Josie — dressed in a purple t-shirt with a white, frilly neck — emerges from the house, skipping along the pathway. After a decent-sized pause — apparently so he can argue that he's not *associated* with her to the appropriate authority — Ben emerges. He wears a t-shirt with an angel rendered on the front in black and white. Beneath, he wears a pair of black jeans. And trainers so battered they would be grounds for his parents to be reported to Child Protection Services.

With the message from AA still fresh in my mind — not to mention the *outrage* . . . at having thought that I'd made it clear I was out of this thing — I pull away from the curb, nearly skinning a cyclist who whizzes by. He shouts out some obscenity over his shoulder, and, as a consequence, almost crashes into a parked van just up ahead.

"Where're we going tonight, Mum?" Josie asks, sitting in the passenger seat.

Ben remains silent, sulking in the back.

I got a text at the eleventh hour asking me if we could meet up a different day; if he could skip out and do something else. All I needed to do was remind him of that shoplifting incident, and that, as far as I am concerned, he's grounded till he turns eighteen.

That shut him up in a snap.

"Dunno," I reply, "I was wondering if you'd like to swing by Mark's house" — I think about the message I got through from AA; and then glance at the clock on the dashboard; realise that I have time to make it over there if I'm quick — "but maybe we should go for a drive first? Take in the sunset? Something like that?"

When Ben speaks from the back seat, I can hear the sneer in his voice. "Maybe next time we get together you should submit a plan in writing fourteen days beforehand."

I glare at him in the rear-view mirror.

He meets my eye for a few seconds . . . and then cowers.

A boy should know better than to challenge his mother.

I swing the car through the London streets. Night has fully set in now. All that holds back the dark are streetlamps and head-lights of advancing cars. My heart is beating strongly, but evenly. As we close on Parisianer Hall, I glance up and about, realising that I can see AA standing on the street corner. He wears an oh-so-subtle overcoat with the collar tugged up. I scan the street quickly, looking for anyone else, and seeing that AA is apparently alone, I make an assessment then act.

I flip the indicator and then pull into the side of the road.

I turn on the hazard lights then tell the kids I'll be right back.

This time — *glory of all glories* — I don't get any smart talk from Ben.

I've managed to keep him honest with those threats of dobbing him in to his father.

Decided that this will be quick, that I won't dawdle longer than is absolutely necessary, I approach AA.

A north wind blows along the street. The leaves of the elm trees — which mark the perimeter of Gonderberry's property — rustle. I begin to regret not having brought anything more substantial than a woolly jumper; the wind just *rips* right through.

"What's this?" AA asks, referring to the car, and my two kids within.

I shrug. "Didn't think this would take long."

AA narrows his eyes. "Well, that was a hell of a presumption to make." AA's expression transforms. He smiles and waves, over my shoulder.

When I turn, I see Josie is at the car window, waving to him.

Ben remains hidden in the darkened interior.

AA fully focuses his attention back onto me. "We've been talking," he says. "Thinking this whole thing over. What the best way to proceed will be."

"And?"

AA performs a strange, seesaw-like motion with his head. "This is it."

"This is *what?*"

AA blinks a couple of times then gazes off along the street, as if there might be someone he's communicating with. When I follow his gaze, indeed, I make out Amy — lurking in one of the bushes. As I take further stock of my surroundings, I note the motorbike which is surreptitiously parked up against the curb. I assume the rider sat on top — wearing a helmet with a tinted visor — is Tabby. That's what I gather from the red hair which unfurls over her chest and down over her shoulder.

I turn back to AA.

AA — apparently — decides this is the time to explain himself. "We were thinking about how to handle the case, and we decided, well, since Paula wants to continue covering our expenses, that we should look into things a little more." He cocks his head to one side. "We thought it would be *presumptive* to assume that you really meant what you said — that you *really* don't want anything more to do with this case." He gives me a sly wink and a smile. "Come on, Anna, you know as well as *we* do that this has got your interest piqued. If you like, think about it this way . . . this is the chance to clear Cuthbert Gonderberry's name once and for all; a chance for us to *show* Paula Stevenstar there's no reason for her to be concerned; that Gonderberry's innocent."

By the time I've thought about it, I already know AA has won the argument. With a kind of flawless logic . . . or at least 'flawless' for my wracked, old brain to handle. "Okay," I reply. "What do we need to do to end this?"

AA nods to the car. "First things first, someone will have to be on childcare duties."

"You mean you're planning on something involving me?"

"Wouldn't have asked you here otherwise," AA replies, then makes for the car. "Keys."

I hesitate, then say, "They're in the ignition."

"Perfect." He clambers into the driver's seat, and I listen to his voice as he enthusiastically greets Josie and Ben . . . the two of them seem pleased to see their 'Uncle' AA. Whenever he shows up it's because there's some sort of fun and games afoot.

Before I really know what's hit me, AA fires up the engine, and pulls away from the curb — apparently off to take my kids on a trip around the block. As I watch the car — *Mark's car* — disappear around the corner, I reflect on just what I'm doing.

How I've *allowed* AA to convince me to do something which, by all accounts, everything within me has resisted. No time to think *too hard*, though, because I note Tabby — in full biker's garb — trundling over to me.

———

By the time Tabby has flipped up the visor to speak to me — by the time the car carrying my kids has disappeared around the corner — I know that I am just as stuck on this job as the rest of us. Tabby informs me, in short, no-nonsense style, that I'm to go up to the buzzer at Gonderberry's gate and — *simply* — speak to him.

She hands me over a device which she explains to be an audio recorder.

She instructs me on how to switch it on — and off; if it comes to that.

I think about turning down the offer, telling her it won't be necessary, but she's already shifted on before I can utter so much as a word.

From across the road, I catch Amy's eye.

She gives me a smile and a thumbs-up.

Of course, I understand how the argument goes — how they've all decided that *I* shall be the one to do the talking with Gonderberry. I'm the one who owned up to what we were doing . . . or dropped us all in it; depending on your point of view . . .

In short, it's my mess to clean up.

As I approach the buzzer, I'm surprised at how calm I feel.

All the same, I can't help wondering why they didn't bother

to inform me just what they had in mind for tonight. If I'd known, I might've gone for something a little . . . *showier* . . . than a jumper and a pair of well-worn jeans.

Then again, perhaps they wanted me to come across as authentic.

I guess 'being authentic' is something which can't be underestimated when you've gone and lied as comprehensively and *obviously* as the four of us have.

If I didn't expect a battalion of security to drop on me the first time I stood at Gonderberry's gate, then I'm *certain* one will do so now.

I think about all the technology these days; how they have computer programs which can recognise facial patterns. Surely after our previous visit Gonderberry will have tightened things up; he will've made sure we won't get within a *ten metres* of his front door.

However, as I feel another chilling breeze blow through me, I'm surprised to hear the voice on the other end of the intercom.

"Yes?"

Chapter Twenty-Two

Somehow I expect to find Gonderberry wearing a tracksuit, perhaps with a towel wrapped around his neck. Everything seemed *too* perfect last time around. If I'm *really* going to commit to this job then I don't want to just brush about the edges.

I want to get to the centre of what makes Gonderberry who he is.

Tonight, however, if I was hoping to find Gonderberry in something approaching 'normal' garb then I'm destined to be disappointed.

He wears a pastel-grey suit with a saffron tie knotted over the top of a white shirt. For a second, I wonder if I've caught him in the middle of a dining engagement, but I establish — almost right away; from the lack of lighting; the lack of *conversation* — that he is alone.

I can't help wondering if it's by choice or by design.

The latter seems more likely from the warm welcome he gives me . . . and that's despite the circumstances in which we first met.

If only he knew the *reason* why I'm here.

That I want to find out whether or not he's a murderer.

"Good evening," he says, smiling wide.

I take in his features again . . . the smoothed-down hair; the penetrating blue-green eyes which seem to peer right into my soul; that childlike innocence which lingers across his face. He arches an eyebrow. "Have you decided to extend your visit?"

I stare back at him for a long few moments, judging his tone, trying to work out if he's *truly* forgotten about my declaration when we left the last time. He only manages to hold his straight-faced expression for another few seconds. He cracks a smile. "Please," he says, "do come inside — I'm sure you had a good reason for doing what you did and I, for one, would be extremely glad to hear it."

———

Instead of the small library at the corner of the house, he takes me to what turns out to be a — *quite sizeable* — sitting room . . . although I'm not sure if 'sitting room' is really the correct term given that the room is easily the entire size of Mark's house.

There's an open fireplace with flames roaring about a whole pile of logs.

I restrain the urge to let out a girlish *squeal* when I feel the solid wooden floorboards give way to something softer:

A bear rug.

When I look up to the mantelpiece, I can't help but note the ominous outline on the wallpaper where a picture frame clearly used to hang.

"Something to drink?" Gonderberry asks.

"Uh, okay," I reply, finally catching myself.

"Red or white?"

"Sorry?"

"*Wine*," he says, with a smile.

This catches me further off guard. Just what *is* this? What am I *doing* here?

"I . . . don't drink," I get out, without thinking it through entirely.

Apparently not hearing my response, he pads across the room, to a glass cabinet. As he peels back the door, he speaks to me over his shoulder. "I always leave a stock up here — always proves a good idea to have a bottle in easy grabbing distance."

My chest tightens as I observe him pouring out a pair of glasses.

The wine — I can't help noting — has a *blood-red* tone.

When he brings my glass over, I take it from him, then hold it tight in my fingers wondering how little I might be able to get away with drinking. However, Gonderberry studies me closely, wily to my games . . . wanting to *ensure* I have a deep, long gulp.

"Cheers," he says, still smiling, holding up his glass.

I clink mine against his.

I postpone bringing the glass to my lips for as long as I can manage, but in the end I know there's no option but to take a sip.

So I do.

The flavour is surprisingly sweet — *surprisingly warming* — and I recall, instantly, why I gave up drinking all those years ago; that it could so easily turn into a crutch . . .

When Gonderberry brings his glass down, he gives a pout of satisfaction. "A good vintage, don't you think?"

Although I have the urge to ask for a glass of water — feeling as if the wine has dried out my mouth and throat — I hold back;

tell myself that I need to play the deferent, polite guest. "Oh, yes," I reply.

Gonderberry gestures to the sofa before the fireplace, and I follow him over.

We sit down.

Some part of me expects him to shuffle along the cushion — to bring himself *inappropriately* close . . . but he holds his distance. When he crosses his legs, he does so in what I take to be such a *camp* way that I wonder if his many well-broadcast relationships with members of the opposite sex were all carefully orchestrated by someone of Brian Mathewson's skillset.

"So," he says, swilling his wine in the glass, peering into it as if he's about to tell my fortune. "You were going to tell me about that act you and the others put on." He glances up; pinning me with those never-still, beautiful eyes. "What was that *about?*"

I feel a gentle warmth in my gut, and a — *not unpleasant* — sinking feeling. But I know my alcohol tolerance — or lack thereof — has nothing to do with my decision to spill the details. To tell the truth.

"We're private investigators. We're being hired by someone who wishes to find out about your fiancée — about Isla Darrington."

Gonderberry doesn't react right away.

He merely continues to stare into my eyes.

Finally, his gaze breaks away and it returns to his wine. He continues to swill the contents about the base of the glass. "Yes, I thought as much." He gives a gentle smile, but I can't help noting the slight twitch to his left eye. "It seems that just about *everyone* has an interest in my private affairs. The cost of fame and fortune, I suppose."

Unable to show much genuine empathy, I hold off replying.

And I shift my focus elsewhere.

Down to the bear rug.

I've never been one of those people who starts jabbering away when nervous; I'm very much the other type. The kind which just *clams up* . . .

Gonderberry knocks back his wine, sets the glass down, and then rises from his seat. "Well, would you like to see the murder weapon?"

———

My heart thuds hard in my chest.

I can't quite believe what's happening.

That I'm actually headed downwards — *again* — into the basement of Cuthbert Gonderberry's home. The air is as I remember it: damp, and with a chilly draught.

I continue to cling to my glass of wine, though I haven't taken another sip since the first. For some reason, it makes me feel stronger — *more confident* — to be holding onto something. Maybe some part of me still begs for a lethal weapon to have and to hold.

Always nearby.

The enclosures are as I remember.

I feel a skittering sensation pass across the surface of my skin.

My blood turns cold.

Without missing a beat, Gonderberry leads me through the room — past the enclosures — to the one which I noted the first time; the one which is covered with a black velvet cloth. As he slips me something approaching a smile, I realise he has tears in his eyes.

My heart beats harder still.

I wish the ground would simply open up and that I would drop right down . . . into a never-ending emptiness.

Gonderberry rolls his shoulders as if he's preparing for some athletic endeavour, and then, with a swift, smooth movement, he grasps hold of the cloth and tugs it away.

My heart hangs at the back of my mouth.

Slowly, I take in the details.

There's a tree branch within, and a pool of water at the base of the enclosure.

However, that's not what draws the eye.

What *does* draw attention is the Burmese python draped over the branch. Its beady, *honey-coloured* eyes peer out from beneath glass. I take in the form, the yellow body, with the splodges upon its scales. Almost like an *alien* creature.

And it stares right back at me.

When Gonderberry turns to me, he has a genuine sadness in his expression. "I asked them to return her once they were through with the investigation."

I blink away my daze, wondering if I've missed the thread of the conversation while I've been taking in the snake; absorbing that it's truly *real*.

"I couldn't think what to do," he continues. "But, in the end, I couldn't be parted from her, either; that was why the obvious solution hit me. Why I decided it was for the best to have her stuffed . . . and to leave her down here."

It's only now that I pluck up the courage to take a step or two closer and realise the python isn't moving . . . that it isn't notice-ably breathing . . .

"A Burmese python," he says. "*Very* particular, too . . . an albino."

Gonderberry continues to stare through the glass.

What must be going through his mind, I really have no clue.

And I don't think it particularly prudent to ask, either.

Realising that we're standing close — so close that I can feel Gonderberry's body heat — I act on instinct. Allowing my wine glass to dangle down to my side, I reach out and give his shoulder a squeeze. He glances back at me briefly, a slight smile lining his mouth, and then he shakes his head. "Such a shame. *Such* a beautiful creature." He sighs. "Still, I suppose we all have to go *some* way . . . that's just nature's course."

Remembering myself, I remove my hand from Gonderberry's shoulder.

I look at my wine glass then subtly lay it down beside one of the enclosures, where I hope Gonderberry won't discover it for quite some time. So he won't have the opportunity to realise I didn't *finish* my serving.

Having come this far — having found myself in *this* situation — I realise that there's nothing else for me to do. So I decide to blurt it out.

"What happened?" I ask. "That day . . ."

Gonderberry peers into the glass enclosure, to the python hanging off the branch. "It's a mystery," he says, his voice sounding far away. "A *real* mystery."

———

I'm thankful Gonderberry has the presence of mind to realise I was feeling uncomfortable down in the snake pit. Unfortunately, though, he doesn't seem to have the same presence of mind where wine is concerned. He asks no question about what became of my previous glass, acting almost out of reflex by going to the cabinet and pouring out another couple of servings. This time, though, there's no clinking of glasses.

"I was always so careful," Gonderberry says. "About *everything*, but especially with my animals." He breathes in deeply, taking the air right down to the pit of his lungs in a way which makes me wonder if he's an ex-smoker; if he misses the habitual inhalation of smoke and tar. Again, he swills his glass of wine, peering into the red liquid slopping about. "I have a system — *always have done*. Whenever I open up an enclosure, I'm certain to hang the opened lock from my belt." Here he indicates his suit trousers, and the — *surely hand-crafted* — belt which he wears there. "It works as a reminder," he says. "And although it's only happened a couple of times, I have *always* remembered . . . in the end."

"And . . . this time?" I ask.

He sucks in then gives a sigh. "I . . . don't know . . . when the police arrived on the scene — when they came to *investigate*" — he adds a touch of venom here — "they said they located the padlock hanging from the enclosure. The lid was left open." He shrugs, widens his eyes. "I truly can't remember . . . *truly can't*."

Here I can't help but feel that he is honestly remorseful.

That — at least as far as he can fathom — he's telling the truth.

Does that mean anything?

Does *my* perception mean anything?

"I was out that evening," he says. "Meeting with a *producer*, actually." He swallows — *hard* — then takes a quick swig of wine. He shakes his head again, either at the bitterness of the taste or at the bitterness of the memory. "I knew something was wrong the second I crossed the threshold. Everything was so . . . *silent* . . . and yet, at the same time, I could tell there was something . . . *something* in the air."

Although he doesn't elaborate any further, I understand exactly where he's coming from. And just what he means when he says 'something'. He means there were *screams* in the air . . . I've always believed there's something about a human scream which just hangs; which just *lurks* for hours and hours afterwards.

Almost as if it leaves an invisible imprint on the world itself.

Maybe we're as crazy as one another.

"It was just like that night . . ."

Gonderberry trails off, his voice growing quieter as he utters each word.

My heart beats hard.

I feel the gentle *thump-thump* deep in my stomach.

"The night when I came here . . . when I found . . . I found . . . *the two of them* . . ."

I'm acquainted enough with Cuthbert Gonderberry's life and times to realise he's speaking about his parents' double-suicide. About how Gonderberry discovered the two of them, in the master bedroom; both with a bullet hole to the forehead. From my own reading into the investigation, I recall how the conclusion had been drawn that Gonderberry's father — the *Admiral* — had first shot his wife and then himself.

Of course, there had been many theories bandied about as to whether it was a double-suicide or a murder-suicide.

Gonderberry draws a couple of staccato breaths. He tips back the remainder of his wine, and then, with a well-arrested stumble, crosses the room and serves himself a drop or two more. He speaks to me from the cabinet. "In some ways, I wish I had been punished . . . that they'd found me *guilty* . . . but the police — the *investigation* . . . they described it as an 'accident' . . . they ordered the animal destroyed . . . but they said it was impossible to prove . . . to prove that I was the one who . . . who . . ."

146

"Let the snake out?" I suggest.

Gonderberry holds very still. Then he nods. "This house has known so much misery."

I watch on as he pours the wine right to the rim. He becomes quite studiously patient as he waits for the last drops from the bottle to fall into the glass. "There have been so many times when I have desired to *sell* the place . . . to simply *get rid* of it." He returns to the sofa and sits beside me. When he sits, he almost upsets the wine, but — *against all odds* — manages to maintain his balance. An actor's sense of control. "But then I thought about my *history* . . . about how the house has been in my family for *generations*." He shakes his head, this time with reddened cheeks. "And I simply *couldn't* do it . . . it just seemed *wrong*."

The two of us sit in silence for the longest time.

I wonder what I can say . . . wonder if there's anything *to* say.

I decide the time is right for me to get going. I thank Gonderberry for the wine, and for having forgiven me for the whole ridiculous act which AA put on. He is unnaturally graceful as he leads me into the hallway, to his front door, and says, "Well, I have to admit that it was somewhat more elaborate than the deception I'm used to . . . I can say that much."

Right as I'm about to leave, he calls me back.

"Say, Anna?"

Looking out across the gravel driveway, I can hear the gentle *rumble* of a car engine idling. AA and my kids await.

I snap back onto Gonderberry.

Summon a smile.

For the first time in our acquaintanceship, I actually feel as if I'm something approaching *calm* in his company. And I realise that it's — *almost exclusively* — down to Gonderberry . . . down to his acceptance; to his forgiveness. Perhaps I didn't misjudge him, after all. Maybe I'm the only one of us who has actually got this case *right* . . .

"I was wondering, if it's not too much trouble, whether you might be interested in attending the opening night of my latest play." He gives a wide smile, only slightly enhanced by the glowing red cheeks brought on from drinking. "I think you had a quick leaf through it when you were last here."

"*Antony and Cleopatra?*" I ask, remembering.

"That's right."

My heart bounces. I've never been to a premiere, or an 'opening night', whatever its name is in a theatrical context. "Yes, I'd be . . . honoured."

"Terrific. Then if you'll be good enough to give me your address, I shall send along the tickets by special delivery."

From somewhere, he has produced a notepad and pen.

As he holds the items out to me, I feel an onrush of nerves.

Is this really a good idea?

My mind flashes back to Paula Stevenstar's story . . . about how Cuthbert was completely reasonable before he cropped up in her bedroom bearing a knife later on.

The calm before the storm?

I take the notepad, realising I only have two options.

I can either give him a fake address or a real one.

. . . Or is there a third option?

I glance up. "Is a post office box okay?"

"Sure," he replies, without batting an eyelid.

That settles my nerves. And I scribble down the details.

Hand the notepad back to him.

"Plus one?" he asks.

I think about Mark . . . feel somewhat ashamed that he's slipped my mind.

If only for a few seconds.

"Yes, please."

Gonderberry retreats into the hallway, and out of the frosty night air. "Terrific, then I shall see you there — I do hope you'll come backstage afterwards."

I feel a warm glow despite the cold. "Looking forward to it."

"Goodbye, Anna," he says, bringing the door shut.

As I tread my way along the gravel pathway — headed for the gates — I can't help but feel a skip in my step. It feels as if a murky fog has cleared; as if my conscience has been cleansed. And, what's more, I think I can conclusively bring this case to a close. Though how AA, Amy and Tabby will take the tearing-up of their meal ticket, I don't want to speculate.

It's only then that I note the familiar weight in my pocket. I reach down, feeling the audio-recording device there. My heart sinks. I think about how I ended up on good terms with Gonderberry . . . how I admitted our deception; how I made some sort of an implicit promise that it was all behind us now.

And yet, I was recording the entire encounter.

What a *bitch* . . .

When I reach the pavement outside, I see AA sitting behind the wheel of Mark's car. As I get closer, I see Josie sat in the back seat. The passenger seat — beside AA — is empty.

For a second I'm confused.

Before I totally wrap my head around what's going on, AA emerges from the driver's side. He wears a look of befuddlement. "Anna, I think we've got a little problem."

Chapter Twenty-Three

I feel as if I could strangle AA.

Like — *really* — strangle him.

As I ride in the passenger seat, with AA tipping us around corners at a rapid click, he explains what happened. He tells me about how he took the car for a 'spin' around the block; about how he was trying to strike up a conversation with my kids.

I glance back at Josie, see that she's apparently unperturbed by the unfolding events — if anything slightly *amused*. To be quite honest, there is quite a lot that's *amusing* about AA. Not to mention her mother.

AA goes on to explain how he had stopped at a traffic light, and that they were — *decorously* — waiting for it to change green when Ben suddenly opened his door. And, without a word, sprinted off into the night.

AA assures me he stuck the hazard lights on and pursued Ben on foot. However, as it soon turned out, AA caught a stitch . . . he lost my son to the night-time.

Great.

Just great.

He claims he took a good half an hour to search for him — and Josie confirms this assertion. After a while, though, he decided to return to Parisianer Hall; apparently to toss the ball into my court. After all, Ben *is* my son; *my* responsibility.

AA brings the car to an abrupt stop alongside a small river. He gestures wildly in the general direction in which Ben ran off. I stare into the darkness, as if Ben might be hiding out there. With a sigh, realising there's little option — I can hardly turn up at Arnold's house without *Ben* — I unplug my seatbelt and venture into the night.

AA unwinds the driver's side window, calls out to me.

When I turn, a blunt object flies into my stomach.

I have the presence of mind to make a grab for it.

And to catch hold.

A *torch*.

Now, that *will* come in handy.

———

The river smells about as good as can be expected.

I'm somewhat grateful that the torch's circle of light only illuminates the ground directly before my toes. It sends a shudder down my spine to think just what exactly might be floating along the surface of the river.

Without any real direction, I set off walking, constantly glancing about, trying to work out if there're any clues. Perhaps this whole private-investigator deal has begun to get to me. Maybe I really *have* started to think that I possess some sort of innate *crime-solving* ability. I can't think why it would've passed me by all these years . . .

I start to think about turning back — about simply owning up to Arnold that I managed to lose *our son* — when I again feel something shift in my gut.

I focus on the bridge up ahead.

To the darkness which lurks beneath.

I glance back over my shoulder.

Realise I can no longer make out the car headlights.

Well, this really *will* be the last shake of the dice.

As I tread now, I can feel that the floor is beginning to freeze — that the ice is starting to form beneath my feet. I know that I need to take care so as not to slip and fall . . . to break my neck and take a tumble into the river. That would see me thoroughly stuck up the proverbial Shit Creek without a paddle.

I shine the torchlight into the darkness, beneath the bridge.

I make out the huddled forms; all of them wrapped up in blankets.

Some of them stir.

I catch the eyes with my torch beam.

The smell of body odour, and excrement, and rotten breath hits me.

Someone mumbles something at me . . . something I can't make out.

"Hello?" I say.

There's another mumble from within the bundles of clothing.

I stoop over.

Take a couple of steps.

"Uh . . . I'm looking for someone," I say. "He's a boy. Fifteen years old. My son."

Now standing hunched-over before the bodies, I turn my torchlight over their faces.

In turn, they hold their forearms up to shield their eyes.

Someone mumbles a response but it doesn't make a lick of sense.

I need to find *Ben*.

I scan the row of bodies, get to the end, and then return to the beginning.

Finally, I settle on one in particular.

Realise that I recognise the face.

Not to mention the washed clothes.

"Ben?" I say.

He remains huddled as he is for a long few seconds. Then — *finally* — willing to admit he's been rumbled, he shifts his attention up in my direction. He holds my gaze.

"Come on," I say, "we're going home. It's late. School tomorrow."

He continues to stare back at me.

It sends a shiver about my collar.

Just the way he looks at me . . . *like a stranger.*

Reluctantly, Ben lifts himself up from the others — from those bodies all massed together.

I back out of the bridge and allow him to pass by.

As he does so, he says nothing at all.

No explanation.

Nothing.

I guess that's teenagers for you.

I take one final look at the huddled-up bodies as I go after Ben.

He trudges along the riverbank, hands stuffed into the front pocket of his hooded sweatshirt. We say nothing to one another until we return to the road . . . to the waiting car.

I exchange glances with AA in the driver's seat, and then turn back to Ben.

Before he can skulk off, I reach out and grab hold of his sweatshirt sleeve. He doesn't resist. But he continues to stare off in the other direction.

"Look at me," I say.

He doesn't react.

"*Look* at me!"

Finally, he relinquishes.

He turns.

Meets my eye.

"What were you doing?"

Ben says nothing.

He stares back.

Not a challenge . . . but he's not backing down either.

"*Tell* me," I say, this time with a touch of desperation.

Ben seems to pick up on the fact that we're not going anywhere until he gives me something by way of explanation. He puffs a sigh out, sending the air streaming from his nostrils and mouth in the form of steam. When he replies, I can hardly make out his words, almost as if he's become like one of those homeless people beneath the bridge.

"What?" I say.

Ben takes another deep breath — surely intended to be another sigh.

I increase my grip on his sleeve.

Finally, he relents.

"I wanted to . . . to see what it *feels* like."

"How what feels like?"

"You know," he says, giving a shrug and looking back off to the river.

"No, I don't."

"Like them . . . like *those* people."

"Like a *homeless* person?"

"Yeah."

I allow the words to settle.

I try to work out what to do . . . just what I'm *supposed* to do.

Then I catch myself.

"What's the matter? What's going on?"

Ben shrugs.

I think — *really think* — before what I say next.

It's time for me to be a grown-up for once.

Yeah, right . . .

"I'm going to tell Dad about what happened."

This gets Ben's attention.

He *gawps*.

Eyes wide.

Lips parted.

Neck stretched.

"But, you said . . ."

"Shut up. It doesn't *matter* what I said — I'm your mother, I get to make the rules."

Ben's mouth flaps open and shut, like a banked fish . . . but then he seems to fathom that I'm telling the truth. And there's *nothing* he can do about it.

"Get in the car," I say.

He allows his shoulders to droop.

Gives a shake of his head.

And — I'm fairly certain — I overhear him utter, "It's not fair," beneath his breath.

I allow myself a faint smile at this *teenagerism*.

Do they get this stuff from a phrasebook?

Once I get back in the car, AA slips me a sidelong glance but — *wisely* — says nothing at all. That's when I feel the uncomfortable object still in my jeans pocket.

The audio recorder.

I slip it out then dump it in AA's lap.

That's enough sleuthing for me . . .

Chapter Twenty-Four

I get the call through from Amy about two weeks later.

As I stare at her name spelled out on my mobile phone screen, I can't help but think of how long it's been since we spoke last. And how I assumed that, well, this whole thing had just blown over. However, what most surprises me is that I get a call rather than a message through the encrypted chat app we all have installed on our mobile phones.

"Tickets have arrived," she says.

" 'Tickets' ?"

"Yeah, through the post office box."

My mind skims back.

I think about my last meeting with Gonderberry.

It returns to me . . . what he said about sending me tickets to the opening night of *Antony and Cleopatra*. It'd completely slipped my mind.

I switch my attention back to Amy. "What's the date?"

"This Friday," she replies, and then, apparently unable to contain herself. "You really *do* know how to get yourself on the inside track, Anna."

"Yeah," I reply, "I guess I do." I glance out of the bedroom window, to the garden.

It's a rare sunny day, and Mark is outside, sawing at some planks of wood.

What their eventual use will turn out to be is anyone's guess.

Or, well, my inexpert eye can't tell.

Amy says that she'll leave the tickets up in Sex Flat; where they'll be neat and safe.

We've sort of reached an understanding whereby none of the others come to Mark's house unless it's one-hundred-per-cent necessary.

I spend a few joyful moments peering out through the bedroom window — taking in Mark toiling over those planks of wood — and then, when I can take the sight of him working up a sweat no more, I head downstairs.

I stand out on the patio, take in the sight of my man — glistening with sweat; and rippling with muscles — as he puts his back into the physical task at hand. I eye his bandaged up fingers; bound together. From the times when I've been in to visit his workshop, he's been in an obvious state of frustration at not being as dexterous as usual . . . as he's *accustomed* to being.

He glances at me.

Gives me a wide smile.

"Come to help out?" he asks.

"No. Actually, I thought I might invite you to the opening night of a theatrical production."

"An 'opening night' ?" Mark replies with a slight scowl, as if

I've just uttered a phrase in a foreign language. "You mean, like, renting a tux?"

I shrug. I hold myself still, bleeding the moment out as long as possible before adding, "It's starring Cuthbert Gonderberry."

Mark mouths, *Wow*. His saw hangs down at his side, forgotten for the time being. He blinks several times, cocks his head to one side; something apparently striking him. The smile — or the look of *excitement*, whatever it's meant to be — slips from his face. "But Friday's parent-teacher evening," he says.

It feels almost as if he's punched me in the gut.

I think it through.

Of course, this means that it'll be Ben's parent-teacher evening too, although it's always been Arnold who attends them in Kate's company.

"That's unfortunate," I reply, and then, "Maybe I can get tickets for a different night — for a performance next week."

There's a long silence.

Finally, Mark breaks from his static pose. He scratches the back of his neck. "Actually, to tell the truth, I never was all that much of a fan of . . . uh . . ."

"*Shakespeare?*" I suggest.

"Yeah," he replies, cracking a slight smile. "I mean, it's one thing to see Gonderberry in a film, but, I don't know . . . these *plays* they all take like three or four hours, don't they?"

Not having all that much knowledge myself, I restrain the urge to answer. That old adage about allowing people to *think* you a fool — rather than opening your mouth to confirm it — has always held true.

"So," I say, "what I'm hearing is, '*Thanks, but no thanks*' ?"

Mark gives me a sheepish grin . . . a grin *uncannily* similar to one of Nathan's.

"Okey doke," I reply, then head back into the house. "Just thought I'd ask."

I've set one foot inside the house when Mark calls to me.

I turn.

Mark stares at me, his expression serious now. "I was . . . I don't know . . ." He flaps his hand through the air. "Forget about it," he says, finally, turning back to his sawing.

I hold still, wondering whether or not I should follow up, then decide that I'm probably better off leaving things as they are.

————

I get to Sex Flat soon enough, and find the tickets on the mantelpiece of the long-neglected fireplace. On my way out, I nearly break AA's nose.

AA grins wildly, seemingly having forgotten that more introspective mood which he put on when he lost my son. "What've you got there?" he says, nodding to my hands.

Suddenly feeling somewhat self-conscious, I reply, "The tickets — for the opening night of *Antony and Cleopatra* starring Cuthbert Gonderberry."

AA screws up his eyes as he examines the ticket. He glances up. "*Plus one.*"

"Want to come?" I ask.

"I wouldn't want to presume. I wouldn't want to do you out of a hot date."

"My 'hot date' doesn't do Shakespeare."

AA breaks into his familiar grin. "Oh, goody. Pick you up at six?"

"Six'd be fine."

I don't really want to hang around for too much longer; don't want to pry into the exact reason *why* AA is present here today.

And he seems just as willing to let me go.

———

Out on the street, I'm in the process of filing away my ticket for Friday's show when I bump straight into someone. I'm midway through apologising when I think to look up; to take stock of who it is.

First, I take in the overcoat; the collar turned up so that it covers everything but the tip of the nose. One of the Middle-Eastern men I noticed playing dice down here, several times before . . . once when I no doubt should've been concentrating on the details of Paula Stevenstar's story.

The man stares back at me, mostly because I haven't said sorry.

I cast a glance down at the pavement.

To the dice there.

I see now that they have a rug which they throw the dice upon.

When I turn, I note the other Middle-Eastern man lurking nearby, casually glancing off across the road. I suppose he's on the lookout for police.

"Twenty pound," he says, and then repeats himself. "Twenty pound."

I glance up, to Sex Flat, half expecting to see AA peering down, slipping me something like an amused, fatherly gaze . . . watching on as his daughter goes through with some act of stupidity. And what I do *is* stupid, but it seems that my mind is made up.

I fish through my handbag, uncover a bundle of notes.

As I surface, I can't help but notice the Middle-Eastern man's features have lit up at the sign of so many twenties stuffed in there. Lots of opportunities.

He takes the twenty-pound note from me, making a show of rubbing it, holding it up to the light, and crinkling it. Finally, apparently content with the state of my money, he pockets the note and produces a pair of dice. "Even pairs," he says, "you win. One hundred pound. No pairs, you lose."

I just about manage to figure out what he's saying.

And I quickly calculate my odds.

Realise that they're not all that good.

Is it three in thirty-six?

Something like that?

Hypnotised, I watch on as the man sends the dice tumbling onto the rug at his feet.

My heart hangs in my throat as the dice roll over.

Reveal a pair of fours.

Feeling somewhat bemused, I turn my attention back to the man.

He gives me a broad grin.

Spreads his arms, as if there's nothing he can do.

Then, without delay, he produces a bundle of twenties and prises out five notes:

One hundred pounds.

Just like he claimed.

I take the notes.

Mostly because of the show he put on when taking my own twenty-pound note, I take great pains to check each one of the notes for its authenticity. They all seem real enough.

When I look back, I see he's still flashing me a beaming grin.

I smile. "See ya."

"Take care."

Leaving him behind, I pad my way up the road, away from Sex Flat, and back to Brent Cross Station. I can't help but feel strangely positive at this turn of events.

I just made eighty quid.

Chapter Twenty-Five

The night before parents' evening — a Thursday — Arnold calls me up and asks me around for a 'chat'. I manage to negotiate neutral territory, and we agree on a pleasantly anonymous café tucked into a shopping centre on Bond Street.

I know what this is about, of course.

It has everything to do with the bombshell I dropped regarding our son.

I came to my senses eventually, deciding that I was being an idiot to keep Ben's arrest a secret from Arnold. When I returned Ben the night we went to visit Gonderberry's home — when Ben took it upon himself to go running off — I spewed the whole deal to Arnold; along with the details of me holding out on him . . . when the time comes to tell the truth, you just have to own up to everything. And take the *blame* for everything.

That night, he was rendered somewhat stunned by the outpouring.

He hadn't got much past the shock by the time I retreated from the doorstep — with Kate lurking in the background, on the staircase. In a way, I suppose it was a cop-out, even if I managed to sell it to myself as doing the 'noble' thing. How many times have I dropped elaborate messes into Arnold's lap and then just let him *get on with it*?

More times than I can count, that's for certain.

I arrive ahead of Arnold — there's a first time for everything — and I set myself to the task of ordering from the expansive menu. When I ask for a 'coffee with milk' the barista takes pity on me, not bothering to pin me down to a more specific brew. The drink I end up with seems to be more froth than coffee, but I'm in no mood to complain.

It'd only start the questions all over again.

Once I'm sat down at a table by the window — so that I have an unobstructed view of the surroundings; of those who might be approaching the café — I allow myself to relax and just take gentle sips at my coffee. I have to admit that I've been excited all week about the prospect of attending the opening night of *Antony and Cleopatra*; for all of the rounds I've done in high circles, I've never actually attended the opening of anything before.

Maybe there *is* something to this private-investigator malarkey.

Arnold arrives soon enough.

He wears a close-fitting, grey denim jacket over the top of a white shirt with a frilly collar. I note that he's recently had a haircut, a close shave about the sides while he's left it a little longer on the top. It looks just like a haircut kids these days go about with.

Whatever the case, I have to suppress a wry grin.

Arnold leans into me, planting a kiss on either cheek.

His skin is smooth.

At least he hasn't bought into the whole 'beard' fad.

He orders at the counter, not missing a beat as he jabbers through some near incomprehensible jumble of options, or flavours, or preparations; all those hallmarks of the *serious* coffee drinker. Me? I just like something that'll give me a good *kick* in the morning.

Once he's ordered, Arnold *umms* and *ahhs* over the upsell — the barista offering him something from the selection of the various pastries and biscuits which adorn the glass cabinet. Finally he settles on a chocolate brownie, and then, as he's about to hand over his money, he changes his mind; instead going for a slice of carrot cake, muttering something about being *healthier* . . . maybe he thinks carrot cake counts as one of his five portions of fruit and vegetables. Someone should probably put him right someday . . .

Once he's sat down opposite, and he's scoffed his way through three quarters of his cake before thinking to offer me a bite — I politely decline — he takes up his serious posture; shoulders arched, hands clasped on the table.

Ready for the Big Chat.

"I thought we should talk before I speak with Ben's teachers tomorrow."

I glance out of the window, to the street outside.

There's a multitude of Christmas shoppers, all bundled together, a mishmash of shopping bags and seasonal clothing and a sense of *snappy* festive cheer in the air.

I've never been one for sentimentalism, but it even gets to me.

Elicits some *emotion* in me.

"What're you planning on telling them?" I ask.

Arnold avoids my gaze — a well-worn tactic. "I thought, at

166

the very least, we should let his tutor know . . . just so he can be on the lookout; so he can *keep an eye* on Ben . . ."

I allow this suggestion to hang in the air a few moments. "You do realise that his form tutor will immediately report the information to the head teacher, don't you?"

Arnold holds himself still. "Why would they do that?"

"Because they *have* to . . . regulations."

Arnold dabs at a crumb of carrot cake on the otherwise-empty plate. He sucks on his finger, clearly savouring the sweetly sensation. "You think we should ask the police to tell his school?"

My eyes nearly bulge from their sockets. "Do you want him to get kicked out?"

Arnold switches his attention out of the window, to the shopping centre, and to the people plodding past, all wrapped up in hats and gloves; thick scarves coiled about their throats like — *it strikes me* — Gonderberry's python.

"What're we going to do?" Arnold murmurs, mostly to himself.

"I suggest we keep it to ourselves for the time being. Tomorrow night, when you go to the parent-teacher conference, probe the issue . . . ask them whether they've noticed any *unusual* behaviour."

Arnold blinks a couple of times.

Clearly absorbing this fact.

"You really think that they'd go over our heads?" he asks.

"Listen, they're not just dealing with *one kid*, they're dealing with the entire school. Of course they will do whatever's best for the other kids. You need to be subtle . . . you need to *talk around* the subject; make it sound like he's being rebellious at home, something like that . . . don't tell them he's a criminal."

"He's *not* a criminal," Arnold says, sounding more than a little defensive.

If there's one thing about parents and their children, it's that the former take any criticism of the latter completely to heart. And being a parent myself — and once having been a child — I'm qualified to comment.

"He *stole* from a *shop*," I say. "*Stealing*. Criminal behaviour."

Arnold absorbs this statement.

Holds it up for consideration.

Then he says, quite decided, "Okay — I'll do my best." He pauses. "But, from the sound of things, you'd be better off coming along."

I feel myself sinking in my chair.

"Just the two of us?" I ask.

Arnold shakes his head. "I've already told Kate that she can come. It would be . . . *complicated* to suddenly tell her that she can't."

"Then it's a non-starter," I reply.

I look about the café, attempting to find something to distract me. Unfortunately, the café is bereft of much by way of distraction.

I decide to take more dramatic action.

I reach back for my coat, hanging off my chair.

Arnold takes the hint, rising up.

I manage to press on a smile. "Let me know how it goes," I say.

As I sidle past the table, I find myself standing before Arnold, and unable to avoid a pair of kisses — one on each of my cheeks.

"Will do," he replies.

I duck out of the meeting without any further drama . . . or brother-sister kisses.

When I get back outside, back onto Bond Street, I feel the festivity begin to bleed its way back into me. I start to forget all about mine and Arnold's meeting.

Maybe this isn't going to be such a bad Christmas after all.

Chapter Twenty-Six

The opening night of Cuthbert Gonderberry's *Antony and Cleopatra* finally rolls around. The house is buzzing with activity as Mark and Nathan sway in and out of one another's way; getting ready for the parent-teacher evening. The two of them head out a little before I do — something which I'm deeply grateful for given that, when AA comes over, it affords me a little time to get his opinion on my get-up.

It's not positive, unfortunately.

"Anna, really," he says, looking over my shoulder at my reflection in the full-length mirror. "You look like somebody's *grandmother* — "

"All right," I shoot back. "That's enough with the hurtful comments."

"I wasn't finished. I wanted to say that you look like somebody's grandmother's *dog*."

"Oh, thanks, that's much better."

He smirks.

I take in my appearance another time.

I settled on an emerald dress — one which I bought about six months ago for one of Mark's networking meet-ups. I thought that I'd done a reasonable job with my choice, and that the green flat shoes I'd picked out were the perfect match.

But apparently not.

As AA digs through my wardrobe, I run an eye over his outfit and find it impossible to come up with anything negative to say. Then something strikes me. "At least I don't look boring."

AA continues to paw about in the wardrobe, apparently feigning that he didn't hear my remark. I have to admit that, when it comes to men, their appearance being *boring* is really the least of it all. Seemingly, the entire point of male formal dress *is* to look boring . . . I mean, how're you meant to jazz up a tuxedo?

. . . Don't answer that question; because I'm sure there *are* ways . . . *plenty* of ways.

Finally, AA digs out a red satin dress which he soon couples with a pair of *towering* high heels. To be honest, I didn't even *know* I possessed such clothes. Then again, AA seems capable of miracles when it comes to dressing up . . .

He unceremoniously tosses the dress at me.

I take it from him.

"Hurry up!" he says. "You're going to make us late."

I disappear into the en suite bathroom while AA continues to prowl about my wardrobe; apparently holding up my other clothes for inspection.

Once I've put on the dress, and examined myself in the somewhat *small* bathroom mirror, I pluck up the courage to emerge, where I find — *unsurprisingly* — AA waiting, arms folded across his chest, a discerning look on his face.

He rounds me a couple of times. I feel him pinch me in a

couple of tender places. When he arrives back in front of my face, he looks me in the eye, gives me the faintest hint of a smile and then nods his approval. "Looks like you're all ready for the ball, Cinderella."

"Don't call me Cinderella."

His smile cracks wider. "My, oh, my, you *do* have some *panache*."

I scowl in response and the two of us head downstairs, and out the front door.

———

On our way to the theatre, I can't help but notice AA constantly checking his mobile phone. Although I have the urge to tell him to give it a rest — at least while he's driving — he's bombing along the road at such a speed that I'm afraid that it might serve only to distract him. That he might flinch and jerk us directly into oncoming traffic.

As it turns out, we do arrive without being killed in an automotive accident.

AA takes us down into some underground car park I never knew existed.

Royal-red, Routemaster buses hum along the road. Black cabs worm about in their wake. I take stock of the private-hire cars . . . generally white with tinted windows. Whoever decided that sort of design was *subtle* really needs shooting. But, then again, I suppose 'being subtle' is the very last thing on most celebrities' minds.

A light drizzle has begun to fall, and I can feel it seeping in through the overcoat I'm wearing. It sends a chill through my blood, and makes goose pimples pucker my skin. I'm all too aware of my exposed shins and thighs, let alone deeply preoccupied in attempting to avoid the many cracks and holes in the pavement.

"That's it," AA says.

I glance up.

See the venue for tonight's performance:

The Auburn Theatre.

Its name stretches about the periphery of the marquee which surrounds the entrance; all illuminated with bright-white bulbs. I suppose that on summer nights, those bulbs serve to light up all the bugs buzzing about in the twilight air; tonight, though, the bulbs bring attention to the tumbling raindrops.

Although I've become accustomed throughout my life to seeing Cuthbert Gonderberry's face just about anywhere, it is odd to see it here tonight — about a hundred feet tall and stretching up the side of the theatre. If I hadn't met him in person, I would've thought that whoever designed the poster had invested an ungodly amount of time in performing some sort of devilment with Gonderberry's eyes . . . his irises make it seem as if he belongs to some alien species: one blue, the other green. His straight-edged jawline, and the tussled — and yet somehow *perfect* — hair seems only to underline the whole unreality of Gonderberry's image.

More than ever, he looks like a Hollywood actor.

His star glows just that little bit *brighter*.

When I take in the poster a second time, I realise that the leading lady — Asha Tumbleton who is to play Cleopatra — is relegated to a corner along with the other — *clearly secondary* — cast members.

As if keen to display some sort of fatherly — or *beau-like* — behaviour, AA loops his arm and instructs me to take hold.

This almost feels like the old days; back when we were off performing undercover.

The only difference, I suppose, is that the two of us are very much off-duty, and — *technically at least* — unemployed.

Just inside the doors, the ushers check our tickets.

I believe something's wrong when one of them radios to a member of the management.

I look at AA.

And AA looks back at me.

There's no need for words, our expressions are all that's required.

We're telling one another that we're exposed . . . *unarmed* . . . if we come across trouble tonight then there'll be nothing we can do.

However, as it turns out, a member of the management — a youngish man dressed in a tuxedo — leads us away from the lobby and up a staircase maintained off limits by a red, velvet rope. I sneak a final glance over my shoulder at the lobby before it disappears from sight; taking stock of the ornately carved ceiling, and the polished-up, walnut bar counter.

The man leads us along an upper-floor corridor, and then through a velvet curtain.

Only when he holds back the curtain, and gives something like a bow, do I realise that he's showing us to a box. I take in the half dozen seats laid out on the balcony, and can't help thinking to myself if this is really as luxurious as it seems.

We'll be watching the entire performance at an *angle*.

Still, at least I get to stare down on all the plebs beneath . . .

The man takes mine and AA's coats, then, with another bow, promises he'll return to take our drinks order. Feeling a little as if I've been caught up in the winter's gales which're blowing outside, I settle down into my seat, and turn my attention to the stage.

It's pretty much as I imagined, which is to say that there're the wooden floorboards, and then a red curtain which provides the backdrop; no doubt, concealing whatever delicate, mechanical workings are taking place out of the audience's sight.

When I cast a glance down at the seats below, I realise that it's not even half full yet.

I look to the other boxes jutting out from upper floors and realise that they're still entirely vacated. I suppose it's not the done thing for the moneyed classes to arrive *early* to something so fleeting and *base* as entertainment. I only recall that I brought my mobile with me at all when my handbag begins to rumble vigorously. I dig out my phone and see I have a new message . . . and not just *any* new message, but one from Amy through the Assassins' Anonymous app.

I tap it open and check it over.

Looking good!

That's all it says.

My mind whirrs to catch up with reality.

Finally I twig — looking down to the commoners' seats — that Amy is standing up and waving away. I slip a glance to AA, who flashes his eyebrows and maintains a stern expression. Then, in mock disgust, he turns away from the waving Amy and in the direction of the stage; pouting. A stickler for manners if nothing else, I can't help but give Amy a dainty little wave, and it's then that I notice Tabby sitting beside her. She smiles up at me.

My chest tightens.

And my gut sinks.

I lean into AA — still placing all his faux enthusiasm on the vacated stage before us. "What've you got planned?" I ask.

He continues to stare at the stage, pretending he hasn't heard me at all.

I give him a solid punch on the upper arm.

He flinches. Shifts in his seat. Glares at me. "Are we on a *school* trip or something?"

"Don't know. *Are* we?" I gesture down at Amy and Tabby. "What're they *doing* here?"

AA shrugs. "It's a free country — you can't stop people from going out and enjoying a bit of the Bard on a Friday night."

"But why *tonight* . . . why *opening* night?"

Again AA shrugs.

I give him another punch.

He sinks his teeth into his lower lip and hisses.

The voices over our shoulders bring me around from the melee.

I glance back to see the man in the tuxedo escorting what appears to be a *high-class* couple into their assigned seats in the box. The couple are in their seventies — or perhaps even older. The gentleman wears a jacket with a tail, which he needs to flip upwards before taking his seat. The two of them give me and AA a gentle nod by way of greeting and what appears — at least to me — like a *calculating* smile.

I wonder if they saw that impulsive punch.

Hardly becoming behaviour for a — *relatively* — young lady . . .

I keep my voice down low now, although I'm certain to communicate my seething tone to AA. "You want to speak to him after the show, don't you? You want *all* of us to go backstage after the show."

"Only fair, isn't it? I mean, why should you have a monopoly on *Cuthers* . . . if it hadn't been for me then you wouldn't have got to meet him at all."

I guess he has a point, and that's the reason why I decide to pull my punches for the time being. I shift my glance about the theatre, taking in the box on the other side, and realising there's another familiar face settling in:

Paula Stevenstar.

Our *client*.

All of a sudden, I find it difficult to sit still . . .

There's something just . . . *off* about this whole experience.

Something which makes me want to leave.

And perhaps if I hadn't been *personally* invited backstage by the show's star after the performance, I would do just that.

Paula gives me a casual wave, and I wave back.

AA leans into me. "Paula says, 'Good work', by the way — you know, getting on Cuthers' inside track . . ."

That's when I feel my anger frothing to the surface.

But I contain it.

Control it.

"Why do you think I'm playing the game?" I say, in a whisper. "What makes you think I'm not *sleeping* with him?"

AA shrugs, then says, in an obnoxious voice which is supposed to be heard by anybody in the same postcode, "Because, my dear, I know you — if you were *sleeping* with him, you'd have a *naughty* glow."

I resist the urge to turn around and apologise to the elderly couple. I've always found that when couples apologise for bickering in public, it only makes things worse.

So I just smoulder away in silence.

I can hear a bell ringing — calling the audience in from the lobby — when I feel my mobile begin to vibrate again. I shift my attention onto its screen, take in the incoming call.

It's Mark.

I glance about, wondering if I might be able to sneak out before the performance starts. But, when I look over my shoulder — when I see another, slightly younger, but no less *high class* couple arriving — I decide I'm just going to have to ignore Mark for the time being. Most likely he's just checking in.

I do the 'proper' thing and hang up, slipping my mobile back into my handbag.

The bell sounds another few times.

People continue to stream in.

Before long, everyone is in their seats, chatting excitedly.

From some of the conversations, I overhear references to Cuthbert Gonderberry. And to his 'innate ability' or his 'natural-born talent' or his 'astonishing presence'. I wonder just how many members of the audience have actually been in the same room as him before; let alone *talked* to him. And I kill that thought right there, realising that I'm beginning to sound more and more like some tiresome *celebrity* spotter.

When the curtain draws — and the whole audience is struck with a *hush* — I have to admit that I'm just as affected by the spell of the stage.

———

By the time the bell rings for the intermission, I can feel myself tingling all over.

It's quite something.

Gonderberry is quite something.

And since I can only understand just about every other word, that's an achievement.

I look to AA, unsure quite what Etiquette dictates we do during the interval.

While the audience streams out, headed to the lobby, I glance over to the box opposite. I note Paula Stevenstar is having what appears to be a decorous conversation.

With half a mind on Mark's phone call just before the performance started, I excuse myself, and shift out between the couples. The usher stands at the entrance to the box. He gives me a deferential smile and a half bow as I pass by.

Out on the staircase, I set about searching for the women's toilets.

I find them guarded by an officious-looking female usher.

No doubt here to keep the Great Unwashed out.

The female usher makes no sound as I pass by.

The toilets are everything I hoped they would be: polished marble, gleaning floors, and a quietly soothing orchestral sound-track bumbling along in the background.

There's a window, too, which looks out across the West End.

For a few seconds, I'm rendered stunned by the many — *many* — lights which glimmer. When I reach up and latch the window open, a fierce chill sneaks in. It sends a freezing sensation through my blood. It also lets in the traffic noise: shouting, car horns. I swiftly shut the window again.

One of the toilets flushes.

I turn in the direction of the sound.

Realise that one of the cubicles — if it can *really* be called that — is occupied.

Not really wanting anybody to overhear my phone conversation, and not wishing to be judged by some Duchess or Dame, I wait patiently for the cubicle door to open.

And, when it does, I get a nasty little shock.

It's Amy.

"Hi Anna!" she says, and then rushes for me, like some mad, out-of-control puppy.

She squeezes me too tightly about the middle.

Once I've prised her free, I cock my head to one side and take in her outfit.

A single-strapped sapphire-blue dress. It really brings out her eyes.

. . . I wonder if AA gave her some tips ahead of tonight.

As always, she smells lightly of strawberries; only this time there's a touch of *spice* about those strawberries. Perhaps she dabbed on a little something extra . . .

Unable to hold back any longer, I blurt out, "What're you doing here? These bathrooms are supposed to be for the audience in the *box* seats."

Amy gives a ducklike pout, as if offended by my bluntness. But, really, she knows me. So there's nothing for her to be offended by. She rolls her eyes. "I . . . was . . . *invited* by Cuthbert Gonderberry."

"What?"

"Uh-huh. Tabby was, too."

Feeling a touch dejected — though not all that sure why — I find myself saying, "And why're you down *there* . . . why don't you have a box seat?"

"The usher said there weren't any more places." She gives a wily grin. "He was *extremely* apologetic. Still, he said we are perfectly entitled to come up here — to use *these* toilets."

I just stand there, feeling like a lemon. "Uh-huh."

Amy's eyes suddenly sparkle as if she's been hit by some invisible lightning bolt. I blame it on the inexhaustible energy of *youth* . . .

"Aren't you *excited*, Anna? You know, to go *backstage* . . . to meet all of the *ack*-taws?"

She's near enough bouncing on the spot now.

She clearly wants to wrap her arms about me again . . . but seems to realise on some subconscious level that it would be a Very Bad Idea Indeed.

"Yeah," I reply. "I *guess*."

"Come on, then," she says, reaching for my hand.

"Uh, I'm just going to make some phone calls, okay? I'll see you after the performance . . . when we go backstage?"

Amy gives me a wide-eyed glare of overexcitement before promptly turning on her heel and heading out of the toilets. Leaving me in peace — *finally*.

I waste no time and whip out my mobile, guesstimating that I have about two minutes *max* before the play continues.

I dial up Mark.

Hold the handset to my ear.

And listen in.

Finally, he picks up, though he gives a distracted, "Hello".

Driving probably.

"How's it going?" I ask.

There's a long pause on the other end of the line. "Are you still there? Are you still at the play?"

"Yes. Why? What's wrong?"

Mark mutters something out of earshot, speaking to someone else.

Nathan?

"Listen," he says, "we'll talk later, okay. Don't worry — it's nothing to worry about."

My mind rushes. "Mark, what's the matter?"

More blabbing on the other end of the phone.

And then the line goes dead.

I continue to hold the handset to my ear for another few seconds . . . unable to quite let go. On impulse, I call Mark back, but there's only a busy tone. I glance up, look around at my surroundings, to the toilet. I can hear the bell ringing off in the lobby. Suddenly the performance doesn't seem so important . . .

I try Mark one more time and then return to my Contacts list.

This time I go through the names until I reach Arnold.

I hold off for a moment, wondering if I'm overreacting.

I tell myself that Mark could've sounded hurried for *any* reason.

That he could've sounded *like that* because of something in the road . . . a car accident up ahead, perhaps?

I hit Call.

My heart really begins to pound.

In the background, the bell has ceased.

I suppose the play is about to recommence.

I turn my attention back to my phone.

Watch as the notification bobs across my screen:

Placing call . . . please wait . . .

The ringing seems to go on for an impossible length of time.

I wonder if I'm *ever* going to get through to Arnold.

And then, finally, right at the last, I hear Arnold's voice.

A slightly bedraggled, weary, "Hello?"

"Arnold?" I say. "What's *going on?*"

He doesn't reply right away.

Like Mark, he's speaking to someone in the background.

It's only then when I realise something eerie; that it's *Mark's* voice.

"Arnold!" I scream out.

"It's Ben," Arnold replies. "Ben and *Nathan*."

My voice is reaching breaking point. "What about Ben and Nathan?"

"They're . . . *gone*."

" 'Gone' ?"

But, already, the phone has gone dead.

And someone is knocking on the toilet door.

Chapter Twenty-Seven

As I hear the knocking on the toilet door, I'm caught in two minds.

Something tells me I should rush right out . . . that I should leave the theatre — *no explanation; no fuss* . . . but what would that achieve?

Arnold told me, in no uncertain terms, that Nathan and Ben are *gone.*

My mind fights to catch up to that fact.

Try as I might, I can't reconcile it.

I call Arnold again. And then, when I clearly can't get through, I try Mark once more. No answer. I just go right through to voicemail. I leave a message, imploring them to call me back as quickly as possible. To give me some sort of explanation.

The knocking at the toilet door continues.

"Madam?" I hear from the other side. "The show is about to start."

The tone is slightly matronly — with just a touch of admonishment.

As if I've been clocked as Not Quite Belonging here.

I pace back and forth, mobile in hand, trying to figure things out.

From nowhere, a plan forms in my mind.

I decide there's no choice but to go with it.

Home . . . *Arnold's* house . . . *Josie.*

Decided, I become a flurry of action, shifting my way towards the toilet door, almost knocking the female usher flat as I go. Before I know it, I'm bounding down the staircase, the usher calling out after me . . . wanting to know if there's something wrong.

My luck seems to be in because a trio of taxis lurks on the curb of the Auburn.

I jump into the first one, instruct the driver where to go.

The driver is diligent, pulling away quickly and without preamble.

He seems to sense my panic . . . seems to *understand* that a woman dressed up for a night at the theatre leaving early can only mean an emergency.

We arrive outside Arnold's house about fifteen minutes later.

On the ride over, I attempt to call up Arnold and Mark — rotating the two of them . . . always placing a call to one or the other.

No answer.

Just voicemail notifications.

Once I've paid the driver, I dive out of the cab, hurdle my way up the path to the front door. I hang about on the step for the longest time, trying to get my thoughts straight.

Trying to get my *story* straight.

In the end, I know there's only one option.

I reach up and ring the doorbell.

Listen to it reverberate within the house.

I step back from the doorstep, for the first time thinking to take in the façade, to see if there's *anybody* home. It's then that I see Josie's bedroom light switched on. I take in the orange glow; can just about make out her silhouette in the drawn blind as she sits upright at her desk . . . working away studiously. I turn back to the front door.

Jam the bell down again.

Then step back.

Look up at her window.

She hasn't moved.

It's then it strikes me that Arnold and Kate have her trained . . . that they've instructed her *not* to answer the doorbell to strangers when they're both out.

Feeling hysterical, my smile splits my cheeks.

Of course. Of course, of course, of course.

What an idiot!

A thought strikes me, and I glance down at my feet.

I sift through the pebbles, discarding ones which seem too large — capable of *breaking* glass — and then discarding those which seem too small — not loud enough to make a *noise*. Finally, I come across the perfect pebble. I sling back my arm and then launch it upwards. I miss. I crouch down again, locate another pebble. I repeat my action.

This time I *hit*.

I study Josie's window, imploring her to open up.

She remains at her desk, her silhouette present there.

Unmoving.

I decide that more basic tactics are called for.

I cup my hands around my mouth and bellow, "*Josie! Josie!*"

Finally, she stirs from her desk.

She stands up.

And comes over to the window.

My heart flutters as she peeps out from behind the blind and then unlatches.

She peers down.

"Mum?" she says, a questioning tone in her voice.

"Open the door, Josie!"

Josie considers this a moment.

I wonder if Arnold and Kate have given Josie any *more* training . . . something along the lines of never — *not under any circumstances* — opening the door to Mummy.

Because Mummy might be the most dangerous person *yet*.

Apparently decided, one way or the other, she backs away from the window.

Brings the blind back down.

———

Soon enough, I'm standing in the hallway, staring at my daughter.

She has pinned her hair into some sort of bun in the centre of her scalp so that it sprouts out and tumbles down the side of her head. I don't think I'll ever fully understand fashion, but it's certain that I will never begin to even get to grips with fashion as dictated by a twelve-year-old. Acting on impulse, I lurch forward and grab hold of her.

I pull her into my chest.

Give her a squeeze.

All of a sudden, I feel like Amy.

When I let Josie free, she stands back with wide eyes . . . with the kind of expression which says, in no uncertain terms, *All right, just what the hell's going on?*

"Have you spoken to Dad?" I ask.

" 'Dad' ?"

"Yes, Dad — *Arnold!*" I add, as if this is going to aid mutual understanding. "Did he tell you about Ben — about what *happened* to Ben?"

Here Josie furrows her brow. "What's happened to Ben?"

"I . . ." — it sinks in then that *I* don't know precisely what's happened — "he's run away. Ben *and* Mark's son, Nathan."

Josie continues to look at me like I'm crazy.

Perhaps I *am* crazy.

I lock eyes with Josie again. "Listen," I say, "if there's anything at all — anything which you've overheard Ben talking about . . . if you have some *idea* about where it is that he's run to then I would very much appreciate you telling me."

Realising Josie looks panicked now — that I'm surely scaring her — I decide to soften my tone . . . or at least *attempt* to. I take gentle hold of her arm. "You won't be in trouble." Realising that I'm gripping a tad too hard, I let off my hold. "Just tell me what you know."

Josie eyes me closely, then shifts her attention to somewhere about an inch above my head. "I . . . ah . . ." She stares at where I hold her. I let go. "That boy, *Josh* . . . he's . . . well —"

"What? *What* is he involved with?"

"Ben never talks to me. But I see things. I hear things, when I'm at school. Sometimes at night he speaks on the phone then sneaks out later, without Daddy or Kate finding out."

My heart beats at the back of my throat.

I feel almost like I could throttle Arnold.

How could he be so careless?

How could he allow our child to become so *reckless* under his own roof?

. . . Of course, my logical mind kicks in soon afterwards, reminding me of my own choices — of my *own* abdication of parental responsibility.

"And? What else?"

Tears sheen in her eyes. She sniffs, becoming overwhelmed by this situation; the constant stream of questions. "I think . . . I think it's a . . . a . . . *gang*."

"A 'gang' ? What're you *talking* about?"

"Josh, he's one of the boys in charge . . . Ben and Nathan, they're both . . . both . . ." Here she finally breaks down into tears. Her throat constricts with her panic. I restrain the urge to reach out and take hold of her, knowing that my touch will be too rough.

Finally, she gets herself together without my intervention. "They're *both* in the gang. They have to do things . . . if they *don't* do the things then they get into trouble." She shakes her head. "They get *beaten up*."

My thoughts swish in and out of my consciousness, like waves. I try to make sense of them, try to get them into a logical order, but there's nothing I can do. Not now . . .

"Where are they, Josie?" I say, meeting her eye, and placing my hands firmly upon her shoulders. "Where have they *gone*?"

Josie meets my eye and mumbles, "Look in Ben's sock drawer . . . near the back . . . there's a folded-up piece of paper there."

I hesitate, concentrating on Josie for another few seconds. And then I shift away, taking hold of the banister and bounding my way up the stairs, making a bee-line for Ben's bedroom. When I get there, I waste no time taking in the milieu —

absorbing and analysing Ben's latest collection of posters, and other assorted paraphernalia . . . all those items which garnish little clues to the teenage person being formed into an adult. I make for the sock drawer. Tug it open. Ditching any sort of decorum, I tip it over, sending socks tumbling onto the carpet. A folded-up piece of paper falls at my feet.

I scoop it up, unfold it.

I immediately see what it is.

A list of train times.

A map.

An *itinerary*.

I look over the details, thinking about what it means.

Straight away, I see they're on a train headed for Dover, and that they have been for the past half an hour or so. As I scan further down the page, I see there are ferry times, too . . . the two of them are planning to cross the English Channel.

France?

The itinerary offers no further solutions.

I turn to see Josie standing in the doorway.

Tears trace her cheeks.

I try to put on a smile but it disintegrates before it's even started.

"Are you coming for the chase?" I ask.

She nods in reply.

As I venture out the door, I take her by the hand.

My mobile phone rumbles in my handbag.

I reach to answer.

Chapter Twenty-Eight

W hen I pick up the phone, I hear Mark's voice on the other end.

"Anna? The reception's better here . . . I've got signal."

"What's going on?" I reply, my voice hurried, as I glance up and down the street, desperately hoping a taxi will *just happen* to pass by.

In the background, I hear a female voice conferring with a male one.

I realise Kate must be with them.

Mark continues, "When we got there, everything happened so quickly. There was a short reception in the main hall . . . all the parents taking their seats. While we were listening to the headmaster, Nathan told me he had to go out; that he needed the toilet." He pauses, draws a shallow breath. "After about five minutes, I began to get nervous . . . when I finally got up, went to look out in the corridor, I ran into Arnold. We swapped stories.

Realised that the boys had pulled the same thing on us . . . that they'd . . . they'd both . . ."

"Run away?"

"Uh-huh. Kate told me" — my gut twinges to hear her name — "that when she looked to the chair, where Ben had been sitting, there was a folded piece of paper. It had *bus* times on it. We gathered they were headed north; that they wanted to catch a bus to Edinburgh. That's where we're headed . . . we're on the motorway . . . trying to catch up. I think if — "

"That's not where they're going! That's *not* where they're headed!"

Off in the distance, by some miracle — at least for a Friday night — I spot a black cab.

I nudge Josie and she takes my hint. She hails the cab, and it reluctantly trundles in our direction. As the cab pulls up at the curb, Josie opens the door. We leap into the back seat. I give the driver a murmured greeting then turn back to the call in progress. "They're going to *Dover*. They're planning on crossing the Channel . . . to head to *France*."

I hold my breath, waiting for Mark to say something.

But he remains silent.

I realise the problem.

Mark called me the best part of two hours ago.

They're already a long way up the motorway — going in the opposite direction.

It'll take them the same amount of time just to get back here.

To where they started from.

"Look, I'm here — *with Josie* — the two of us are going to head to Dover; see what's happening. If you like, you can keep travelling up to Edinburgh; it *could* be where they're headed . . . who's to say?"

Mark remains silent.

I feel my heart thrum in my throat.

"Anna," he replies, finally. "I'm sorry."

For a long few seconds I'm totally beleaguered.

Why's Mark apologising?

I'm the resident apologist . . . there's barely a day which goes by *without* me needing to apologise for something or other.

"What?" I reply, my tone deadened now. "*Why?*"

Mark swallows hard. I hear the sound of his Adam's apple bob in his throat. "I spoke to Nathan . . . I *knew* more about this . . . the day, when I cut myself, in my workshop . . . it was because I had my mind on him . . . on what was *going on* . . . but if I'd known; if I'd known that Ben was involved too . . . it would've been, well, *different.*"

"I don't understand."

Mark takes a moment to collect himself.

I decide that since he's clearly driving right now, it would be idiotic of me to provoke his already fragile emotions any further. This situation is grim enough without having another murky veil draped over it.

"I'll explain. *Later.*"

And then he hangs up.

When I channel back into my surroundings, I realise we've come to a standstill.

That the taxi is parked up beside the curb. And that the taxi driver is glancing back over his shoulder. "You sure about that?"

"Hmm?" I reply.

He jerks his thumb at Josie. "She says you wanna go to bloody Dover . . . you absolutely *sure* about that?"

I glance to Josie.

Her frightened eyes meet mine.

I reach down and squeeze her trembling hand.

Then I turn back to the taxi driver. "Yes, I'm sure."

The driver flashes his eyebrows then turns in his seat, muttering something about bloody women . . .

Chapter Twenty-Nine

W e make rapid progress.

I communicate to the driver — in no uncertain terms — that we're in a real rush, and that I'd really appreciate him getting us there just as quickly as he is able. Thankfully, we understand one another. He puts his foot down.

As we bomb along the motorway, I wonder whether I should pump Josie for more information, but decide to leave things alone for the time being. Instead, I think to say, "This isn't your fault, you know? Nobody expected you to say anything about it."

Although my sentiment is a good one, that's clearly *all* it is, because Josie promptly bursts into tears. As I take her in my arms, I catch the driver's eye in the rear-view mirror. He shakes his head at me as if beleaguered by my Sadim touch.

To be honest, most days I'm just as beleaguered.

The sea air floats in through the ventilation vents. I take a moment — with midnight approaching— to breathe it all in . . . to *try* and calm my jangling nerves.

I have to admit that when I left the house tonight — when I headed to the opening night of *Antony and Cleopatra* — I never expected to end up in Dover.

Much less that I would be in hot pursuit of my live-in lover's child and my *own* son.

We pass a weathered 'Welcome to Dover' sign.

"Any ideas where to, exactly?" the driver asks.

"Train station."

As we head along empty streets — houses with cars parked up on the pavements outside — I note the castle all illuminated and growing up out of the hill. I wonder if times were simpler centuries ago . . . if teenagers were such a complete nightmare as they are in modern times. At least these days we don't allow people to cavalierly go around with swords hanging from their waists . . . that's progress of a kind, I suppose.

The train station is appropriately deserted for midnight, and I glance about hoping to catch sight of Nathan or Ben, or both. I imagine them to be lugging oversized rucksacks; somehow having subtly snuck their belongings along with them to the parent-teacher evening. But I can see neither.

Finally, on the cusp of giving up, I spot a man in a uniform. He yawns as he trudges away from the now-closed station gate.

I wind down the window, letting in the freezing cold seaside air.

I call out.

Ask whether he's seen a pair of boys of Nathan and Ben's descriptions.

He squints at me from behind his round spectacles then scratches his near-bald scalp. He tells me he did see a pair of boys and points off in the direction he saw them going.

I thank him then turn to the driver. Without missing a beat, I say, "Ferry terminal."

He doesn't drive away from the station.

I try to keep myself calm.

Try to tell myself that if I wanted to — if I *really* wanted to — I could break his neck just as easily as I can click my fingers.

He looks at me over his shoulder, with something like a discerning glare.

Only now do I note that he's older than I first took him to be; that the skin about his eyes is more leathered, and that his irises are that *watery blue* which seems to afflict people as they get older. He peers out from behind the lenses of his glasses.

"I'll drive you to the terminal," he says, "if that's what you want." He pushes his glasses further up the ridge of his nose with a practised prod. "But, if you don't mind me saying, I think there's somewhere we should check first."

"Where?" I reply, glad for any help.

He says nothing. He just disengages the handbrake and pulls away.

Chapter Thirty

My heart hammers against my ribs as the car climbs the gentle slope.

The White Cliffs of Dover.

What strikes me the most is how there're no trees . . . how only long, unkempt grass grows up out of the flattened terrain. I can see a white lighthouse up ahead.

The driver sucks at his teeth as the tarmac road turns to dirt. He eases off on his accelerator as he bumps us through the rutted surface and closer towards the edge of the Cliffs. I feel my whole body going rigid as I try to make some *sense* of the darkness ahead.

The driver stops. "This is as far as I go."

I look to Josie. "Stay here."

She makes no response.

She simply sits where she is.

Even then — with a world of peril threatening to tumble upon me — I think about how she's *so much* more easily handled than Ben.

Once I get outside, the chilling air hits me. I regret not having reclaimed my jacket on the way out of the theatre. There didn't seem to be any time. No time *at all*.

I dip my fingers into my handbag.

From within, I withdraw my mobile.

I glance at the screen, seeing I have half a dozen new messages on the Assassins' Anonymous app. I don't check them right now. I use the screen to illuminate my path.

After a few steps, I ditch my high heels, treading the dirt path with bare feet. It's a clear night; the stars all glittering in the heavens above. The cold is almost impossible to stand. I force myself onward. The horror of what I might be about to uncover is too much to bear. So I *don't* think.

Finally, as I hear the gentle *slosh* of the waves beating in against the shore down below, I realise I'm nearing the cliff edge.

I suck in a breath, feel myself tremble.

My heart seems to hold still.

Ahead, I see a pair of figures.

Nothing more than silhouettes in the moonlight.

Standing at the edge.

I repress the urge to shout out.

I take care.

One step at a time.

Gently.

Slowly.

Softly.

The two figures continue to stand at the edge.

When I come within a dozen or so steps, I stop.

And I stare.

I realise I'm going to have to say something sometime, and decide there's no time like the present. "Ben? Nathan?"

They remain still, absorbed by the sight beneath.

By the *prospect* of what lies just ahead.

And why wouldn't they be?

The view is as majestic as the fall is deadly.

I take a step forward.

"What's going on, boys?"

One of them turns to glance over his shoulder.

It takes me a moment to realise it's Nathan.

Finally, it's Ben who speaks. He continues to stare down. "We've had enough. We don't want to run away. We want it to be over with."

"You want *what* to be over with?"

"The gang. The one at *school*."

I remain silent.

Think back to what Josie said.

It sounds consistent.

And I exercise my patience.

Stay still.

"It's the first *I've* heard of it," I say.

Ben smirks. "You don't know *anything*. You even *met* Josh."

I think back to the unpleasant specimen who attended that film with me, Josie and Ben, and who Ben — I couldn't help noticing — seemed incapable of being parted from.

Maybe my people-reading skills need some work.

That's a real surprise . . .

"It's how they've been treating us," Ben continues. "Making us *do* things for them . . . making *me* do things." He glances to Nathan. "If I don't go along with what they say then they hurt Nathan . . . *blackmail*."

My heart skips a beat.

I think back to the conversation with Arnold in the café.

The one we had ahead of the parent-teacher evening.

I was so blasé.

I blew the concerns out of the water, as if they had no importance.

As if it *wasn't* a big deal . . .

Well, it's certainly a big deal *now*.

I decide it's time for me to arrest control of this situation.

To get the boys away from the cliff edge.

"I've come to take you home." I shift a glance at Nathan. "To take you *both* home."

Ben's smile widens.

I can't help but note the maniacal glint in his eye.

"No," he says, "you don't get it — there's no going back. Not for us."

"Why? Why *not?*"

Ben looks to Nathan, and Nathan looks back to him.

For the first time, I recognise the rapport between the two of them.

The *mutual* understanding.

I wonder how long this has all been in the planning.

How long the two of them have plotted this . . . *suicide pact*.

Ben looks back down the cliff edge.

My heart leaps into my mouth.

For the first time in this exchange I truly feel that he *will* jump.

That he *will* take the final step.

But — right when I'm certain he's about to topple forward — he leans back.

Turns to me.

"They wanted me to do something bigger," he says. "*Much* bigger. They said that if I didn't do it . . . if I didn't do what they *wanted* then they would kill Nathan." He sniffs. I can't tell if it's from the obscenely cold weather or from the emotional turmoil.

Perhaps a little of both.

"They said that if I *ran* they would kill Nathan."

I look to Nathan, his wide-eyed stare. He says nothing.

"And this is the solution?" I ask, only realising after I've said it that my words are dripping with sarcasm. There's a time and a place for sarcasm, and right now clearly *isn't* the time.

Ben shrugs.

I glance over my shoulder, wishing that someone more diplomatic — Mark, Arnold . . . even *Kate* — might turn up out of the gloom.

But not one of them does.

There is *someone*, however.

It takes me several seconds to fathom just who . . . and then to make sense of the sight.

Josie.

With her gentle, girlish steps, she treads the cliff path. She passes me a tentative glance, as if afraid of reprimand; afraid that I'll tell her off for disobeying my orders. If only I could instil such reverence in Ben or Nathan.

She studies the scene for a long moment. She stares out across the sea — across the still surface of the water; to the lights on the coast of France. "It's a very big world," she says. "There's a lot of it to see." She looks to Ben and Nathan — both of whom are rendered stunned. "Why do you want to give it all up just because of some *boys*? Why do you feel that you *need* to do what they say? Why won't you just ask for help?"

My heart completely stops.

My whole body goes cold.

I feel a skitter pass up my spine.

Then I look to Nathan, and to Ben.

They continue to stare down over the edge.

I realise now that tears line both of their faces.

Finally, Nathan speaks up. His voice is quiet, but he manages to project it loudly enough to make himself heard over the breeze and the gentle wash of the waves. "If we don't . . . *do it* then what will you think of us . . . what will *happen* to us?"

I glance to Josie, and realise that now it's time for me to take over.

Hopefully I won't mess up her good work.

"Nothing," I say. "I understand — I *understand* what it's like to feel enthralled by someone; to feel as though there's no escape . . . as if the only solution . . ." but I don't finish that thought. When I speak again, my voice is firmer, more even-handed. "Let's go home," I say. "We can talk about this later. We can *fix* everything later."

The two boys continue to stare over the edge.

To the sea beneath.

And then, without warning, Nathan turns.

He treads back towards me.

Shoulders hunched.

Head bowed to his chest.

Without another word, he passes me by, heading along the dirt track, off to the waiting taxi; its headlights beaming like rays of moonlight through thick cloud.

Ben stays where he is.

Now, though, I see something different in his face.

The unmistakable appearance of thought . . . of *calculation*.

I think about my words again.

Wonder if there's anything else left for me to say.

Anything that I can *utter* which might make him change his mind.

There is one thing.

So I say it.

"I'm sorry — *so sorry* for everything."

Chapter Thirty-One

On the way back, in the taxi, nobody says anything. I fire off a text message with the simple words:

Got them. Coming home.

We perform a quick drive-past on Arnold's house, but, seeing none of the lights are lit, I head back to Mark's home. I guess they decided to drive all the way up north; all the way to Edinburgh.

I make myself busy, with my cat Lizzie purring her head off, oblivious to the context of the situation, and glad only for the company. She rubs herself up against my leg as I set up Ben and Josie in the spare room of Mark's house, lingering for surely far longer than is necessary on the landing outside . . . waiting for both of them to drop off to sleep.

Seeing light glimmering from beneath Nathan's bedroom door, I knock. He gives me permission to enter. When I look him over, he's still fully clothed, sitting on his bed, with his knees tucked up to his chest. He eyes me nervously as I tread further inside.

I think about bringing the door shut behind me, but decide against it.

From what I've learned tonight, there don't seem to be all that many secrets which Ben and Nathan — or *Josie*, for that matter — *don't* share.

"Are you going to be okay?" I ask, grimacing internally at my idiot tone.

Nathan gives a slight smile. Whether he's gently mocking my attempts at sincerity or just reacting with hysteria to the night's events, I really haven't much of a clue.

Whichever one it is, I'm glad to have him home.

To have *brought* him home.

"Try to get some sleep," I say. "I'm sure your dad will be up when he gets in. Let me know if you need anything."

I head back out of the room, bringing the door closed behind me.

———

I wait in the sitting room, vaguely aware that it's well past three in the morning. I browse through my mobile, the Assassins' Anonymous app catching my eye once more and proving to be irresistible. I tap it and then suck a sigh in through my teeth.

There're messages from Tabby, Amy and AA.

All of them, obviously, want to know what's up.

Why I skipped out so suddenly.

AA makes some remark about having 'picked up my coat'.

Further messages go into detail about the backstage visit, and the various wonders which accompanied the experience. Amy talks about 'unending streams' of champagne flowing while Tabby waxes lyrical about the 'beautiful, hunks of man flesh' . . . AA, on the other hand, seems to be all business, at least in the last message he tapped out and sent me — before he, and the other two, gave me up as a lost cause:

Paula says he's going to do it again.

I skim the message over.

Think about it.

Try to analyse.

Of course by 'he' AA means Gonderberry, and by 'do it' he means *murder*.

Still, though, I haven't quite managed to get myself past the mental block that he has even murdered in the *first place*. From my interactions so far with Gonderberry, I simply haven't seen any evidence which suggests this mean streak . . . which suggests that he's anything other than a human being like the rest of us; albeit with a Hollywood career, a marvellous home, and a rather *odd* snake-collecting hobby.

Is this just like those witness statements which come out in trials; the ones from the ignorant loved ones who claim that the acts simply don't *fit* the person 'they know'?

I suppose I should know better.

I should know that human behaviour can change at the merest *flip* of a switch.

Strangely — as I turn AA's message over in my mind — I feel a touch of anger directed at Paula Stevenstar; directed at her for implicating Gonderberry in all of these acts based on nothing much more than a whim . . . than a — no doubt — alcohol-affected memory from nearly twenty years ago.

It wouldn't stand up in court, that's for sure.

Then again, when did I start caring about courts?

When did I start caring even the *tiniest* bit about the laws of the land?

I hear the *grumble* of an idling car engine in the road outside.

This is followed by the *crunch* of tyres over the gravel driveway.

I get up from my seat, giving a yawn.

And I go to greet the others at the door.

Chapter Thirty-Two

O f course, in the week which follows, all hell breaks loose. It's just as would be expected when a pair of teenage boys get it into their heads to go jumping off a cliff.

Once we finish with the police, a battalion of therapists descends upon us, wanting to know the ins and outs of our 'backgrounds'. Drop by drop, they bleed facts out of the boys. How the gang at school functions. How Josh and others recruit kids and then force them to do their bidding by threatening to cause harm to another student.

In Ben's case, when the gang got hold of him, they decided to use Nathan as leverage.

If Ben ever said no to something which was proposed, all they had to do was pick on Nathan in some way; cause him some physical harm . . . and Ben would soon change his mind. As it turns out, as Ben continues to spill the beans, he was involved in far wider ranging — *far worse deeds* — than stealing a packet of biscuits from a local supermarket.

Although he won't own up to the exact details, worried about the gang coming after him, he alludes to various warehouses — factories — which the gang would target.

I listen in on the stories, feeling as if some secondary reality is playing out.

When the therapists inevitably centre in on Ben's exact role — on his exact *value* — to the gang as a whole, Ben will only mention that he is a 'natural-born thief' . . . although he says it without a hint of arrogance. Just a simply stated fact. He explains that the only reason he and Josh were caught at the supermarket was because of some higher-up in the gang deciding they themselves needed to be punished. Whether or not Ben has been picked out for punishment in the same way as Nathan — elected as a kind of voodoo doll for one particular member — remains to be seen. Ben won't open up about that particular aspect.

Nathan, of course, is entirely innocent.

Just a bystander caught in the cross-fire.

When he was first picked on by gang members, he believed it only to be bullying, but, as things transpired, as he did some digging of his own, he soon realised it was a more complex matter than that. And once he discovered just a little, Ben came to him and told him *everything* . . . information which Nathan, in turn, relayed to Mark, though without mentioning Ben's name out loud.

As I allow the implications of the entire thing to hit me, I think about how stupid I was in asking Ben to watch out for Nathan, when, of course, he was looking out for Nathan the whole time. How could he *not* look out for Nathan?

My heart pounds as I think things through.

As I try to work out how I was so blind.

Did I just *not care*?

How could I have been so *oblivious* not to notice my son . . . to notice *Nathan* was falling into such great trouble?

How could *Arnold* and *Kate* allow it to pass them by?

I've always thought of the two of them as being attentive to every last one of Ben and Josie's activities; in school or out. And maybe that's a lesson I should've learned long ago.

That I shouldn't trust anybody.

Not even myself.

As I brew some coffee for myself and Mark — currently slaving away in his workshop — I'm in no mood to hear my mobile buzzing its way across the kitchen counter. But, all the same, I leave the coffee-making alone for a moment.

Turn my attention to the backlit screen.

Another Assassins' Anonymous message.

From Amy:

Letter for you from CG.

I blink a couple of times.

With everything that's been going on — with the fallout surrounding Nathan and Ben's aborted suicide attempt — I'd almost completely forgotten about Cuthbert Gonderberry. *Almost* put him right out of my mind.

I turn my attention again to the opening night of *Antony and Cleopatra*, and how he had been so intent on me coming backstage following the performance. That he clearly so sincerely wished for me to meet him afterwards. It does ache a touch that I blew him off, but, at the same time, I know that I have a good reason. Well, more than that really . . . I have an *ironclad* motive for ducking out.

But that doesn't mean I shouldn't explain myself.

I text Amy back:

What does it say?

She replies right away:

Really, Anna, you think I'm so low as to open your post?

I allow myself a wry smile, then finish up making the coffee.

Sure enough, approximately five seconds later, Amy chimes me with another message:

There's another pair of tickets inside. He wants you to come this Friday. It'll be his last of the run before he leaves for America.

I blink a couple of times.

Try to absorb the situation.

It's admittedly surreal that I am on familiar terms with Cuthbert Gonderberry; the A-list film star. And yet, I'm curious . . . why's he so keen to meet me?

He met with the others backstage, after all; and they had the chance to apologise, or whatever it was that he wanted from them . . . perhaps to merely show that there were no hard feelings. What makes *me* so special?

I finish up brewing the coffee, pouring it into a pair of mugs — one for me, one for Mark. When I'm about to take Mark's coffee through to his workshop, my phone rumbles again. And I go to check on the Assassins' Anonymous app:

Meeting in SF this afternoon. 3 p.m.

Perhaps it's a testament to this job's hold on me that I actually glance up at the kitchen clock to check what the time is. Seeing that it's just after eleven in the morning, I know I have *oodles* of time to make it to Sex Flat.

Again, I wonder if I can pull out of this investigation.

And — *once more* — I realise it has me held tightly in its grasp.

No chance of escape.

So, I take the coffee through to Mark, tell him my plans, and set about getting myself ready for the afternoon meeting awaiting me.

———

I arrive to Brent Cross ahead of time, and can't help noticing that the Middle-Eastern men are there again. That they're wearing those same thick, winter overcoats. Given the cold snap we had over the weekend, they seem only appropriate now; rather than slightly exaggerated as they seemed in the preceding weeks.

I check the time, and realise I'm well ahead of schedule.

Time enough for a little *play*.

The Middle-Eastern man greets me with a friendly smile and reaches back to nudge his friend gently in the chest. His friend looks me over, then smiles too.

"You come to make me poor?" the man says.

I shrug, smile back. "Dunno, we'll see if my luck holds."

I hand over a twenty-pound note.

He goes through that whole rigmarole of checking it against the weak sunlight, creasing it, folding it, and then finally pocketing it. Then he flashes his eyebrows at the rug which lies on the pavement, at their feet.

Without further ado, he rattles the dice in his fist before sending them tumbling across the rug. The two of us — oceans apart in language and culture — stare at the dice as they gradually come to rest. Pairs. Even numbers.

"Bah!" the man blurts out, as if decrying the heavens themselves.

"Tough luck," I reply, with a smile.

Shaking his head, he counts out my winnings.

He hands the money over.

"Congratulations."

"Thanks," I say, and then begin to walk off.

I'm only a few steps away when a rather naughty thought strikes me. I turn around. "Out of interest, what happens if I hand over a hundred . . . you know, instead of *twenty*?"

The men exchange glances.

Then the first man gives me a shrug.

"More winnings," he says, with a wider smile still.

I think this proposition over, and then, deciding that I *am* now running late, I bid them farewell and head for Sex Flat.

————

When I get upstairs, AA, Tabby and Amy are all there.

All three of them looking somewhat pensive as they splay themselves across their chosen seat. I feel almost as if I'm invading some pristine scene.

"What're you so happy about?" AA says.

I just beam back. "I'm up a hundred and sixty pounds on those guys outside. It's easier than it looks — *free* money."

Tabby arches an eyebrow. "Yeah, but are you sure it's *real* money?"

On impulse, I dip my hand into my jean pocket and pull out the wad I won just now.

I toss it at her.

She accepts it with a grimace, clearly unimpressed by my carefree gesture. She peels through the notes; her quick, detail-oriented eyes taking stock of the whole bundle.

"I don't know how they make it work. How they actually think they can make *money* from it . . . but it seems to work just fine for me . . ."

Finished counting, Tabby hurls the bundle back.

I catch it without a flinch.

Deposit it in my back pocket.

"The odds'll be about one in ten," Tabby says, looking so bored that she's clearly on the cusp of yawning. "They'll be making about double whatever they pay out."

My brain *aches* to even consider what she's saying.

"I've won twice now," I put in, as if it means anything.

"The technical term is *Beginners' Luck* . . . why not give it another eight tries and see just how well you do . . . see who comes out on top in the end."

I sink down into one of the armchairs, content with the satisfying bulge in my pocket. I vaguely wonder if this is how men feel when they have an erection . . . if so then it explains an awful lot about how the world works.

"So," I say, "what's on the agenda for today?"

AA straightens himself up in his chair, pulls back the sleeve of his jacket and inspects his watch. "Paula will be by in a little while. She'll be coming to give us another expert opinion — to highlight her current fears."

I look about their faces, and realise I have to say something. "Did someone put something in the water? Why's everyone so glum? You all look as if you're *not* the kinds of degenerates who get invited to the opening night of plays starring Cuthbert Gonderberry."

This time it's Amy who speaks up. "The reason we're down, Anna, is because we're not getting anywhere with this case." She shakes her head. "Actually, it's worse than that, it seems that our client *herself* is making more breakthroughs than *we* are . . ."

"And I guess that's not a good look for professional private investigators?"

"No," Amy replies, succinctly.

Tabby pipes up. "What happened on Friday — why'd you duck out? If what we heard on the tape is anything to go by, then you could've got some valuable info out of Gonderberry. As things are now, though, someone else might have to *die*."

"What 'tape' ?" I ask.

Tabby rolls her eyes. "The one *you* recorded when you went to visit — *remember*?"

I think back to visiting Gonderberry alone.

It feels a long time ago.

And I'd completely forgotten about the audio recorder.

Somehow — even though I was complicit in the whole routine — I feel as if they tricked me into doing what I did.

"He killed his parents," AA says, without missing a beat. "That much I'm sure about."

His tone is so dry — so matter of fact — that this feels almost like a dream. Almost as if someone has replaced Happy-Go-Lucky AA with AA the Grouch. Whoever knew people could get so hot under the collar about an unresolved mystery?

Tabby refocuses on me. "Why *did* you pull that disappearing act?"

My chest tightens.

I'd hoped that particular question would drop away.

But apparently my luck doesn't hold while constrained by the realm of Sex Flat.

"It was a personal thing," I say. "My son — "

"Her son tried to kill himself," Amy puts in.

My mouth latches open.

Amy meets my eye briefly then adds, "Her boyfriend's adopted son too," as if this helps.

At the very least this admission hushes the entire room.

Seems to clam up everybody.

"Well," Tabby says, "I guess that's as good an excuse as any."

"Did they manage it?" AA asks.

I cock my head to one side, finally losing the smile I won along with that eighty pounds. "What do *you* think?"

I would ask Amy just how she found out about this personal matter, but I know that the answer is most probably a monotonously simple one; that she just called up Mark's house and outright *asked* him why I skipped out. That's one of the many — *many* — drawbacks of allowing business and family to intermingle.

It makes keeping secrets almost impossible.

Judging that I can safely steer the conversation back to the case at hand — back to what we're actually *here* for — I say, "I don't trust her — Paula . . . and if we're honest about it, what this all comes down to is who we trust; whose word we take over the other . . ."

AA decides to take up the mantle. "Anna, just look at the evidence — look at *Gonderberry* . . . how many bodies have you seen dropping dead around him? Look me in the eye and tell me that it's simple coincidence."

Just as he instructs me, I look him steadily in the eye and say,

"I don't think it's coincidence, but I don't think that he's to blame either."

Although nobody says anything, the entire room might as well give a group *groan*.

I can *hear* it inside my skull.

They all *think* that I've gone and 'fallen' for Cuthbert Gonderberry . . . that he's somehow got to me with his Hollywood charm. That I've somehow been transported into the body of a hormone-crazed thirteen-year-old girl.

"Let's just hear her out," Tabby says. "Hear what she has to say."

I can't help thinking I've heard this before.

But I know better than to argue.

———

Paula shows up wearing a mink coat with a purple feather boa blazing from the collar. Given the circumstances — our sordid, seedy surroundings — her dress seems only appropriate. As she treads about us, dealing each one with a kiss on either cheek, I catch a strong whiff of lemony perfume. My heart dips. And my stomach clenches tight.

She turns her attention onto me, cocking her head to one side. "What happened to you, my dear, on opening night?" She cracks a smile, showing off whitened teeth . . . there's something predatory in the gesture. "Get cold feet?"

I resist the urge to look to the others.

I keep my expression straight.

Serious.

And I answer her question by looking her in the eye.

"A personal issue came up," I reply, answering honestly.

She pouts, then takes a seat in one of the armchairs, though not without giving the upholstery a good looking-over, and a swift sweep of her palm to remove some piece of lint or dust mote. Once sat down, she assumes that odd, slightly girlish pose as she did the time before, when she related her personal history with Gonderberry. She presses her knees together and clutches her hands in her lap.

I wonder to myself if this is something which is taught in finishing schools.

Those institutions devoted to preparing girls for *high* society . .
.

AA starts things off. "What makes you think Cuthbert is thinking of *killing* again?"

When I shift a glance at AA, I'm glad to see he looks somewhat discerning, as if he's just as sceptical as me.

Paula remains where she is, stony. Silent. Then, slowly, she raises her head, looks over all of us, and then says, "It's just *small* things . . . *signs*."

"What 'signs' ?" Tabby puts in.

I can't help but notice how *grating* her tone is.

Maybe my scepticism truly has sunken in further with them that I anticipated.

. . . Now, shall I use my new-found powers for good or for evil?

Paula closes her eyes tightly, as if summoning some image into her mind's eye so that she can better describe it for us. Next, she reaches up and touches her fingers to her temple. She gives a shake of her head. ". . . Got a . . . I've got a . . . *terrible* headache."

I look about Amy, Tabby and AA, who all wear expressions of concern. And, I'm pretty sure, looks which silently say, *All right, Anna, maybe you were onto something.*

Paula remains like that for another few seconds before Amy thinks to ask her if she'd like a glass of water. Paula recovers slightly at the question, giving Amy a beaming, actress's smile. I don't suppose that the tap water from Sex Flat is really the sort of quality which Paula is accustomed to, but she drinks long and hard, not stopping until she has drained the glass. She thanks Amy then looks about us all, that same somewhat delirious smile on her lips. "I get so . . . *dehydrated* sometimes."

I'm still not convinced as to what I should make of this act — or whether it's an 'act' at all. The only thing I can do is steer the conversation back around to the reason why we're all here. "What're the *signs*?" I say. "How do you know that Cuthbert is ready to kill again?"

Even as I utter the words, I can't help but think how wild they sound.

I guess that I've already made up my mind so fully that I can no longer stretch my imagination to consider any other possibility. Isn't that one of the many weaknesses which is always pointed out in TV detectives? That they jump to a conclusion far too quickly.

Elementary, my dear Watson . . .

Paula takes a profound breath, causing her birdlike body to puff up. She looks over at me. "You're the most closely associated with Cuthbert." She glances at Amy. "From what I've heard, he's invited you to his final performance of the run; as his own *special* guest."

I stay quiet, unsure what to make of Paula's insinuation . . . but only just.

Paula continues, "This is how he treats *everyone*, at least from what I have seen from the outside. He draws them in close, takes them in his confidence . . . shows them how *generous* — how *forgiving* — he is, and then he turns violent . . . he turns *lethal*." She turns away from me, gazes absentmindedly down into the street, then says, mostly to herself, "Those men with the dice are back again."

I look to the others, thinking the matter over. Then I turn back to Paula, still looking out of the window to the street outside. "You think he wants to kill *me*?"

Paula meets my eye. Gives a tiny smile. "I'm afraid so, dear."

Even though it's clearly a ridiculous thing to suggest — even though I know that *even if* Gonderberry *did* attempt to kill me I'd easily fight him off — I can't help the chill which passes through my bloodstream. Just to know that someone — *somewhere* — might be out to have me killed. But I've lived my life like that; why should it come as such a shock now? I guess my life is doomed to forever be a glut of questions; and a drought of answers.

"What do you suggest?" I say, looking her back in the eye.

She keeps up that same smile for another few seconds and then — slowly but surely — it disintegrates. She blinks several times, as if clearing some delusion from her vision. "Why, my dear, I thought that would be obvious." She looks about the room, to the others. "This is your big chance — *for all of you* — to catch him in the act . . . to bring him to justice." When she speaks the final words, her voice takes on a deep, open tone . . . one of those voices which I suppose would be more at home on the stage than in some anonymous, dingy flat. "Once and for *all*."

Chapter Thirty-Three

I have to admit, as the day of the performance creeps up, I begin to find myself lending credence to Paula Stevenstar's suspicions.

What if she's right?

What if I'm being blind?

What if I'm refusing to see something *obvious?*

In my line of work — in my previous line of work — I always thought that I was well-acquainted with the margins of society; with the psychopaths, sociopaths, and any other –path you'd care to mention. All I have is my gut feeling . . . the one which tells me in strong terms that Gonderberry is innocent. That, as unfortunate as his presence about the periphery of these crimes has been, he has been nothing more than an observer.

Wow, maybe I *am* fooling myself.

The day before the performance, with Mark shoving Nathan in and out of the door — to police interviews; and then to psychiatric sessions — I realise that I have a message awaiting me on my mobile:

Gonderberry wants to meet you.

I send a message back, telling Amy — *in straight terms* — that I'm going to see him the following night. Friday. Backstage.

She sends me another message.

Claims he's insistent.

I think things over, wonder if there's some way I might be able to duck out of this potential engagement. As I do think it over, Lizzie wraps herself about my legs, purring her little cat head off, and brushing her thick fur against me. I bend down, hoist her in my arms, and cuddle her to my chest.

I stare out of the kitchen window, into the back garden. All the trees long ago lost their leaves, of course, and the skies are a gunmetal grey. From the nip in the air, I feel there's a chance of snow later. That'd really put a cap on all the Christmas lights that have gone up; the festivity which has already begun to soar through the air.

Lizzie gives an elongated *purr* as if she's offering some well thought-out counsel on my current dilemma. I interpret her purrs as telling me to give Gonderberry one last look-over. That I owe it to myself to be *sure* about him.

Before I truly draw any real conclusions.

————

I turn up at the gates to Parisianer Hall in a thick overcoat. I can't help thinking — as I inspect my surroundings, as I take in the other mansions which overlook the road — whether I might be taken by neighbours as a prostitute. I suppose it's something they're well-acquainted with here. Raggedy, wrapped-up women turning up on the doorsteps of multimillion-pound homes.

By request, this time I have no audio-recording device.

I don't even have any backup.

I told AA, Tabby and Amy to stay at home . . . threatening them that I would again refuse to attend the backstage proceedings tomorrow night; that I would finish my involvement in this case — as Paula Stevenstar might put it — *once and for all.*

I glance about, still not quite able to believe that I *truly am* alone. But, if Amy, Tabby and AA are out there somewhere — *hiding in the bushes* — then they've put on a good disguise.

Just after I've announced myself, and Gonderberry has ordered the gates open, another thought strikes. I dip into my pocket, remove my mobile, and then place it beneath a rock at my feet . . . I wonder if that's where Gonderberry leaves his key when he goes out.

With the afternoon turning to evening, I stride my way up the driveway — gravel crunching beneath my feet. The bare branches of the surrounding elm trees sway in the gentle breeze. I'm almost certain that I feel a snowflake brush my cheek. It sends a skitter down my spine; somehow connecting me to all those childhood memories . . . all of those times long ago past; all of those memories of seemingly divine White Christmases.

Gonderberry greets me with a wide smile, and a couple of kisses — one for each cheek, just like with Paula Stevenstar. Tonight, he has on a rather more reserved red polo shirt over a pair of smart black jeans. He has on a pair of ankle high boots which have been polished to a shine, and which look as though they'd be perfect for mountain-walking . . . and which — *just as likely* — have never made it outside the city limits. "There's some-thing I'd like to show you."

I wonder if he's going to lead me once more into the sitting room, but, instead, he leads me downwards, to the basement; where he keeps his 'collection'.

It's then that my senses begin to tingle.

When all those paranoid remarks which've been skittering through my brain finally come home to roost. I can't quite shift the feeling he's leading me down into the basement so he can silence my screams.

So he can be sure the *neighbours* won't hear.

Everything is just as I recall.

That dry, rotten scent.

I feel the many beady, snake eyes glaring out at me.

Those sleek scales reflecting the high-wattage bulbs.

Dozens of lashing tongues.

This time, Gonderberry has left the enclosure with his stuffed Burmese python uncovered. Gonderberry leads me to another enclosure. When he turns to me, his eyes are wide with childlike excitement. "I would like to introduce you to the *true* star of the show . . . the one who *really* makes the production a spectacle. The world-famous *asp* with whose venom Cleopatra departs her mortal coil. Beautiful, isn't she?"

I take in the thick, blue-grey stripes wrapped about its body.

And the hood which sags down over its head.

Some recollection strikes.

Something familiar.

Something I learned at school, perhaps?

"A cobra?" I blurt out.

Gonderberry cracks a smile. "Why, yes . . . that's *right*. An Egyptian banded cobra, in fact. An *asp* by any other name." His voice purrs. "She's performed beautifully; such a *placid* creature, completely unfussed by the lights, by the people. I wonder . . . would you like to hold *her*?"

My whole body goes rigid.

Unconsciously, I whip through a mental checklist, thinking through what has led to this moment, and unable to stop myself coming back to Paula Stevenstar's comments; about how Gonderberry works his way into his victims' confidence before *striking* . . .

But then another detail occurs to me.

"No venom?"

Gonderberry shakes his head. "That's right — nothing to worry about." He flashes me another smile. "She won't bite." He glances back in through the glass. "Docile little thing."

I take in the snake as it slithers leisurely along and I can't help wonder if I *won't* turn out to be the first one she bites.

I take another moment to consider.

One way or another, this will all be over by tomorrow night.

At the end of the meeting, Paula Stevenstar laid it all down . . . she presented her ultimatum. That the investigation will come to an *official* end if we fail to uncover anything further about Gonderberry; anything which might arouse reason for suspicion.

"So?" Gonderberry says. "How about it?"

———

I have to admit, I never imagined the first snake I would end up holding — if I ever ended up holding a snake at all — would be a cobra.

I'm surprised at the length, how 'she' is about a metre and a half in length. I'm even more surprised, however, at just how cute

. . . yes, *cute* . . . I begin to find her. After I've got over the fear she's not going to whip her head into my arm and sink her teeth into my skin.

Her blue eyes match her stripes and her body is elegant, and sleek.

The feel of her muscles, as she clenches onto my arm, is a sensation I've never quite felt before. I no longer feel skitters in my stomach.

I realise I've become accustomed.

And I start to *understand* how someone can become a fan of snakes.

I start to *understand* Gonderberry.

My heart raps my throat when I hand the snake back into Gonderberry's care.

He takes her from me, holding her for a long few moments, stroking her head, before replacing her within her enclosure. When he settles the lid back down, an almost wistful expression has appeared in his eye.

Nostalgia?

He turns to me. "My father never understood my habits. He never understood my *obsession* with theatre . . . with *acting* . . . and" — he gestures to his surroundings — "he never would've understood this . . ."

I try to find something within his words; something which might imply, one way or the other, whether or not he's guilty of his mother and father's deaths. But, if he is guilty, then he's playing his cards out in the open.

Why bring up his father at all?

Then again, perhaps if he does plan on killing me he feels he can treat me with a certain degree of confidentiality.

Once we're through with meeting the cobra, Gonderberry

walks me — *almost absentmindedly* — through his house. I find my head spinning as I attempt to keep up with Gonderberry's conversation while paying attention to the odd detail he points out — the heirloom; the priceless oil painting; or some prized architectural feature. As we head along, I search for more clues, more signs that the others' suspicions might prove correct.

But I pick up on nothing.

By the end of my visit — or what feels like it, with the night-time having long ago draped itself down upon the mansion — I realise I haven't learned anything I didn't already know. But it's been a pleasant evening, all the same.

The two of us stand on the doorstep and I wonder if I might be able to — *somehow* — bring up the case which brought us together. If he is ever going to open up then surely this is the time. And yet, as he looks beyond me, to the gardens, those blue-green eyes of his absorbing the entire landscape, I know I just can't work up the nerve.

That we've made Gonderberry suffer long enough.

"Anna?" he says, as I think about saying goodbye.

I turn back to him.

We haven't spoken for a few minutes so his voice sounds strangely alien.

"I'd like to ask you something."

"Okay."

He looks me in the eye. "I wish to lay everything on the table, so to speak."

My heart throbs a little harder.

"I know who you are," he says, and then, with a slight shake of the head, he looks away. "I know who you *were* . . . I mean, when Brian Mathewson was on the scene."

If this was a cartoon my mouth would gape open.

With a smile, he says, "I was Brian's client, too — just like *Paula* was."

He adds *something* to Paula's name when he speaks it; some sort of twist . . . but what exactly it means, I can't quite say.

I feel as if I'm sinking.

As if this whole . . . *thing* has been rumbled.

I glance about — panicked — wondering if it was really so bright to insist on going it alone tonight. To not bring along any backup.

"Don't worry, Anna," he says, with a chuckle in his voice. "I knew about this — I *knew* what was going on all the time." He shakes his head. "I hope you didn't think me *so* naïve . . . *so* out-of-the-loop that a bunch of 'Belarussian' tourists might wind up on my doorstep."

I feel myself blushing.

Because I know I *did* take him for naïve.

At least to begin with . . .

"I have my own contacts," he says. "Those who run in Brian's circles would be negligent not to ensure their own survival; not to watch their own backs. There was a time when . . . well . . . let's just say there were certain *demands* made of me; certain *demands* which would've gone away if the person making them had just *happened* to disappear."

It's not difficult to read between the lines.

To know that we could've easily met under different circumstances.

"Paula, though," he continues, "she has *always* been a funny one." He draws breath. "Not wanting to sound like a complete paranoiac, I believe that she's been out for me for many years. Why, I'm not so sure. But every one of my performances, she's *there* . . . in the audience. There was even a time when she showed up on a film set. A *most* unpleasant scene."

I wonder at what to say next, and then I settle on the logical thing.

And if it means betraying my client — biting the hand which feeds me — then so be it.

"Paula believes you tried to kill her," I say.

Throughout our encounter thus far, Gonderberry has seemed to be entirely in control — entirely *at leisure* . . . even as he delivered the revelations he just has . . . now, though, he looks distinctly uneasy. I wonder if I might've said too much.

I wonder if this might be the straw which breaks the camel's back.

I wonder if this'll prove to be the motive for my murder.

I switch back to Gonderberry.

He stares into mid-air, gathering his thoughts. "Well, that's simply . . . *outrageous*."

Again, I think it over; wonder how much to say.

And I realise there's really nothing lost by me simply spilling the beans.

I tell him about the meeting with his parents, and then about what happened afterwards; how he feigned he was over the issue . . . only to pull a knife on her in their bedroom later.

"No," he says, "I mean, that's . . . granted I was somewhat *put out* following the meeting with my parents, although, truth be told, I was wound so tight I'm sure I said some *daft* things . . . I'm sure I put Paula under the microscope unduly. But I got over myself eventually. There was always something about my parents which just . . . well, I don't think there's any other way to describe it . . . they would drive me *insane*." He draws a deeper breath. His shoulders sink. Then rise. "Do you know what my father said to me the first time I was handed a starring role?"

I shake my head.

"He said it was, 'All in a day's work for a pansy.' "

"Different time, I guess."

"Tell me about it. I have little recollection of that evening — the one with Paula — I do remember I lost her sometime in the early morning . . ." He closes his eyes tightly, making an effort to concentrate on the memory. "Granted, I had a lot to drink that night. I didn't return home until it was light . . . until the next day. Until Paula was *gone*."

The two of us stand on the doorstep for the longest time.

We're from utterly different worlds.

From *utterly* different contexts.

And yet, Gonderberry has opened his veins.

How can I possibly *not* believe him?

Chapter Thirty-Four

"That's it," I say, into the phone. "I'm not going."

AA remains silent on the other end.

Apparently thinking.

Plotting.

I stare out through the bedroom window, down to the frosted lawn, and then to the frozen pond. There was a dusting of snow overnight. Nothing significant. Only enough to make everybody's lives just a little more difficult. When I woke this morning, I thought I might've been teleported to Lapland overnight.

When I turn around, I see Lizzie lying on the unmade bed, tucking her paws beneath her belly, warming them. She looks up at me, gives me a slow blink, and then drifts back away to sleep. So much for feline assistance with this particular phone call.

With this particular *problem*.

"Are you going to tell him?" AA finally responds.

"No. Why *should* I?"

"Common manners?"

I'm sick of this . . . I'm sick of rising to the bait . . . I'm sick of being drawn into deeper — *darker* — mysteries each time I turn around. Because now, and I'm certain of it, Paula Stevenstar has been playing us all for fools; using us as some elaborate extension of her own ego . . . for being ditched all those years ago — via some misunderstanding — by the man who became the Great Cuthbert Gonderberry.

"Don't you want to see this through?" AA says. "Don't you want to prove her *wrong*? Prove she's *deluded*?"

"What good will come of it? You do realise that deluded people aren't exactly the type who're open to reasoned argument, don't you?"

AA stays quiet.

And I scratch a score up for me.

How many it'll take to win this little exchange, there's no way of knowing.

"It just seems . . . I don't know," AA continues, fumbling over his words. "As if it's lacking in *closure* . . . as if it's lacking that last little *act*."

I roll my eyes at the forced metaphor.

One thing's for certain, I'm looking forward to getting theatre off my brain.

I never was *passionate* about the Arts.

"He's *invited* you, Anna. Don't we owe him something? Some show of grace? One final apology for everything we've done?"

I think about all that's happened in the past few weeks. "I'm tired of apologising."

"Yeah, well, next time we'll take greater care — find an *apology-free* case."

" 'Next time' ?" I almost choke on the phrase.

"Sure, you'd never believe how word gets around — how

many people are *banging* on the door wanting to contract our services."

I look out the window again, inspecting the horizon, and the pinkish light which is rising. The weak winter sun. I sigh. I turn my attention back to the phone. "I'll go tonight," I say, "but I'll have to think about the rest."

"Of course. Take all the time you need."

When the silence between us has stretched out long enough, I hang up. Judging by the fact that AA doesn't ring back, I suppose he's said all he needs to. He's done all the convincing he has the heart to do.

The ball's in my court, now.

Or — in Thespian terms — I'm in the spotlight.

———

I gear up for the evening ahead.

Meanwhile — downstairs — Mark and Nathan go through some exercise assigned by one of the therapists; one of these exercises which involves an awful lot of going through hypothetical situations — talking through how *one* should act.

Some of those involved in the gang have been arrested, while others are on the run. Ben and Nathan need to learn to live in fear for a while . . . as the police round up the ringleaders and bring them to justice. The exercises — *apparently* — are a means of tackling that particular problem. Oftentimes, in the past few days, I've wondered whether I should offer Ben my services, but in the end I decided he will be choking as it is what with the pincer movement courtesy of Arnold and Kate. The kid'll be lucky to be allowed out of the house alone by the time he turns eighteen.

Not that I'm taking the situation lightly.

It's *perilous* . . . and Ben is my son . . . but that won't change the situation as it is.

I scrub at my fingernails with a brush, attempting to get shot of the dirt. After a good ten minutes or so of trying — and with my hands now a rosy-red — I give up and shove the scrubbing brush to one side. I glance down at the gun lying on the floor of the shower stall. A simple 9mm. I examine it with a critical eye; think about what I'm doing . . . and *why* I'm doing it.

Why? Why? Why?

. . . Isn't that just the story of my life?

The gun is clean.

Before I buried it in Mark's back garden, I placed it within a resealable plastic bag.

Even so, I took the whole thing apart . . . made sure everything was in good working order. I'm nothing if not a responsible gun owner — most of the time.

Let me tell you, it was some trick for me to wait for Mark to toddle off to his workshop and then set about digging up frozen ground. After about fifteen minutes' effort, I'd near enough convinced myself I was going to get caught.

Or that I was going to serve myself with a heavy dose of frostbite.

Thankfully, though, neither of these grim eventualities played out, and so now I stand in the bathroom ready to arm myself for the night's activities.

I err on the side of caution, going with the same outfit which AA picked out for the previous night. I reason this away by telling myself that Gonderberry didn't get so much as a glimpse of me . . . he won't realise I've worn the same dress two weeks in a row . . .

As for AA, Amy and Tabby, well, they can laugh like drains if they want.

I really don't care.

In the end, there doesn't seem to be any sensible way for me to conceal my sidearm about my person, so I drop it inside my handbag. I can count on one hand the amount of times when I've had my handbag looked through while out in public, but, all the same, I locate a velvety black pouch to conceal the gun within so as to thwart the most superficial of searches. That done, I check myself over in the mirror, and can't help thinking that I don't look too bad . . . I mean I don't *look* as crazy as I obviously am.

With a quick farewell to Mark and Nathan — still going through their exercise in the sitting room — I catch the cab which rolls up on the curb outside.

And head to the Auburn Theatre.

———

I arrive to the theatre much later than I did last time.

I suppose I'm learning how to act in high-class company.

One day they'll make a lady of me . . .

The same usher appears at my elbow when summoned, however, instead of leading me to the box as he did the previous week, he takes me through a ground-floor side passage — one which runs alongside the theatre lobby. Before I've quite caught my breath, I realise what's happening . . . he's taking me backstage.

I fly into one of those female panics, something gripping me from within, urging me to glance about frantically for some mirror to check out my reflection.

But, of course, in this dingy tight side passage, there *are* no mirrors.

Pretty soon, though, there's an abundance.

And all of the mirrors have those exposed, high-wattage bulbs surrounding them.

For some reason it puts me back in mind of Gonderberry's snakes. Perhaps actors are cold-blooded; maybe that's what separates them from us regular human beings . . .

The usher continues unfazed.

I feel myself assaulted by the powder which mists the air — all of that concealer being applied. None of those occupying the stools before the mirrors so much as turn to look at us. They remain busy, taking stock of their looks.

We head down another narrow corridor, where the usher pauses outside a door. 'Cuthbert Gonderberry' is written on a plaque; framed by a Hollywood-style star.

My heart flutters in my throat.

It's strange, even now, even after having met him many times over, I have the same star-struck reaction to seeing his name. Although my logical mind can separate reality from fantasy there's something in my subconscious which just won't allow me to believe this is actually happening.

The usher knocks decorously then turns the doorknob and leads me inside.

I have to say, as I take stock of the dressing room, I would've thought that someone of Gonderberry's calibre — someone with his *profile* — might've been afforded something more in the way of trimmings. Something more luxurious.

However, it is what it is.

There's bare brickwork and a rickety-looking window high up in the wall.

The floorboards underfoot look as if they're near-rotten.

Across the room, there's a white plastic garden table set up with an assortment of treats; most notably a large silver tray featuring chocolates, champagne, and other goodies.

Beneath the table, I can't help but note the wicker basket — the sort which I would more normally associate with Bazaars in the Middle East; at least from what I've seen in cartoons or in films. I know that, within, Gonderberry's snake awaits.

Ready for tonight's performance.

The famous *asp*.

Gonderberry himself sits before the mirror. He wears his Roman-style tunic and armour. A royal-red cape draped over his shoulders. All decked out in gold, it seems easy to believe that he's a general, or even a *king*. His *face* fits the outfit.

I think about his blood line and wonder whether he does indeed have kingly blood lurking there somewhere. It wouldn't surprise me.

Gonderberry is currently in the process of working mascara onto his left eyelash. When he gets through, he looks to me in the mirror. We exchange glances. He smiles. "I thought I would invite you backstage before the show tonight so you wouldn't have the chance to duck out."

Although his words sound a mite cutting, his tone is warm, friendly.

And I take it for what it is.

"I was wondering, what would you think of watching from the side of the stage?"

"I . . . uh . . ."

He smiles again. "The boxes are all full tonight, but I thought I might be able to resolve that little problem by making it out to be a charming gesture. What do you think?"

"I think . . . that would be *wonderful*."

A bell sounds in the near distance.

I realise that the play's about to start.

Now fully dressed as Mark Antony — mascara and all — Gonderberry rises from his chair. He pads across the dressing room, to the goodies. He plucks a grape from a bunch and tosses it over to me.

I respond a little belatedly, but I respond nonetheless.

Catching it.

"This is the part where you say, 'Break a leg', or words to that effect."

Examining the grape — a purplish shade — I feel somewhat playful. "I was thinking of something more along the lines of, 'Macbeth'."

Gonderberry gasps out loud, and reaches to his throat as if he might be choking. He staggers back a few steps until he butts into the wall.

An apology is on the tip of my tongue.

I'm all too aware of the concerned usher standing at my shoulder.

Finally, though, Gonderberry cracks a grin. Then slips another grape — concealed in his fist — into his mouth.

"This way, madam," the usher says.

I turn around, head out of the dressing room.

Right as I'm on the point of leaving, I look to the basket, down on the floor.

A skitter passes up my spine.

Maybe some fears are just impossible to get over.

———

I stand at the side of the stage, feeling somewhat out of place.

I dare a couple of glances out around the curtain, to the audience, but soon wind my neck in, worried that I'll spot either AA, Tabby or Amy . . . Paula Stevenstar wouldn't be much better, for that matter.

Since I've already seen the first part of the play — having ducked out at the intermission last time — I can't help but wonder if my attention is going to slip . . . however, I'm pleasantly surprised to find that I remember hardly anything. Just like the time before, I'm mesmerised by the spectacle.

I recall her name, the actress who plays Cleopatra: Asha Tumbleton.

She matches the version of herself on the poster; what with the hair all held up in a towering, black knot; and the dark, distinctive, curling lines beside her eyes.

I find myself holding my breath when she stands on the stage, unable to quite believe my eyes. When Gonderberry enters, I can hardly contain myself. Down here — on the stage itself — they seem so much closer . . . so much more *real*.

Once the interval rolls around, I turn side on, wanting to keep out of the way of the many stage hands all buzzing about behind the closed curtain; arranging props, getting everything in its right place for the next scene.

It's then that I hear a familiar voice in my ear. "Anna?"

I turn.

Find myself staring at Mark Antony.

Even in the dim light of the backstage, I can make out the glistening layer of sweat upon his brow. He sniffles a couple of times, perhaps because of the cool, night air which blows in from some opened door. "Enjoying it so far?"

I walk alongside him, managing a smile as I match his pace. "Of course."

"Good — that's *good*."

Somehow I supposed that career actors would grow somewhat world-weary and cynical after having taken part in so many different performances. But Gonderberry still seems to possess his youthful enthusiasm; his *passion*.

When we reach his dressing room, there're half a dozen assistants waiting. All of them are female except for one effeminate-looking man.

I stand back, not wanting to get in the way.

As the assistants go to work on Gonderberry, I listen to him issuing instructions with regards to his snake, in preparation for the scene . . . the scene in which Cleopatra — Asha Tumbleton — will poison herself with the asp . . . and thus join Mark Antony in death.

It all sounds decidedly melodramatic, and yet I can't help but feel a touch *antsy* about the whole upcoming performance. As if something might go differently; as if there might be some sort of a *change* to Antony and Cleopatra's doomed fate.

Why do all the happy stories have to be funny?

Why do all the sad stories have to be tragic?

I guess these are the rules set down by minds much grander than mine.

When the bell begins to sound in the theatre once again — the punters being called back to their seats in the auditorium — I slip off to one side, keeping myself from getting under anybody's feet. Even so, I get more than my fair share of bitter looks from the assistants, and I can't help wondering if they might be furious at my mere presence there . . . and my — *apparently intimate* — relationship with Gonderberry.

If only they knew that it was all professional.

That it was business . . . and nothing more.

I slip out of Gonderberry's dressing room and drift along on the tails of the assistants, reassuming my place at the side of the stage.

———

As the second half of the play unfolds — as the tension mounts — an itchy sensation sets in beneath my skin. My heart thumps in my throat. I wonder if it's just the play . . . or if there's something else involved too.

We're about an hour into the second half — with the climax rapidly approaching — when I feel my phone vibrate in my handbag. Just like any normal woman, I fumble past my concealed handgun and dig it out, taking care not to allow the glare of the screen's backlight to play out across the stage . . . or to light me up like a Christmas tree.

It's a message on the Assassins' Anonymous app.

From Amy:

Snake is venomous!

My heart bounces up into my throat.

I glance about.

Is this a joke?

I look to the audience.

I can't pick any of them out.

No sign of Tabby, AA, or Amy . . . although I realise that — sitting up in her box — Paula Stevenstar is scrutinising the stage; no doubt searching for some piece of 'evidence' to fuel her delusions. When I switch back to the stage, I see that Gonderberry has just succumbed; that several others dressed in Roman costumes carry him away . . . headed for the other side of the stage.

I look to Cleopatra — to Asha Tumbleton.

Tears streak her cheeks, her makeup in clumps; in muddy, uneven rivulets.

She faces the audience, the spotlight pinning her where she stands.

I back away.

I disappear into the backstage darkness.

I need to find Gonderberry.

That same thought pounds through my temples.

Got to find Gonderberry. Got to find Gonderberry. Got to find Gonderberry.

I come to a dead-end.

A simple, undecorated brick wall.

I feel a draught.

Another message comes into my mobile.

Again from Amy through the Assassins' Anonymous app:

End performance. Get the snake. Venomous.

Thoughts flash through my brain.

I try to get them straight.

. . . *Fail.*

I shove my way through hordes of people, all of them travelling in the opposite direction. Then I spot him. He smiles. He laughs, alongside others. His fellow actors, all of them dressed, like him, in their Roman garb.

Anger twists my gut.

I pace towards him. "Cuthbert! Cuthbert!"

He turns to me, alarmed.

It seems I've struck the appropriate tone.

When he recognises me — *sees* that it's me — his features soften.

And he leaves the others behind.

He grins as he approaches, but I'm in no mood for niceties.

I grab hold of the front of his tunic.

Dragging him back in the direction of the stage.

"Anna, Anna!" he blurts out. "What is this . . . what's going *on*?!"

As the two of us arrive at the side of the stage, I keep my voice hushed, then I turn into him. He's the only chance of getting things clear now; the only chance of getting things *straight*. "That snake. You said it wasn't venomous."

"It absolutely *isn't*."

"You're *sure*?" I say, my tone probing; eager for answers.

This time he turns into me, his eyes wide. "Yes."

I shake my head as I watch one of Cleopatra's servants — a *clown* — lay the basket down beside her. The two of us watch on as the speech continues, and then, as the actors begin to tumble — feigning death — Cleopatra steadily approaches the basket.

I reach into my handbag.

Get hold of my gun.

Withdraw it from the velvet pouch.

Hold it down at my side.

Slowly — *gently* — Cleopatra draws the snake from its basket.

I look to Gonderberry — intently observing the scene. His eyes pass over the animal. He turns pale. "That's not mine — that's not my *snake*!"

The snake wraps about Cleopatra's arm. Cleopatra speaks in

the Shakespearean tones which float over me like warm waves. I keep my head cool — and my concentration clear.

My heart beats steadily.

Even though I haven't held a gun in months, this feels natural.

It feels *right*.

I line up the sight as Cleopatra brings the snake up to her throat.

I take a step.

One more.

And feel the bright spotlight.

All the *eyes* upon me.

And then I squeeze the trigger.

Chapter Thirty-Five

There are screams.

Panic erupts.

From somewhere — the lobby? — the bell clangs.

The gunshot continues to ring about my skull.

My eardrums hum.

I feel as if my trigger finger is burning.

Red hot.

I take in the scene slowly.

Wonder if I somehow missed.

I absorb Cleopatra.

How she stands stock-still.

Mouth wide open in a silent scream.

Realising I'm still pointing my gun at her, I bring it down to my side, release the magazine, and allow the pieces to drop at my feet . . . to fall into the darkness of the stage.

Just another prop.

I turn on my heel.

Head out — into the darkness.

Away from the theatre.

———

Rational thought fails to return until I'm a good five minutes away. And then it feels as if my brain is numb . . . as if my *whole body* has gone numb.

I hear sirens in the near distance.

I know I have to move quickly.

That I can't afford to dawdle.

Easier said than done in my current get-up.

High heels don't make for effective running shoes.

All the police need to do is recover the weapon.

Dust for fingerprints.

And work out it was me.

This time there'll be no Brian Mathewson to offer protection.

It only strikes me as I take long, loping strides down yet another backstreet that I have no destination in mind. No general sense of direction. I *feel* a car engine before I hear it. When I turn my head, I'm sure I'll find a police car — blazing blue lights at my heel. A pair of well-to-do armed officers shouting: *Get down! Get down!*

However, when I turn my head, I realise it's an estate car.

It takes me another second to realise that it's *AA's* car.

The one he ferried us to Cuthbert Gonderberry's house in.

I stand stunned, unable to quite believe my fate.

And then — *suddenly* — I break free of inactivity.

Rush to the opened back door.

Hurl myself inside.

And thank all the gods in the world for the dependability of friends.

———

Sitting amongst the others, I half expect them to make a beeline for Mark's house.

Instead, though, I realise they're headed for Brent Cross. That we're all going to our meeting place. That we're headed for *Sex Flat*.

I snap to my senses in the back seat, realising it's Tabby who's driving. She makes gentle adjustments to the wheel as she makes rapid progress. She is a purveyor of the art of no-frills, anonymous driving.

I take in AA — sat in the passenger seat. He grips the roof handle, uncomfortable placing his faith in someone else's driving skills. Amy sits beside me, in the back seat. Despite everything — *despite everything that's just happened* — she is grinning her head off like it's Christmas Day.

"All clear, I think," Tabby says.

"You *think?*" AA shoots back.

Tabby arches an eyebrow. "I was trying to be modest — there's not a cat's chance in hell we were followed. Too much panic. We were too quick." She glances up in the rear-view mirror, meeting my eye momentarily. "Anna was too quick."

I recognise the street now; the one on which Sex Flat is located.

The pavement where the pair of Middle-Eastern men stand during the day.

Without warning, Tabby takes a sharp left, diving the car down a steep ramp.

My eyes need a moment to adjust to the dim lighting.

To realise we've arrived in an underground car park.

It's near deserted.

She parks us up in one of the bays, swiftly turns off the engine and drags the keys free of the ignition. We all just sit there — in the car; in silence — with only the *tick-tick-tick* sound of the engine cooling down.

———

I find it almost impossible to stay still.

I can't *sit* . . . that's for certain.

None of the others say anything — all of them apparently content to stare at me as if I'm some piece of minimalist theatre.

"I was seen," I say, finally managing to catch my nerves. "The usher . . . the audience . . . Cuthbert Gonderberry himself, for Christ's sake!"

I take a deep breath.

My head is humming.

Everything seems to be out of joint.

Finally, I look to the others, wondering how they can remain so calm at a time of such great stress. Then again, I don't suppose *they* were the ones who fired a shot from an illegal handgun on a stage before hundreds of people.

I take another breath.

When I look up again, I realise there's a cup of coffee being thrust into my chest.

Amy holds it, still grinning that same grin. "Drink this."

I'm of half a mind to grab the cup and toss its *boiling-hot* contents at her face.

But I restrain myself.

Deciding to be *reasonable*.

I take the cup, look down into the black liquid.

It looks just like crude oil.

I take a sip. Another.

At first, I can't taste anything except for the bitter, burned coffee beans.

But then I grow accustomed.

Realise that it's working its magic on me.

Bringing me back to the Land of the Conscious.

I take another deep, cleansing breath, and then — with a steady eye — absorb the others surrounding me. They all have somewhat smug expressions pressed across their faces. I tip back the remainder of the coffee then allow the cup to droop down at my side.

"What?" I say. "What *is* it?"

"Oh, Anna," AA says, now smiling pleasantly. "You'll never believe how lucky we got."

———

I'm not quite sure if I take a seat in the armchair of my own accord or if Amy helps me down. I *can* be certain I'm trembling all over; that I feel as if my toes and fingertips have gone numb. My whole body feels as if it continues to shake with the kickback of the pistol. I guess it *has* been longer than I can remember. I look to the others — to AA. "So," I say, aware that my voice is still shaking all over the place. "How *the hell* did you know it was the wrong snake? How did you know it was venomous?"

AA exchanges glances with Amy, and then Tabby.

'Smug' seems to be understatement of the century.

AA decides it falls on him to play educator. He meets my eye. "Well, don't do yourself down. It was because of your whim that we decided to follow a different line of enquiry."

"And what 'line of enquiry' was that?"

AA shrugs. "We decided to set up a periphery — to see who was coming and going. Although we weren't convinced Gonderberry *wasn't* responsible for the murders; we did have the notion that he perhaps wasn't working alone. After all, it would be quite a big deal to get away with killing three people without some *grand* help."

My chest tightens.

If only they'd been there while Gonderberry stood next to me, while he told me, with complete surprise, that it wasn't his snake. Just before I fired the pistol, I heard the *gasp* at the back of his throat. I am certain he was telling the truth.

Could he *really* be that good of an actor?

Or a good enough actor to fool *me*?

I turn to the others. "And who did you see?"

AA looks to Tabby, who decides it's time for her to pick up the story. "I was stationed in the car; just across the street." She gives a wry grin. "Feigning some sort of mechanical emergency . . . oil in need of changing; something like that." She rolls her eyes. "You wouldn't *believe* the sheer quantity of knights in shining armour keen to help out a damsel in distress. That was *most* annoying. Anyway, I was keeping an eye on the back alley of the theatre — on those who were coming and going from the emergency exits." She narrows her eyes. "There were more people than I ever would've thought — let me tell you — and security was just about the most lax I've seen anyplace."

"But?"

"*But*, I did pick out someone. A man. He was carrying a *suspicious* item.*"

"What was it?"

Amy picks up the story. "Tabby got in touch, told me to . . . I don't know . . . subtly *bump into* the man . . . see what it was he had."

"It was a rectangular shape," Tabby says. "Covered with a dark sheet. That was what grabbed my attention — that was what made me think this wasn't right. It made me think of that covered enclosure back at Gonderberry's house . . . down in that snake pit of his."

My heart beats a little firmer.

Of course, they heard all about the stuffed python — the 'murder weapon', as Gonderberry himself phrased it — when they listened back to the audio recording I made.

"And?" I say.

"Well," Amy continues, "I was stationed in the back alley when I got the message from Tabby — that I was to get a better look." She shrugs. "It wasn't a masterstroke, I just trod down the alley then shoulder barged the man. The sheet tumbled down. I saw the snake inside." She smiles. "Of course, I apologised about the mistake, helped the man fumble the sheet back over the enclosure. There was something about his manner which was unsettling. How he glanced about — all hyper — as if he had been caught doing something naughty." She grins wider, shaking her head. "It would've been comical if someone's life hadn't been on the line. Before I could say anything, he disappeared past the usher. He had *credentials*, whoever he was."

The room slips into silence.

I turn my focus down, to my shoes.

They look as if they've been through the mill this evening — several flecks of mud; stains from the many dirty puddles I trotted through.

I wait for someone to take me home.

Chapter Thirty-Six

In the bedroom, I help Mark take the bandages off his fingers. I make all the appropriate, sympathetic noises men require when it comes to 'wounds'. As I unwind the latest bandage, I hear my mobile buzzing away on the bedside table.

An unrecognised number.

I think about treating it the same way I *usually* treat unrecognised numbers . . . that is by waiting to see if they'll leave a voicemail. But something — *call it intuition* — screams for me to pick up.

When I do, tentatively leaving Mark to apply the prescribed antibiotic to the now-exposed, healing cut on his fingers, I recognise the voice instantly.

Cuthbert Gonderberry.

"Anna?" he says.

I shift a glance at Mark . . . as if I'm *consciously* trying to make this seem more illicit than it actually is. All the same, Mark takes the hint, giving me a smile and a wink as he treks out. I wait till the bedroom door has clicked shut before replying to Gonderberry.

"I . . . *hello*," I finally say, deciding to start all over again.

" 'Hello' yourself," Cuthbert says, sounding somewhat jovial. "You have no idea what pains I had to go to in order to get my hands on your phone number."

"Really? How many people did you have to kill?" I catch myself before he gets a chance to respond. "Sorry, assassins' humour."

But Gonderberry doesn't seem to find this uncouth at all. He just chuckles away on the other end. "That was quite some display you put on. It was a shame you ran off so quickly — before any of us had the chance to thank you."

"Shooting guns in public places isn't a good look these days."

Gonderberry laughs. "You should know the police confirmed your suspicions; the snake was indeed venomous . . . and I was able to confirm the smaller matter of it not belonging to me." He draws a sigh. "As you might imagine Asha is somewhat nervous about continuing in the role of Cleopatra, but I'm sure — in time — she'll get over it . . . or perhaps just steer clear of forth-coming productions. She would like to thank you, also, I am certain."

I don't think to mention the fact that Asha could easily be six foot under by now if my aim had only been ever so slightly off.

"I did go to the trouble of keeping this out of the papers, as far as I could manage." He pauses for a second, and I imagine him in one of the upper rooms of his house, perhaps looking out over the expansive grounds. "How are things with your client?" he asks.

"Paula?"

Gonderberry gives a mock gasp. "Dearie me, I thought you of all people would value client confidentially far *higher* than that."

I wince. He's caught me off guard. He's called me up while I'm 'off-duty' — while I'm at home — but I know that's no excuse.

"What I wanted to ask, Anna, was whether you might happen to have any sort of *availability* in the near future."

" 'Availability' ?"

"You see, following this latest episode, I am *quite* certain that . . . how should I put this without sounding paranoid? . . . Someone has it *in* for me."

I feel Lizzie coil herself about my leg. "That's funny, I was thinking the same thing."

"Then you agree to help out?"

I hesitate, wondering whether I'm not about to throw myself into some cesspool.

"I can assure you the compensation will be *quite* worthwhile."

And it's then, with a wry smile on my lips, that I know he's got me.

———

I think long and hard before informing the others about Gonder-berry contacting me.

In the end, I bring them into the loop, realising it's just as much because I don't want Mark getting strange ideas; that I want to be able to reach for the trusty card of this being 'work', and to have witnesses to fall back on.

Well, that and the fact that someone could've quite easily died without their involvement during that fateful performance of Antony and Cleopatra.

When I sit them down in Sex Flat and explain mine and Gonderberry's suspicions, they seem to be far more captivated than they were previously. I bring up the subject of Paula Stevenstar. When her name brings on a profound silence, I decide to pin AA down. "Has she been in touch?"

AA shakes his head. "No. And her last cheque bounced."

I allow myself a wry smile. "I suppose she realised we were on to her . . . that she overplayed her hand with that snake . . ."

Amy pipes up. "You really think *she* was responsible?"

I shrug. "Why else is she so interested in Gonderberry?" I look to Tabby and AA, as if hoping for them to bolster my argument. "She clearly wants to see him suffer."

Although Tabby and AA seem more convinced than Amy, I can tell that they're not all the way there yet. That they're going to take *just a little more* . . .

"I'm just saying," Amy continues, "we shouldn't jump to conclusions. Let's find out who's responsible for the snake-changing trick . . . and maybe even the loose python."

"Not to mention his parents," Tabby pitches in.

"Yeah," Amy replies, glancing at me. "Only once we've pinned down those responsible can we emphatically say that Paula Stevenstar was or *wasn't* involved."

My stomach sinks.

This all feels as though it's becoming more and more complicated.

That — instead of resolving — the mystery is becoming foggier and foggier.

And, what's more, I'm not convinced the four of us are even in the right place to solve it. Don't the police set up entire departments to handle this sort of thing . . . or is that only on TV and in films?

I sit still, in the armchair, looking down into the sun-streaked street; seeing those Middle-Eastern men continuing to play that dice game. And that's when it strikes me. I look up to the others. "Let's see this through — for better or worse — like we agreed."

Chapter Thirty-Seven

We all arrive outside the gates to Parisianer Hall.

Having been granted access, we tread up the driveway.

I take my chance to study the others' faces.

To try and divine what they *really* think.

The only person smiling — as always seems the case — is Amy.

She beams, and beams, and beams . . . how she was ever police escapes me; because if there's one thing which I've observed of police throughout my life it's that smiles — *genuine smiles* — tend to be at something of a premium.

Tabby and AA are much more reflective, clearly thinking things over as the gravel crunches beneath our shoes.

Gonderberry, as always, looks squeaky clean. Today, he wears an untucked, crisply pressed white shirt over a pair of blue jeans. He has his sleeves rolled up to his elbows. This is probably what qualifies — for him — as 'scruffy'. My heart quickens when I meet his eye, and then again when he leans into me, planting a kiss on each of my cheeks. To my horror, when he steps away, I realise I'm blushing . . . *Jesus is it really this bad?*

Am I becoming besotted?

If I am then it's happening remarkably subtly.

Without me so much as noticing.

And it's *hardly* that Gonderberry is even my type . . .

I much prefer Mark's Rugged Carpenter to Gonderberry's Wizened Thesp.

As always, Gonderberry is hospitable. He serves us each a glass of wine, despite the fact that it's closer to midday than midnight. My whole body goes rigid as I hold my own glass, peering down into the dark-red liquid and wondering how I might be able to dispose of it surreptitiously. As the conversation goes on, I realise that it's somewhat easier to *not* drink when there's company. Nobody really notices your glass . . . unless it's *empty*, that is.

While we're speaking in the sitting room, I can't help but feel somewhat jealous of the others. I begin to regret having brought them here . . . having to *share* Gonderberry with them. And I have to admit that I feel like a *complete* idiot even as I think it.

Once we're beyond the niceties — and the tying up of loose ends surrounding *that* night at the theatre — we get down to the facts of the matter. To finding whoever it is who's — *apparently* — been framing Gonderberry.

"Now," Gonderberry says, placing his glass down on a nearby mahogany table, "I fear I might have uncovered the motivation — the *reason* behind all of this . . . *silliness.*"

The frivolous way he refers to the murders as 'silliness' chimes with me.

It sets off some alarm in my head.

And then I remind myself of all he's had to deal with.

The loss of a fiancée.

And the loss of his parents.

I assure myself that — deep down — this can be no laughing matter for him.

That he needs to project a façade of calm.

Gonderberry blinks rapidly, regarding his near-empty glass of wine. "It's funny," he says, shaking his head in a way which suggests it's *anything but* . . . "Throughout the years I've done battle. Parisianer Hall — as I'm sure you're all aware — dates back to Tudor times . . . depending on who you believe, the construction was completed in either 1535 or 1538. In any case, we can safely say that Parisianer Hall is closing on five hundred years.

"Parisianer Hall was originally commission by, well, a *Parisianer*. I have reason to believe he was a successful merchant . . . in any case, the original purchaser — this *Parisianer* — failed to keep up with the costs of construction. He fell further and further behind." He smiles with a single corner of his mouth. "It makes really quite fascinating reading, the documents which accompany the construction . . . the financial statements."

I can only take Gonderberry's word for it. When this is all over and done with, I will have spent an ungodly amount of time poring over Tudor-period texts . . .

Gonderberry continues, "The house was — *at one point* — marked for demolition . . . they were planning on simply flattening the property; allowing the ground to grow fallow again. However, one of my ancestor's — a man by the name of Nicholas Parker — rescued the build, putting up the funds to complete the project. Once it was finished, he decided on keeping the original name, and from that point onwards

Parisianer Hall remained in my family." He smiles again; this time with pride. "Until it passed down to me."

The room falls silent.

I slip a quick glance over to Amy, then to Tabby, finally meeting AA's eye.

If this was something we'd been lectured about in a classroom, then I'm certain that our eyes would've long ago glazed over. The four of us hardly have the personality to cope with rote learning. However, given that this is happening in the real world — and that there's a *real-life* mystery involved — I guess we're hooked.

"It's not been plain-sailing — not by any means," Gonderberry continues. "In fact, I happen to know that my father had to think long and hard about whether or not to continue to live in the house around the time of my birth. His career in the Navy had yet to *really* take off. He found himself stalled: Lieutenant Commander . . . the family trust was taking a beating from the upkeep of the premises. And it wasn't just my father who had struggled to keep up Parisianer Hall. It seems — looking back over our tomes of family history — that there was always a moment where it appeared that the only choice available was to *sell* the property. To be through with it once and for all." Here he gives another smile. "As for me, I recall being a struggling actor — soon after my parents' death . . . if it hadn't been for Hollywood knocking on the door then I don't know *what* I would've done. Even so, I recall that I spent the entirety of my first years' paycheques on taking care of the accumulated neglect. As I'm sure you've noticed, I keep an exceptionally light house staff for a property such as this . . . I don't believe in hiring full-time employees; not when I'm so often away. Not with my profession being as flaky as it is."

I draw in a deep breath. Take in the woody scent which hangs about the sitting room.

I peer into the open fireplace, to the flames as they lick their way up the log.

It seems slightly humorous to imagine Gonderberry out the back of his mansion chopping firewood . . . and I can't help wondering just how many people he means by 'light' house staff.

AA leans forward, his eyes sharp, alive to picking up on even the slightest of details. "You were saying you thought you had a reason for people to come after you?"

I silently thank AA for saying what was surely on mine, Amy and Tabby's minds.

That's the thing with actors, I suppose, it's so easy for them to get carried away.

Especially when it comes to themselves.

Gonderberry reaches for his wine. He tips back the remainder then sinks into the sofa. "I'm sorry. Once I get talking about the Hall it'd take wild horses to shut me up." He stares at his wine glass, as if considering a refill. "You recall I told you it was a Parisian merchant — a *Frenchman* — who first commissioned the house? A man by the name of Jacquot. Well, throughout the years, there has been quite an *odd* procession of the merchant's family members attempting to purchase the house. And these offers always seem to come right when we are at our most vulnerable — right when we need to make a quick buck. Why they have their heart so set on this house escapes me, but they keep coming back. Every time they sniff an opportunity." Gonderberry shifts about on the sofa as if struggling to get comfortable. "There have always been stories — a *curse* surrounding the house." He smirks. "I've never believed in things like that myself, but I've never allowed myself to underestimate the power of human want . . . the effort which will be exerted when something is kept from a human being's grasp."

Unable to take it anymore, I leap in. "You're saying the descendants of the man who commissioned Parisianer Hall might be behind . . . the murder . . . the *murders*."

Gonderberry stares into mid-air.

He seems to drift away to another place.

Far away.

Then — as if woken by the *snap* of fingers — he returns.

He looks to me. "That's precisely what I'm saying."

———

We all remain quiet as we sit around Gonderberry; all of us trying to get our heads around what he's just said — trying to understand the bombshell he's just dropped.

"I've never told anybody these concerns." Gonderberry makes eye contact with each one of us in turn. "This is something which has *never* escaped the walls of the house."

He drifts into silence again and I wonder if he might be about to snap; if he might be ready to command us from his house. But, instead, he says, "I'm sure Paula couldn't rightly recall exactly what it was she had said to so stoke my fury. Indeed, I cannot be blameless in my role. There was no way that she could've known . . ."

Apparently eager to hear the rest, Amy says, "Know what?"

Gonderberry snaps his head up. Sears Amy with his stare. "As we were walking up the driveway — approaching the house — she made some quip about it looking as if the place was haunted . . . I told her to be quiet, to not say anything about that to my mother or father. But what did she do? She brought it up . . . my parents, they were superstitious. Deeply so. To be quite frank, I hardly blame them, what with all the *past stories* of horrors which've taken place here. I have no reason to believe it *wasn't* suicide. Neither can I stretch myself to believe that those who wish to lay their hands on Parisianer Hall would be so obvious as to go bumping off the heirs themselves."

From the fireplace, a burning log spits.

I feel a burst of heat.

It singes the hair on my cheek.

"You must understand that those who wish to lay their hands on the house believe this to be their ancestors' *spiritual home*. They will stop at nothing to lay claim to it."

Another silence.

Tabby speaks up. "Why not just give it to them?"

Again, I believe that Gonderberry might fly into a rage; that he will send us packing in a storm of fire and brimstone. Instead, though, he remains straight-faced, seemingly unmoved. "Believe me, dear, I have thought of doing so many — *many* — times over the course of my life." He tucks his chin into his chest then clutches his hands together, as if praying. "But there *is* such a thing as tradition." His tone cools. "Over my *dead body* will they have this house — over my *dead body* will they achieve what they seek through intimidation." He continues to stew for the longest time, and then I note the tear streak free of the corner of his eye. It rolls down his cheek. Before he can get hold of himself, he is openly weeping.

Amy is the quickest to respond. She jumps up from her armchair; throws her arms about him, squeezing him tightly.

I feel an *odd* pang of jealousy.

Can I just *get over* myself?

When Amy's got the situation under control — she seems a

veritable expert at handling crying people — she gives him some room. And Gonderberry duly opens up.

"What nobody knows — what I had the media *suppress* — was that my fiancée . . . that Isla, was pregnant at the time." He swallows hard, his Adam's apple bobbing in his throat. "They know that I am the final heir . . . that they have only to wait for me to die then they can buy out the Hall; they can *have* their desire."

Tabby speaks up. "Aren't you afraid they might have you killed? And that no one will know the secret?"

It's the question we all want to ask.

He sucks air through his nostrils and his whole body seems to inflate, giving him a sort of presence which I recognise as his 'stage appearance'. "I believe that they would never do something so obvious as to bump off the heir. They haven't in hundreds of years. In any case, I'm telling you all now, aren't I? I'm telling you all this — *all of this* — because I feel I can trust you. Am I wrong?"

Nobody says anything.

Finally, he looks at me. "I told you, Anna, about how I wanted to have someone killed — one of their family members . . . to *avenge* my parents' deaths." He grimaces. "But, no, I won't do it — I *won't* sink to their level." He puffs up further still and arches his shoulders back, as if delivering an epic speech. "I'll tell you one thing, though. If they want this house then they shall pry it from my *cold, dead fingers*."

Chapter Thirty-Eight

That evening I go to Arnold's house to check in with my children.

As I previously assumed, Ben is very much grounded. It's a strange mixture in terms of his treatment; given the fact that he's both the victim and the guilty party . . .

Goodness knows *I* can empathise.

I get through with the dramatics as early as possible. Like I already decided, I keep my distance from Ben, not prying too much into the 'procedures' and 'support' going on . . . I'm sure Arnold and Kate have those arenas very much sewn up.

When I get back home — back to Mark's house — I greet the two of them briefly. Just like Ben, they're going through with the psychiatrists' exercises; all of these *routines* which're designed to ease anxiety.

I get online at the first opportunity — cup of tea in hand; cat in lap — and do some more research into Parisianer Hall. Sure enough, it doesn't take much searching to find the answers I'm looking for . . . or, more exactly, the various strange goings-on which've been reported. One of the links I follow is entitled 'speakingforthedead.com'.

There turns out to be an entire page dedicated to Parisianer Hall.

I skim through the annals of the strange goings-on, taking stock of the various beats in the story; the reports of ghostly sightings; the appearance of blood on freshly washed laundry. Then there's the case of the *human* bones discovered in the wine cellar.

They'd been picked clean.

All of a sudden, I begin to understand just why Gonderberry doesn't want to hire full-time staff, and it has nothing to do with his finances. When I last checked Gonderberry's net worth it stood at well north of fifty million pounds. He wants to be able to keep a close eye on anybody who enters the property. On anybody who sets foot in Parisianer Hall.

At first, this puzzles me, when I think about how he so flippantly accepted an anonymous group of 'Belarussian' tourists. But then the penny drops. He knew all along who we were. He's been in charge the whole time.

I continue to look over the webpage, reaching the part where the murders begin.

The first — I note — took place in the early part of the seventeenth century.

Not a family member.

The son of one of the gardeners.

He fell from a great height . . . right down onto the patio.

I skim onwards, picking out the murders — roughly one every ten years.

Finally, I reach the latest ones.

The suicides of Gonderberry's parents.

And then — at last — the death of Gonderberry's fiancée.

Of course, it says nothing about the baby she was carrying . .
.

Mark calls me away to come and eat something. It's only when I sit down at the table that I realise how ravenous I am. I'm grateful for the thick and cheesy spaghetti bolognese which Mark has whipped up . . . I also can't help but wonder just what Gonderberry might be eating tonight; if he allows himself the privilege of a private chef to cook up his meals . . . or if — taking his control freakery to new levels — he's actually learned how to rustle up a few dishes by himself . . .

After dinner, Nathan asks to be excused, when Mark does excuse him, he thumps his way upstairs, to his bedroom. The two of us sit in silence until we hear the door slam shut. Mark glances up from his now-empty plate. Although he raises a smile, I can see he's dog-tired . . . I've had more than one night's sleep disturbed by his constant tossing and turning.

If it'd been my house then I might've plucked up the nerve to ask him to go sleep on the sofa. There are limits to my cheek, though.

Even *I'm* not capable of telling a man what to do inside his own house.

"How're things going?" Mark asks.

"Oh, fine."

"I mean, you know, with Ben?"

I wince internally, thinking about how I'm a horrible mother. And then, feeling myself slipping down an overly familiar avenue, I arrest my descent. "He seems to be getting on okay — from what Arnold and Kate say."

That's a lie too, since I make it my main mission in life to have as little interaction with my ex-husband, and his very own live-in lover, as possible.

"You don't . . ." Mark begins, and then his gaze slips away.

I take a leap of faith as to what he was about to say. "Dunno," I reply. "Do you think I should be more involved? Should I be more *hands-on?*"

Mark turns his attention onto me again. Shrugs. "I guess all situations are different." He gives a slight smile — a great achievement given the circumstances . . . given the *context.* "You did stop the pair of them from jumping off a cliff."

"That was Josie, actually."

Mark shakes his head, still smiling.

I guess if you can smile about this then you can smile about *anything* . . .

"Well, you paid the taxi at least."

Not really having anything to say, I collect our plates and head into the kitchen, mentally preparing myself to slot them into the dishwasher. I really can be a domestic goddess when I put my mind to it.

Mark follows. "And . . . work?"

One of the few positives over the course of the past week has been the *lack* of questions pertaining to my work. "Oh . . ."

"Gonderberry? Have you proven he did it?"

" 'Did what' ?"

"You know, killed his *girlfriend?*"

Something sticks in my throat.

Out of nowhere, a tear pricks my eye.

I turn my back to him, concentrate on placing glasses on the upper level of the dishwasher. Finally, I manage a reply. "No, I haven't."

Mark sighs then turns away.

No doubt he thinks he's put me in a bad mood . . . or maybe he's frustrated that I keep him distant from my work; that I don't share every last detail with him.

However, as he pads off into the sitting room, I hear him call back to me over his shoulder. "Cup of tea, please."

I allow myself a slight smile.

Perhaps there will be peace, after all.

When I return to the bedroom later on, I notice I have a message on the Assassins' Anonymous app. It's from Amy:

Got him.

Chapter Thirty-Nine

The building which houses Sex Flat is dark and deadly quiet as I climb the staircase. In the distance, I can hear a police siren. A little closer, I hear loud coughing.

I breathe in deeply before I knock. When I do, I feel as if I'm not entirely prepared for what lies within. I might be a bad person, but I don't make a habit of doing things like this.

Tabby's face appears in the crack at the door. She looks me over then lets me in.

Inside, I see a man bound to a chair. He's gagged, too. His eyes look panicked — something which seems entirely reasonable given the circumstances.

I look to the others.

It's probably the first time I've been up to Sex Flat when everybody has actually looked *alert* . . . rather than draping themselves across various pieces of furniture. Maybe there's something about kidnap which snaps everyone to their senses . . .

AA and Amy stand behind the man bound to the chair.

Tabby brings the door shut on my heel then stands on my shoulder.

The man takes me in with wide eyes.

I can tell he's trembling.

"This is him?" I ask, a little idiotically.

Amy nods. "This is the one who brought the snake in."

I turn my attention back to the man, taking him in properly for the first time.

He doesn't fit my typical image of a *henchman*, which is to say that — in and of his appearance — there's nothing which leaps out. He has no tattoos. Neither does he have any piercings. No scars, either. In fact, to be quite honest, he looks quite fresh faced, and I can't see him being much older than eighteen or nineteen . . . early-twenties would be a stretch. He has dusty blond hair and baby-blue eyes.

Deciding the others have built up my arrival — perhaps wrongly suggesting I'm the one 'in charge' — I do my best to fulfil the role, strolling before the bound man, narrowing my eyes as I do so. I give AA a nod and — as if we share a telepathic connection — he loosens the gag about the man's mouth. The gag falls down to his neck.

"What's your name?" I ask.

"He won't say anything," AA replies, from behind the man.

I shift him a quick, reprimanding glance then take a couple of steps closer to the bound man. "What's your *name*?"

The man meets my eyes. He locks onto my stare.

Unable to look away.

I feel a pang in my gut.

Power . . . *power* over someone.

It's been a long time since I felt like this.

A long time since I felt as *good* as this.

"Jean-Pierre." A bead of sweat forms on his brow. It rolls its way down the side of his eye. He winces. "Jean-Pierre *Allard*."

Both from the name, and his accented English, I draw the conclusion that he's French.

From the looks of the others' expressions, they've caught onto the same idea.

And onto what it might mean.

Tabby begins to speak from over my shoulder. "I found him skulking about Parisianer Hall. He was fiddling with the fence. When I grabbed him — did a search — he had some pliers, a lock-picking kit . . . some *other* items, too. I called up Amy — sent her over a picture. She confirmed him as the man she'd seen in the alleyway behind the Auburn."

Amy picks things up. "It took me a few times to look over the photo. He was wearing a beanie cap that night. But I recalled seeing tufts of blond hair. The face I remembered."

A tingle passes through my gut.

One of those childish sensations that strikes you when the sole of your boot hovers just above an ants' nest . . . and you know it would only take a sudden *downward* movement to change *everything* in those ants' lives.

I look back to the man — *Jean-Pierre Allard*. "What were you doing?"

Eyes bulging from their sockets, he replies, "I am from the family — from the Jacquot family." Tears sparkle in his eyes. "Please, it is nothing I . . . nothing I may . . . I may . . ."

AA seizes hold of the chair back and gives it a hard shake. When he finishes, he looks at me as if he's done good work. As if he's loosened the man's tongue.

In truth, of course, he's done nothing to aid discourse. Jean-

Pierre begins to stutter. "Yuh-yuh-you do not . . . do not . . . uh-uh-uh-understand."

"I think we understand *perfectly* well," Amy replies. "You were the one who delivered the deadly snake — the one who attempted to commit murder."

Jean-Pierre Allard shakes his head over and over again, and then, apparently catching hold of himself, his complexion turned pale, he says, "I am . . . the . . . the . . ."

AA gives Jean-Pierre's chair another firm rocking.

This time it serves to speed up Jean-Pierre.

"In my family, we have a . . . a . . . *chosen one.*"

I exchange glances with AA, who has backed away for the time being.

Jean-Pierre's eyes flicker about the room, as if he might be searching for some method of escape. Yeah, good luck with that . . .

" 'A chosen one' ?" I echo, with the tone of derision that it surely merits.

Jean-Pierre nods vigorously, gasps. ". . . *Yes.* My family, for years . . . for *many, many years* . . . they have desired to possess the house — the Parisianer Hall. It was . . . the . . . the . . . *dream* of my ancestor; of our family. Once a generation, each time that a . . . a boy is born . . . we are given the responsibility . . . to try . . . *try* to pry the property from the . . . the possession of . . . of . . ."

"The Gonderberrys?" I put in, hoping to help out.

Strangely beginning to feel a touch of sympathy.

And I have to remind myself that — as Amy suggested — this man is guilty of attempted murder. If I hadn't intercepted that snake who *knows* what might've happened?

"Why do you act like this?" I ask. "Why do you run about in

the shadows? Why don't you just come straight out and *kill* him — kill Cuthbert Gonderberry?"

Jean-Pierre holds himself very still.

His chest rises and falls with rapid breathing.

Out of nowhere, he gives a smile — an almost *wicked* smile.

"There is a complication," he replies.

"What sort of 'complication' ?"

His smile vanishes. He raises his eyebrows. "Your employer has not elaborated? If anything should happen to the heir *himself* . . . the current heir of Parisianer Hall . . . then the mansion should be placed in the care of a trust — of a public foundation."

I look to AA, as if Gonderberry might've confided this particular detail in him.

But his blank stare reveals he hasn't.

When I look to Tabby and Amy, I see they're similarly beleaguered.

I turn back to Jean-Pierre. "What is it you *want*? What were you trying to *achieve* tonight if you weren't intending to sneak into the grounds and kill Cuthbert Gonderberry?"

Jean-Pierre holds his stare very level — then looks to the street outside. "We wish for a meeting."

"A 'meeting' ?"

"Yes. Almost five hundred years have passed of this . . . *curse* . . . of this . . ."

" 'Feud' ?" Tabby suggests.

Jean-Pierre deals Tabby a long and hard glare, as if daring her to say something further. As if he would be able to do anything at all in retribution bound to the chair as he is. "Yes, we agree that it has gone for too long now . . ."

I think for a beat then say, "We have to speak with Gonderberry."

———

It feels wildly unnatural to simply turn Jean-Pierre free . . . but that's what we do.

When we let him loose, he doesn't make off quickly, but neither does he dawdle. He seems to know where he's going. I guess he and his family have become intimately familiar with London's backstreets, especially under the cloak of darkness.

From beside me, Amy gives a heavy sigh. "So, they need to keep Cuthbert alive — but they need to dispossess him . . . they need to force him to *sell*."

"That's what it sounded like to me," I reply, watching Jean-Pierre slip from view.

Chapter Forty

W e speak with Gonderberry, tell him of the meeting with Jean-Pierre, and what it is his 'family' wish for. Gonderberry, to my surprise, seems lacking in resolve. From the tone of his voice over the phone, he sounds almost *resigned* to what's about to happen. Or maybe he's just fed up. Perhaps he wishes to live in peace.

Free from this *craziness*.

I can't say that I blame him.

Not one bit.

If the family want the house so badly then *why not* give it to them?

From what I've read of Gonderberry, he possesses 'a lovely piece of real estate' in Los Angeles; touching distance from Hollywood, which is where — as he openly admitted — all the money is.

I wonder how we're going to work out the details of the meeting, but it seems that Gonderberry is miles ahead. He calls me back later that day to set a meeting for the next Saturday night; a 'dinner party' as he terms it.

He informs me that he wishes to bring along *one* of us to the dinner itself . . . and — *surprise, surprise* — who does it turn out to be?

AA slouches on mine and Mark's bed, casually reclining on his elbow. He looks like one of those magazine models all dressed up in a fiercely cut suit, hair beautifully taken care of, his skin gleaning with some high-priced cream or other . . . *just hanging out.*

Lizzie lies on her back before him, and AA casually passes his fingertips across her belly, bringing her out in a fresh wave of ecstatic purrs each time he does so.

Downstairs, I can hear Mark and Nathan speaking to one another over the dining room table. Another one of those therapist assignments.

"What happened to the blue one?" AA asks.

"What 'blue one' ?" I reply.

AA rolls his eyes. "*You* know, the dress you wore to one of those Christmas mixers at Mathewson Media — *aeons* ago . . ."

Just to hear 'Mathewson Media' again sends a tremor down my spine.

I look myself over in the mirror — unsure what exactly is the matter with this pale pink, strappy number I've picked out. As if reading my mind, AA says, "You're dressed for Sunday School . . . You don't look dangerous at all."

I fumble through my wardrobe, looking for something which might be appropriate. "Why do I *want* to look dangerous?"

"Why else would Gonderberry be wishing for you to personally hang off his arm tonight — to take part in the discussion?"

"Because I'm the prettiest?"

I decide to take AA's smirk as confirmation of my assumption, rather than as a slight. When I next back away from the wardrobe, I am holding a simple, black, figure-hugging dress . . . something which I recall having worn to another party. "What about this?"

AA gives me a wry smile. "Perfect."

———

The four of us approach Parisianer Hall. We turn up in one of AA's sports cars. As with our previous visit, Gonderberry allows us in through the gates so we can park at the front of the house. I have to admit that AA's obnoxious-purple sports car doesn't look all that outgunned by Gonderberry's cherry-red coupé. Holding its own, even. Maybe there's a lesson there — something about assassins and actors . . .

Snow lines the driveway, lawn, and the tree branches.

All things considered, it's a very *cosy* scene.

One which makes me want to rush inside as soon as possible and stoke up a blazing log fire. Even through the thick coat I managed to convince AA to *allow* me to bring along tonight, I feel the chill. The tights which I snuck on unbeknownst to AA don't seem to mitigate it one jot. Mercifully — before I turn from Anna to ice cube — Gonderberry throws open the doors. I *feel* the warmth wafting out. When Gonderberry grins at us I can't help but think he's looking as *spruced-up* as ever I've seen him.

His longish, tussled hair hangs down in elegant, ragged curls.

He has on a tuxedo.

And he actually looks like men are *supposed* to look in tuxedos . . . which is to say that the cummerbund about his waist serves not merely to conceal a beer belly but to draw attention to his tight abdomen. "Well, you're the first here," he says, with a wide smile.

Indeed, despite night very much having set in, and the driveway lights now illuminating the grounds, the guests haven't yet arrived. Then again, it's only just after five in the evening. And the invitation doesn't kick in until half past eight.

We haven't arrived ridiculously early due to some faux paus. Quite the opposite. We are here to get things set up. Or, as we used to say in the Army, *to secure the perimeter*.

As part of the condition for the meeting the Jacquots would not agree to come alone. They seem just as paranoid as Gonderberry is . . . although, where Gonderberry has good reason to feel so — after all the terrible things that've happened to his family down the centuries — the Jacquots' uneasiness is harder to understand.

They hold the power. Or *think* they do . . .

I take in Amy and Tabby.

I didn't get much of an opportunity to scrutinise their appearances in the cramped confines of AA's car. Tabby wears a trouser suit the colour of red wine. It has a scooped neckline, playfully — *yet professionally* — showing off cleavage. She accompanies the outfit with a black leather handbag with a silver strap.

Amy has on a gown the colour of white roses. As I take her in, I can't help but flip AA a sidelong glance, wondering if *she* looks as if she's 'dressed-up for Sunday School' . . . maybe it's just a young girl thing: those bitches can get away with anything.

Like Tabby, Amy wears a handbag too . . . and what's curious about their handbags is that they match. The unobservant might believe there was some kind of breakdown in communication ahead of the engagement; that they didn't share their outfits ahead of time.

However, I know better.

All that really matters is what each handbag contains . . .

As Gonderberry leads us into the hallway, Amy and Tabby excuse themselves, heading upstairs. They know their job. And me and AA know ours.

Amy and Tabby will be working surveillance. They will be keeping an ear out both on what happens *within* the house, and what goes on throughout the grounds. AA, meanwhile, will be a roaming presence, or, as Gonderberry hit on with a stroke of genius, 'the butler'.

As for me? I'm going to be arm candy.

And — *yes* — Gonderberry was kind enough to put it in clear terms.

What no doubt differentiates me from the average 'arm candy' is that I have a pistol strapped to my inner thigh; ready for whipping out at a moment's notice.

We agreed the best means of communication is the Assassins' Anonymous app. It seems unnecessary for us to wire ourselves up with walkie-talkies; not to mention *unsubtle* to have a wire snaking down our necks. It makes more sense for us to communicate through our mobiles. Nobody will so much as bat an eyelid at someone checking a *phone*.

AA saunters off into the house, apparently to go and get his bearings. I can't help but feel that I can smell *blood* in the air. Or is it just that my mind has become corrupted with all the horror I've witnessed? All the horror I've wrought on others . . .

Have I gone beyond cynicism?

"This way," Gonderberry says, offering me the crook of his arm.

When I take hold, I don't feel that it's sleazy or weird at all.

I guess these are the many signs which make up a *normal* man.

Would he have turned out normal if he hadn't lived his entire life in this house?

Living with a millstone tied about his neck?

Gonderberry leads me into the dining room.

My heart skips several beats.

And my breath deserts me briefly.

Then I catch it back again.

I take in the white tablecloth, and the silver cutlery arranged at each place. It's one big circular table, and it must be large enough to accommodate fifty — *a hundred?* — people.

Above our heads, I see the glass dome. Tonight it shows off the lightly falling snowflakes, tumbling down through the air. I watch a few of them smudge up against the glass, lose myself in the sight for several seconds. Then I snap back to reality.

Off across the room, I make out the open door into the kitchen.

I can hear the frenzied activity within as the cooks all get to work preparing the courses which will be served in the next few hours.

"Well," I say, turning into Gonderberry. "Looks like you've got everything sorted out."

Gonderberry scopes the table. "It does, doesn't it? The Admiral would've been so pleased. It's funny. It's kind of an appropriate send off for the house . . . a nice way for things to end." He turns back to me, smiling warmly again. "A *big* party."

The two of us stand there for the longest time.

I have no idea what I'm supposed to say.

It feels as though we've failed.

We *have* failed.

We were supposed to bring the killer — or *killers* — of

Gonderberry's fiancée to justice. That is what Paula Stevenstar originally asked of us.

And where has it brought us?

Where has it brought *me?*

"See you in a bit, Anna," Gonderberry says, easing away. He treads off out of the dining room, leaving me to behold the incredible trimmings before me.

———

I begin to feel nervous when I observe the first car trundling up along the driveway.

There's no sign of Gonderberry, or AA, for that matter.

Amy and Tabby seem to be occupied also.

I wonder if I should throw the doors open and greet the visitors. My heart beats hard. Blood rushes to my temples. I get to wondering *just who* exactly will step through the doorway. Famous people? No doubt . . .

Taking the coward's option, I rush up the staircase as quickly as my high heels will allow. I find myself on a landing on the floor above.

I look to my left.

To my right.

Decide that the large double doors at the end of the corridor must lead to the master bedroom. I follow my gut. Pick my way over the plush carpet then bring my suddenly fragile knuckles to knock.

From within, I hear a vague, dampened response.

I decide that's all I need.

I go in.

The master bedroom seems to appear to me from out of my

subconscious, and I suddenly realise that it's because I must've seen it pictured in the various interviews I read featuring Gonderberry.

The cold strikes me.

It puckers up my skin.

Gonderberry himself is standing at a pair of open glass doors which look out over a small balcony. As I tread up behind, I realise the view features the entirety of the gardens, all sweeping out beneath. From here, he can make out the street side of the gate. I wonder if — the first day we came here — he stood on this balcony and observed our fumbling attempts at getting access.

"It's . . . time. The guests are arriving."

Gonderberry continues to show his back to me, and he seems off in his own world.

I wonder if I should back out of the room, but reason with myself that if he'd truly wanted me to leave then he would've told me to do so.

This is *his* house, after all.

When Gonderberry speaks, his voice is tiny, almost without power and yet still carrying to my ears. I think of it as being the voice he puts on when required to perform a 'stage whisper'. "I really loved her, Anna."

I feel my chest tighten.

My heart sinks.

I step closer.

Gonderberry doesn't turn, although he surely senses my approach. "To begin with . . . throughout my life, really . . . my father — the *Admiral* — always told me how important it was for me to settle down — to *pass on* the family name. I know how stupid that sounds. It would only cause more suffering. I would be passing my burden down to the next generation. Condemning my child to a life of misery. And yet, when I found Isla was . . . *pregnant* it was as if a weight had come off my shoulders, as if everything was going to be all right." He goes quiet for a long few moments, screwing up his forehead, the words going dry on his tongue whenever he tries to speak. "But . . . all the while, at the back of my mind, there was this voice *praying* that something would happen; that this . . . this *child* wouldn't need to suffer the same misery." He shakes his head, bringing a clenched fist up to his lips. "When I . . . when I . . . no, it's so terrible . . . *awful.*"

My whole body has gone rigid.

Down below, on the driveway, I hear merry, melodious voices; people who are completely oblivious of what's taking place in Gonderberry's bedroom. Perhaps they wouldn't even care if they knew. Everyone has problems; Gonderberry is simply another.

Finally, Gonderberry stares at a spot just across the bedroom.

When I follow his gaze, I see nothing remarkable.

Only the diamond-patterned wallpaper with fine purple and gold lines.

Was that the place . . . where he found them . . . his *parents?*

Gonderberry lingers over the spot for the longest time before turning into me.

I feel his warm breath up against my cheeks.

His eyes lock onto mine . . . those almost *magical* blue-grey tones.

My heart beats harder.

I know what's about to happen.

And I know I should stop it . . . but it's already too late.

Gonderberry presses his lips against mine. They're soft; then firm — *insistent.* It lasts no longer than a couple of seconds. And then it's over.

My heart flutters up to my throat.

A chill runs through my blood.

Feeling myself shaking all over, Gonderberry takes hold of my hand. Our fingers intertwine. "It's time to face up to this — time to put this to bed once and for all."

Chapter Forty-One

The party passes me by in a blur.

So many faces.

So many *names*.

Most of them are half-familiar; others are so obvious that even *I* recognise them.

Gonderberry introduces me to the guests almost by-the-by, and I never merit anything more than a quick-once over. Never a second glance. Even though I tell myself that this is the perfect situation — that the goal for tonight was that I would be *unseen* — I can't help but feel some ego bruising. I am unspectacular. Forgettable. *Beige*.

It's well past nine when I feel my mobile buzz in my handbag. I dig it out.

A message from Tabby, through the Assassins' Anonymous app:

They're here.

I look around.

Accidently catch Tabby's eye . . . where she stands across the room. She holds her mobile in her hand, no doubt monitoring the systems she and Amy installed via some technical wizardry. I remind myself never to get on Amy's wrong side. She can do more damage with a keyboard than most can do with a ton of explosives.

I look over the crowd, trying to gain my first impressions of the Jacquots.

There are four of them, in all.

Two men, both of them silver-haired. Jean-Pierre stands on their heels. And an elderly woman, who must be in her seventies — *eighties?* — holds tightly to his hand. They all look respectable in their formal dress; the men in tuxedos, and the older woman in a flowing, midnight-blue ball gown. They've come dressed for a *party*.

Gonderberry materialises at my elbow. "Shall we?" he says, taking me by the hand and leading me over to the door.

The Jacquots stand before AA — taking on the mantle of the butler's meet-and-greet duties. They nod deferentially to him then switch their whole attention onto Gonderberry, and then onto me. While the other three Jacquots act just like everyone else this evening, giving me a short, polite greeting, before turning back to Gonderberry; Jean-Pierre remains staring at me. I believe he's going to draw unnecessary attention — *cause a scene* — right at the moment one of the silver-haired men calls him away.

"This way, please," Gonderberry says, pressing on a smile, and leading the Jacquots through the other guests. He makes light quips with other guests he recognises along the way — which is the vast majority.

I feel a touch light-headed as — instead of leading us into the main dining room — Gonderberry instead shows us along a back corridor. The delicious smells wafting out of the kitchen catch my nose. Roasting onions. Frying garlic. Sizzling butter.

Gonderberry leads us into a room not much larger than the library he showed us on our first visit. However, far more thought has gone into the presentation of this room. In reality, it is a small-scale, carbon copy of the larger dining hall.

Gonderberry stands back, waiting for us to take our seats around the circular table.

A pair of candles burn away atop silver holders with some elaborate, sprawling design. I have little time to admire the details, though, because one of the silver-haired men speaks up. His English is excellent, with only the slightest trace of a French accent. "It was our understanding that you would be prepared to sign away the deeds this very evening."

I look to Gonderberry, then back to the silver-haired man.

Gonderberry looks to the silver-haired man who hasn't yet spoken. His English isn't as good. "My apologies, Mister Gonderberry. I believe my lawyer is . . . how you say?"

Gonderberry eyes the silver-haired man who first spoke — the *lawyer*. "Getting ahead of himself?"

"*Oui, oui.*" He taps his temple. "Sometimes he not *think* about the etiquette . . . about the *manners*."

The way the silver-haired man phrases these concepts with an almost serpentine *hiss* sends a shiver through my gut. I suppose that — in the world of high society — manners are of the utmost importance.

A waiter appears in the doorway. Each of us orders. When I glance back up, I find myself on the end of a searing glare from the elderly woman sat opposite. She only looks away when summoned by Jean-Pierre.

I look to Gonderberry, sat beside me, and wonder if he can say something to lighten the mood. Or should I take it upon myself to crack a joke?

———

The meal goes by with a whole lot of silence. Then again, I don't suppose that these people have all that much to say to one another. As Tabby put it, they've been battling out a 'feud' for the best part of five hundred years; why would all that cease merely because they're breaking bread at the same table?

As the dinner begins to come to an end, I believe, from the admittedly *brief* conversations, that I have most of the people pegged. I know who each of them is.

The silver-haired man who spoke with Gonderberry first, is of course the Jacquot family's lawyer. A stern, businesslike man by the name of Monsieur Dubois.

The other silver-haired man is Jean-Pierre's father . . . Monsieur Allard.

By the logic of age difference — and from the short exchanges — I decide the elderly woman is Jean-Pierre's grand-mother. I overhear one of the waiters refer to her as Madame Jacquot . . . it appears she didn't take her husband's surname.

Once dessert is done with — a spritely lemon sorbet which, under any other circumstances, might've left me feeling sparky, light-hearted — it seems that business is very much about to commence. The lawyer — Monsieur Dubois — speaks with one of the waiters who returns with a briefcase. Monsieur Dubois lays the briefcase in his lap and then flips the catches. He digs about within before producing a pile of documents. He places them on the table. "Would you like some *time* to consult with a lawyer, Mister Gonderberry?" He serves me a flippant glance. "I assume that *she* is not your lawyer?"

Gonderberry eyeballs the documents, clearly lost in thought. Finally, he reaches out to take them. He flips through the pages and then looks up once more. "That shouldn't be necessary. But I would like a moment alone — a moment to *reflect* . . ."

Monsieur Dubois cracks what must be his first smile of the evening. "But, of course, Mister Gonderberry. Take all the time you need. There is no one to say that you should sign tonight. This is a *delicate* matter."

Gonderberry takes hold of the documents. Then he rises up out of his chair.

I have a heart-stopping moment when I wonder what *my* role will be.

Should I follow Gonderberry?

Should I remain?

My mobile buzzes. When I look, I have a new message from AA:

Stay put.

There it is . . . I have my orders.

I look up to the Jacquots — speaking amongst themselves in French.

It's funny, despite all the history, all the stories I've heard, I can't quite bring myself to see them as 'evil' . . . they seem so *normal*. Could these truly be the same people who caused so many horrors for Gonderberry's family throughout the centuries?

I feel antsy when ten minutes have passed.

I wonder when Gonderberry will return.

Surely he'll have a change of heart? And then I start to wonder if — *maybe* — he might have a screw loose. Has he gone to 'talk the matter over' with his snakes?

Gone to seek their 'counsel' ?

Perhaps him saying he didn't believe in the supernatural was an attempt to throw me off the scent. And then I realise I can smell smoke.

A scream in the distance.

Someone shouting, "*Fire! Fire!*"

And then AA appears in the doorway — his face bright-red and damp with sweat.

Chapter Forty-Two

The cold is overwhelming when I rush outside. My bare feet touch the freezing gravel driveway. I lost the first shoe only a few steps along the corridor as AA bundled me along. And I lost the other one soon after.

The snow falls heavier now; it chills the back of my neck.

At first I don't see the flames at all . . . and then I can't *not* see them.

They lash at the sky.

Smoke plumes from seemingly every orifice.

Ash hangs in the air, fluttering into my mouth and nostrils.

I look about, to the chattering guests.

Some of them are in shock.

Others laugh drunkenly as if this is the funniest thing they've ever seen.

I just do my best to stand still despite the shivering which racks my body.

"Anna, Anna?"

I turn. See it's Tabby. Amy drags along at her heels. As if it's become her signature greeting, Amy throws her arms about me. "I'm so glad you're okay. I was so worried!"

I look about me.

Realise something.

"Where's *AA*?"

Amy and Tabby look blank.

I glance about. "He was right *here*. He led me *out* of the mansion."

Again, nothing from Amy or Tabby.

Then Amy says, "I'm sure he'll be okay."

I stand still for another second before something grips hold.

And I know I have to go back.

Feeling the freezing, impossibly hard — *impossibly sharp* — gravel digging into the exposed soles of my feet, I bound my way back up the steps to the mansion.

People — *guests* — doubled over and in shock, stumble out of the doors.

It brings something like a war scene into mind.

As if a bomb's just dropped.

And we're dealing with the fallout.

Only I know there was no bomb . . .

I feel raw heat against my cheeks.

Smoke unfurls from within.

Covering everything.

I turn my head.

Take a gulp of fresh night air.

Then plunge back in.

———

I stagger about the hallway, searching for the walls.

Finally, my hand presses up against a firm surface.

Someone grabs hold of me . . . screams for help . . . I work on instinct.

Break their hold.

Give them a firm shove in the direction of the door.

I hear them fall.

Then — through the smoke — someone stoops to pick them up.

Two figures trudge for the exit.

I keep myself low — attempting to keep my head beneath the smoke . . . that's not an easy proposition, though. The smoke is *everywhere*.

It seems to be inside my *brain*.

I spot a discarded sweatshirt nearby.

Make a grab for it.

Then hold it over my nose and mouth.

Guarding my airways.

Keeping my head beneath the smoke.

It's then that I see him . . . *not AA* . . . *Gonderberry* . . .

He wears a gasmask.

An old model. One of those which might've been put to use twenty, thirty years ago.

He's heading for the basement.

Does he plan on rescuing his snakes?

What is he *thinking*?

As I make to pursue him, I note another familiar form.

AA.

Perhaps someone didn't get through to him that he's only *playing* the part of the noble, ever-faithful butler. That he doesn't inhabit the role in real life.

He goes after Gonderberry.

Apparently unaware that Gonderberry has a gasmask. That he can remain down in the basement indefinitely . . . at least until the *flames* get him.

I give chase.

It seems there's nothing else for me to do.

I use the wall to guide my way.

Onto the steps.

Then down.

Down. Down. Down.

Down.

The smoke thickens.

I see his form ahead.

His collapsed body.

AA.

I glance back over my shoulder.

But there's no help coming.

It's all up to me.

As I close on him, I realise his eyes are closed.

I slap him on the cheek.

He blinks away his daze.

Returns to me.

Focuses on me.

His lips form words I can't hear.

Not over my pounding heart.

I offer him my hand.

He holds up his own weak fingers.

I grab him.

Drag him upwards.

He relents.

Gives me some help.

Together, we stagger upwards.

Back up into the house.

To the hallway.

Every step is a fresh hell.

Every step makes me feel like we will tumble back.

Into the snake pit.

I eye the exit.

Four steps.

Three.

Two.

One.

We trip but somehow I wrench hold of AA . . . keep him upright.

Together we stagger on.

Through the hallway.

Then out the door.

And into the night.

————

As I sit with AA in the ambulance outside the burning mansion, I notice a familiar group. They look dishevelled. As if they've been dragged through a bonfire . . . *backwards*.

Then again, I don't suppose *I* look any great shakes.

The Jacquots.

They're hunched over.

Leaving the Hall behind.

Perhaps making peace with the fact that — at the very least — if they won't have the mansion, then *no one* shall.

I say nothing as they pass by.

AA coughs.

I turn to him.

I'm surprised to see his eyes open.

Until a few moments ago, he was out cold.

In a creaky voice which betrays his smoke inhalation, he says, "I went . . . back for . . . *them* . . . to . . . to help them . . . *out*." He breaks down into a coughing fit.

Thankfully there's no paramedic nearby to tell me off.

AA gets himself back under control. "I tried to find . . . to find . . ."

"Gonderberry?"

He nods in reply.

"And you did, only you didn't realise he had a gasmask; that he apparently valued his snakes over his own life."

It's then that I twig I haven't seen Gonderberry yet.

My heart sinks.

I rise up from AA's side.

There's a tug on my forearm.

When I turn, I'm surprised to see AA grabbing me.

And that his hold is insistent.

Unrelenting.

He meets my eye.

Gives me a simple shake of the head.

And I know.

I *just* know.

He didn't make it.

For several seconds, I'm sad to think of the fact, even though it hasn't yet been confirmed. Just the prospect that Cuthbert Gonderberry has ceased to exist . . .

Tabby appears between the open doors of the ambulance. Amy hangs at her heels, with similarly wide eyes. Tabby looks flustered — *panicked even*. To be honest, it's the first time I've ever seen her looking anything close to losing control. "The Jacquots are going!" she says. "They're getting *away*! Don't you see — they set the *fire*! It had to be them!"

I look to Tabby, then give her a doleful shake of my head. "I don't think now's the time for explanations . . . perhaps we should wait for tomorrow."

Chapter Forty-Three

In fact, it turns out to be more like a week later, rather than the next day, when the explanations finally come. At least it gives a chance for the dust to settle. A chance for us to absorb the full facts.

Parisianer Hall burned to the ground.

We know that.

Fact One.

Cuthbert Gonderberry — A-list Hollywood star, fresh from a roundly, well-reviewed run of Shakespeare's *Antony and Cleopatra* — was killed.

Fact Two.

The fire itself was set by Cuthbert Gonderberry . . . it was a planned arson, according to investigators. One which — *they estimated* — had taken the best part of several days to fully put together. Cuthbert Gonderberry never intended to sell up.

All along he intended to burn Parisianer Hall to the ground.

Fact Three.

To be honest, as I powder my nose — or whatever it is I'm supposed to be doing in the bathroom for half an hour — I look myself over in the mirror and wonder how things got to this point. How I got myself so inextricably mixed up in all this.

It all started with AA . . . AA and his *big mouth*.

So big that it doesn't only get himself into trouble but everyone in the vicinity.

When I emerge from the bathroom, I'm startled by Mark standing there. He wears a stern expression. He has apparently left his workshop in a rush . . . he still wears his woodworking apron. "Are you busy?"

I think about the meeting I'm supposed to be going to . . . then make the judgement call that — *just maybe* — I should risk arriving late.

"No . . . why?"

Mark draws a deep breath. "I thought you should hear this from me first . . . before you got a chance to hear it — *I dunno* — on the grapevine."

I begin to feel nauseous.

My heart sinks.

I guess this is the part where he kicks me out.

Oblivious to the scene playing out, Lizzie rubs herself against my bare calves. Unconsciously, I reach down and scoop her up to my chest. If we go then we go together . . .

I realise Mark's holding something.

Right before my eyes.

At first it's a blur . . . then slowly — *surely* — I bring it into focus.

A letter.

I read the handwriting.

It's addressed to us.

That's odd, for a start. Me and Mark get almost *no* jointly addressed post.

I look to him, as confused about this as anybody.

And then it strikes me.

What it *could* be.

That kiss . . . the one with Gonderberry . . . the evening of the fire . . . before he . . . *died*.

Was there some photographer lurking in the bushes?

A long lens.

Are they looking to blackmail me?

But then why did they address the letter to both of us?

Finally, Mark puts me out of my misery.

He hands the letter over.

I slip it free of the envelope.

Expect the photograph . . . but, instead, it's a small piece of cardboard.

A *pink* piece of cardboard.

Gradually, I absorb the details.

A *wedding* . . . then I get the names:

Arnold and Kate wish to . . .

And that's all I need to read.

That's as far as I need to go.

I look back up at Mark.

"Well?" he says. "Are you — you know — okay about it?"

I look at the invitation again and have a strong urge to break out into laughter. But that would be insensitive. Especially when Mark has been so . . . *understanding* of my feelings; when he's done his best to *empathise*.

I meet his eye. "It's fine — I'll be okay."

He gives me a slight smile then places his hand on my shoulder in a somewhat *brotherly* gesture. "Let me know if you want to talk."

I press my lips together, and then, deciding this whole 'brotherly gesture' business needs to be swiftly nipped in the bud, I swoop into him and plant a passionate kiss upon his lips. And I don't let him loose till I'm truly done with him.

I pad towards the door.

"Off out?" he says.

I glance back. "Yeah, that okay?"

"Sure, I've got some stuff to sand down anyway."

A pause settles over the two of us.

He cracks a smile. "Go on then, off a sleuthing you *go*."

I step back into him, press my lips — *hard* — against his, and then go.

———

On the way to Brent Cross, I have time to think about things — to think about Arnold and Kate's rapidly approaching wedding. I should've expected it to happen; it was foolish *not* to expect it . . . they've been living together in pseudo matrimonial bliss for what already feels like the longest time.

And who am I to spoil that?

Why *would* I want to spoil that?

I think back to my last visit to Ben and Josie — the day after the fire — the two of them seemed to be getting on well; they were *balanced . . . happy* even . . .

Ben seems to be going okay after all the gang business,

though he is still jumpy, and has a strict curfew to abide by. But I have faith he'll get through it — that he's got his mother's resilience. That he'll be able to keep on going — put up a fight — when things get ugly. And Josie . . . well, she got lucky . . . she's nothing like me at all.

I hit the road to Sex Flat. The sun streams down — lending little warmth, but a lot of light. I feel it on my cheeks, and it sends thrills through my blood. It makes me feel glad to be alive; if that's even something to be legitimately happy about.

As I'm about to cross the street, to the building which houses Sex Flat, I can't help but notice my two Middle-Eastern acquaintances. Hands in pockets. Jogging from one foot to the other; attempting to remain warm.

Why not . . . *why not* . . .

I stroll over.

There's a noticeable second when they look me over.

No doubt wary.

Asking themselves, *Police? Not Police?*

But their familiar smiles soon return.

I think back to what Tabby said up in Sex Flat — about it being Beginners' Luck . . . well, now would be a pretty good time to prove her wrong.

I reach into my purse, peel out eight twenty pound notes then hand them over to the somewhat disbelieving Middle-Eastern man. I guess he never quite thought he'd have the chance to earn his money back.

He spends longer than ever scrutinising the notes, passing them to his companion when through with his inspection for a fresh pair of eyes. The Middle-Eastern man reveals the dice clasped in his palm. "One throw?" he asks.

I shrug my shoulders, plunging my hands into my anorak pockets. "Sure."

He arches an eyebrow, apparently unconvinced I know what I'm doing . . . but, then again, I guess I really *don't* know what I'm doing . . . at least most of the time.

He throws down the dice.

A six and a three.

I stare at the dice . . . somehow unable to believe.

Then I look to the Middle-Eastern man, and he looks back to me.

For the longest moment, I realise he's not smiling at all . . . and that — *when he lost before* — he was nothing but glad all over.

Why's he so put out now?

Finally, with a reluctant stoop, he recovers the dice. He shrugs. "Sorry."

"No worries," I reply, then cross the road.

Before I disappear into the doorway, I glance back and give the two men a sheepish wave. But they're already looking the other way.

———

Even while I'm climbing the stairs to Sex Flat, I know something's amiss.

Something's *Not Quite Right* . . .

When I hear the door slam, I realise what it is.

I quicken my pace, up the stairs, and find myself nose to nose with our client:

Paula Stevenstar.

She eyes me with great surprise. "Oh! You *startled* me."

I look to the door, to Sex Flat beyond. "Are you . . . uh . . ."

Paula meets my gaze. "Oh, no . . . I mean, this is all over with now. Gonderberry is *dead*." She flashes me an unconvincing smile. "Still, there were some things I wanted to wrap up — some *commitments* I wished to uphold."

I know instinctively that she's talking about the cheque that bounced.

It's funny how some people will just talk all around a subject.

"Are you . . . off now?" I say.

"Yes, yes," she replies, and then makes her way past — grinning inanely.

I wait till I hear the door to the street shut before knocking.

AA opens up this time. He gives me a slight smile and arches an eyebrow.

As I sidle past, I can't help remarking, "You know you look a complete perv when you do that, don't you?"

"A *perv*? You might be so lucky."

With a satisfied smile, I take a seat on one of the armchairs. I shift a glance at Tabby. "Well," I say, "you were right — I went out dead-even."

Tabby rolls her eyes. "You put down *all* your winnings?"

"Yup."

Tabby parts her lips to reply, then seems to think better of it. Finally, she says, "At least you're a proper gambler . . . *all or nothing* . . . the casinos would just *love* you . . ."

I don't know whether to take this as a criticism or a compliment.

Either way, my brief but fiery gambling career is *over* as far as I'm concerned.

I switch over to Amy, realising she's perusing her mobile

phone. "The youth of today, huh? Got their brains all tangled up with the damn Interweb." I look to Tabby and AA, hoping they'll side with my curmudgeonly way of thinking, but the best I get are winces.

Amy glances up. "Something's come in."

" 'Something' ? That sounds awfully specific."

"Look, if you're interested then say so, otherwise . . ."

"Interested in what?" Tabby says, crossing the room then looking over Amy's shoulder. She gives — what I hope is — a mock expression of surprise . . . either that or her face has been replaced by an excellent reproduction of Edvard Munch's *The Scream*.

AA slips me a sceptical glance, and then, crossing his arms over his chest, goes to see what all the fuss is about. Sure enough, when he also takes in the screen, he gapes in surprise. He looks to me — eyes wide. "Anna, you've got to see this."

I hold still for as long as possible.

I look to the sky outside.

I glance back down to the Middle-Eastern men and their dice game.

And then, because I've run out of places to look — and I don't want to depress myself by looking at Sex Flat itself — I turn my attention onto the others.

This is my chance.

The door is *right there*.

I just need to take the first step.

And then I'll be gone.

With a mixture of reluctance and excitement, I hoik myself up from my armchair.

Even before I've drawn up behind the others — before I've

seen what exactly is on Amy's mobile phone screen — I know that I've made my choice.

I'm sticking with these guys.

For better or worse.

THE END

Author's Note

Thank you for taking the time to read one of my books. If you would like to hear about my latest releases you can sign up for my newsletter here: www.aviain.com

Thanks for reading!

AV Iain

Snake Pit
An Anna Harris Novel

www.ingramcontent.com/pod-product-compliance
Lightning Source LLC
Chambersburg PA
CBHW031317280626
47169CB00019B/1789